K-RHO:
The *Sweet* Taste of Sisterhood

Jessie,
thank you for showing
me the value of
keeping it real and
enjoying the path
you choose in life.
La Toya Hankins
6/9/16

K-RHO:
The *Sweet* Taste of Sisterhood

—

by La Toya Hankins

Resolute Publishing
Louisville, KY

ISBN-13: 978-0-9830948-4-5
ISBN-10: 0983094845

First Printing

10 9 8 7 6 5 4 3 2 1

Author's Acknowledgments: Shout out to Sistahs on the Shelf, Rodney Carroll, and all
those who supported my dream of being a published author. Your feedback inspired
me to do better, and I am a better author because you are such excellent readers.
Love and respect to my independent LBGT authors, especially Rashid Darden
for telling our truths—good, bad, and scandalous.

Resolute Publishing, LLC
Louisville, KY 40201

www.respublishing.com
info@respublishing.com

This book is dedicated to my Sisters of the Dove and other members of sororities who support each other and don't let different life choices stand in the way of true sisterhood. This also goes out to my Canadian chap stick who has supported me through this process. You are so very special to me and I'm so glad to have you in my life. Schefflera

CHAPTER ONE
February 1991
Kiara

ANY OTHER MONDAY night, Kiara Michaels' mind would be on the ethics of corporate mergers. Tonight, a different kind of union occupied her thoughts.

Two weeks ago, the heavy purple linen envelope her mother trained her to expect almost from birth landed in the Copper Road University sophomore's campus mailbox. The letter bore an invitation. The women of the Lambda Mu Chapter of Kappa Alpha Rho Sorority, Incorporated had requested her attendance for an interview. She was being considered for membership. Acceptance of the offer required Kiara to deliver three copies of the enclosed application and a money order for $24.95 to the Sanford Student Center at 6:45 p.m. tonight.

Kiara walked briskly out the back entrance of her dorm. The Blueburg, North Carolina cold air slapped her mocha colored cheeks with an icy hand. Shivering she thought, 'why am I doing this? Doesn't being the daughter of a lifetime sorority member count for something? They should just tell me where to show up in my white dress so I can get my sorority handbook, pin and a bounty of crossing gifts. Hell, I have probably been to more national conventions than all the girls put together.'

"Excuse me, are you here for the Kappa sorority meet-

7

ing?" a voice said behind Kiara.

Kiara turned to face a girl who resembled a gazelle. Slender shape, beaming brown eyes and a direct gaze. She wore a royal blue beret leaned to the side of a neat black braided bob. Smiling, the girl waited for a response.

"Are you here for an interview?" Kiara asked walking inside followed by the newcomer.

"Yes, good to know I'm not the only one they are meeting with tonight. Usually, this time on a Monday, I would be in my Comparative Latin American Politics class. But, since the lovely women of the Lambda Mu Chapter of Kappa Alpha Rho Sorority, Incorporated requested my presence, I decided to forgo my educational advancement for a night. I'm Gloria Allen by the way, what's your name?"

Kiara introduced herself. Walking up the carpeted steps to the second floor, Kiara noted Gloria also wore glasses and seemed about the same height. Then again, it could have been the three-inch heels Kiara wore making her eye level to her companion.

Lowering herself onto one of the brown leather sofas in the center of the second floor lobby, Kiara noticed fifteen other girls milling around. Removing her jacket, she unconsciously rubbed the back of her neck. She had recently cut her hair and still felt sensitive about exposing her neck. Her hairstyle choice did not come from a desire to jump on the recent Toni Braxton hair cut craze sweeping campus. It was to camouflage the damage of a dorm-applied perm. The scholarship checks only stretched so far and trying to cut costs, Kiara had gone the budget route instead of the beauty salon. Feeling clumps of the hair, damaged by harsh lye, separate from her scalp when she washed her hair a week ago, she realized some things were worth the price you paid.

"Does one of y'all have a light?" the buxom girl with skin dark as a starless December night asked. She sat with an unlit cigarette in her mouth. To Kiara, she resembled an African queen regarding her subjects who'd failed to amuse her. She wore her raven colored hair in a neat bun and had a serious look on her face.

"Sorry. I don't smoke," Kiara said. Gloria shook her head.

"No matter, I don't think I'm supposed to smoke in here anyway. I just wanted to stir up some trouble while I wait for the sisters to call me in for my inquisition," the girl drawled, checking her brown teddy bear faced watch. "They need to hurry up. My show comes on at nine and I am not trying to miss it because Thelma and 'nem are running behind."

"I totally know where you are coming from with that. I was just saying to Kiara, I am usually in one of my night classes at this time. Dr. Brevard usually lets us out right at the stroke of nine so by the time I get back to my dorm shows have been on for about fifteen minutes. I hate trying to get into a show once it's started. I feel like I'm playing catch up the entire time so I usually don't try to watch," Gloria said nodding her head.

"Listen to me just talking up a storm without introducing myself. My name is Gloria and this is Kiara. What's your name?"

"Donna Edwards, pleased to meet you," she said.

"Nice to meet you Donna. Seems like I have seen you around campus before. What's your major?"

"Social work."

"Cool, mine is Political Science and Spanish. Kiara what is your major?

"Business with a minor in Psychology," she answered.

'Man, this girl asks a lot of questions,' Kiara thought looking around the room.

Gloria continued her fact-finding mission. "Neat. So what dorm do you stay in?"

Frustration creeping in her tone, Donna answered, "Brunswick, and you?"

"Pitt."

"Aw shit, the honors dorm. My girl May-Lynn stays there and I know there aren't that many of *us* up in there. Props to you," Donna said with an approving look.

Blushing, Gloria replied, "Please, it's just a brick building with some people who happen to test well. I think it's neat your dorm is right beside mine. No wonder you look familiar. I have probably seen you coming and going in the morning."

"How about you?" Donna asked Kiara. "Don't tell me you stay in one of the other Coal Campus dorms? You know I think it is sort of silly for Copper Road to divide up the dorms on campus using mining terms. I mean damn, everyone knows where the money came from to build the campus."

"No, I stay in one of the Diamond Divide campus dorms, Greene," Kiara said.

"Oh, the girl jock dorm. What sport you play? My cousin Regina who plays softball stays there, on the third floor. Country as hell," Donna said, shaking her head. "She got written up last semester for trying to cook some collards in a crock pot in her room. You know the rooms aren't wired that well and it caused a small fire. My people, my people."

Relaxing a little, Kiara replied, "I run track. Gina your cousin? I heard about that last year. At least, from what I heard, the greens were off the chain so the situation wasn't too bad."

The three of them shared a laugh. The laughter seemed to help calm the trio's nervousness about the interviews. They each came to this interview with different motivations but hoped for the same outcome. Kiara's purpose was, in a sense, to join the family business. Her mother, two aunts and a cousin were Kappa Alpha Rho members. Kiara's exposure to the organization began almost from the crib, when her mother dressed her in *Future K-Rho* shirts and took her to every sorority function possible. Kiara had been a Rho Angel in elementary school, a Rho-ette in middle school, and a Rho Rose in high school.

Along with her actual love for the organization's mission, Kiara's reason for joining involved the love of her mother. Staring at Donna and Gloria, she reflected. She and her mom never seemed to have anything in common. Her mother never left the house without her shoes and purse matching. Kiara lived in t-shirts and tennis shoes. Dorothy Michaels seemed to own the biggest church hat collection east of Cape Fear River. Kiara kept her hair pulled back in a ponytail, or due to recent circumstances, simply styled. Kiara thought, 'maybe if we shared the same organization we could bridge a gap, which seemed to start when I decided I'd rather climb trees than play with tea sets.'

"So y'all sophomores or juniors?" Donna asked. When Kiara looked at her with a why-you-want-to-know expression, she added, "In a few minutes, those K-Rho sisters are going to be all up in your Kool-Aid so you might as well get used to people being nosy."

"I'm a sophomore," Kiara said looking at Gloria.

"So am I."

"Good, there's nothing worse than being around a bunch of young-acting freshmen or some stuck-up upperclassmen," Donna said offering mints to Gloria and Kiara. After they declined, she placed one in her mouth.

"So I guess you're a sophomore," Gloria said.

"How did you guess?" Donna replied with smiling sarcasm.

Kiara considered the motivation of the two sophomores she just met. Neither had shared what brought them to the interview. She knew K-Rho was selective so she assumed the two had something going for them. Otherwise, they would be in class or somewhere else. At this point, she thought to herself, 'I should focus on me and not them.' Soon she heard her name. Looking at her watch, Kiara realized close to twenty minutes had passed since she sat down. Grabbing her purse, Kiara walked to the door where a girl in purple and platinum stood, and prepared herself for what awaited on the other side.

"Good evening, Ms. Michaels, my name is Ruth Wilson. I am currently the president of the Lambda Mu Chapter of Kappa Alpha Rho Sorority, Incorporated," she said. "I, along with chapter secretary Veronica Whitman, will be conducting your interview. We anticipate the interview to last up to thirty minutes, but out of respect for yours and our schedules, hopefully we will complete the process without extending that timeframe."

Kiara and Ruth often cracked jokes in Abnormal Psychology, however tonight Ruth was all business. Kiara knew she had to respond accordingly if she was to make a good impression.

Setting the digital clock facing her, Ruth started the interview. "Kiara, why do you want to be a member of Kappa Alpha Rho Sorority, Incorporated?"

"My interest in Kappa Alpha Rho Sorority, Incorporated comes from my admiration of the sorority's goals of standing strong, reaching high, and giving back," Kiara said. She struggled not to shift in her seat. Be it nerves, the new wool long sleeve navy dress, or a very good heating system, she was starting to sweat. She knew being a legacy or daughter of a sorority member all but guaranteed her acceptance. Still, anytime she faced an interview she felt a little unsettled.

"Not to speak ill of the other sororities on the yard, but the Lambda Mu Chapter members are the ones registering voters, collecting food and clothing for the homeless and tutoring students at the high schools. I remember when the student union didn't want to bring Angela Davis here to speak, y'all donated all the money from your dances to help pay for her fee. Plus, y'all's step team is all that."

Veronica and Ruth smiled slightly and scribbled Kiara's answers. She hoped praising the chapter's philanthropic and party side would confirm her appreciation and awareness of the group's impact on the Copper Road Campus. Known for being selective, Kappa Alpha Rho's interest process differed from other organizations. Instead of interest meetings, they garnered their interviewees based on attendance at each of their events. Consideration for membership required each of the women to have attended at least three Kappa Alpha Rho events during the previous twelve months. Kiara had attended five.

The Lambda Mu Chapter was also unique on campus for never having any allegations of hazing leveled against it. CRU hosted eleven fraternities and sororities. All of them except Kappa Alpha Rho had been removed at one time or another. Kiara felt based on her experience and stories she had heard from others, if selected for membership, she wouldn't have to worry about being mentally or physically harassed.

"Thank you for your response to the question. What do you think you can bring to Kappa Alpha Rho Sorority?" Veronica asked.

"I can bring a dedication to keeping the name of Kappa Alpha Rho respected on the yard. I also bring a knowledge and appreciation of all that Kappa Alpha Rho has done and a desire to make it all that it can be."

"If I didn't know any better, I would think you had practiced that little speech," Veronica said, lifting her naturally arched eyebrow and looking sideways at Ruth.

Not knowing what to say, she responded, "No, that came from my heart."

When she told her mother about receiving her packet, her mother kindly sent her what she had just said in case the question came up in her interview. Dorothy had given the same response during her interview thirty years ago. Waiting for Ruth and Veronica's response, Kiara's stomach churned. Did it work?

"Kiara, are you seeing anybody special?" Ruth asked in a way suggesting she may already know the answer.

The hair on the back of Kiara's neck stood up. Did they know about Chris? Since becoming a couple last year, the two worked hard at keeping their relationship under wraps. She wasn't ashamed, just cautious. Copper Road University was a Southern school and certain types of relationships were frowned upon. She kept her love life under wraps out of a love of privacy. She also didn't want it to interfere with becoming a Kappa. While on the national level the organization prided itself on its diverse membership, on the local level everyone may not be so accepting.

Crossing her fingers under the table Kiara answered, "Not really."

"Good to know. The process of becoming a member of Kappa Alpha Rho Sorority, Incorporated is very time intensive and often results in less time on social activities. If you are selected for membership, the learning process requires your full attention. Oftentimes those not connected with the organization have a difficult time understanding," Ruth said smoothly.

"I understand," Kiara said.

Veronica and Ruth asked additional questions. Kiara shared what social issues she felt the organization should address through their community service projects and her career plans after college. The two also confirmed they had researched her. Veronica complimented her for winning the conference 800 meter title last year and expressed appreciation for volunteering at the hug-in to raise money for Blueburg's chapter of the American Heart Association. The runner, who lost her father three years ago to a heart attack, smiled at the members' praise. After giving Kiara a chance to ask questions, they dismissed her and advised if there were any additional information needed they would be in touch.

Kiara's nervousness about the interview prevented her from eating her usual four small meals. Instead, only a cup of coffee and a pack of crackers had touched her lips during the previous twelve hours. Now, her stomach signaled it was chow time. Pondering her dining options, Kiara saw the smoking sophomore from the lobby coming out the small study room to her left.

"Hey Donna, how did it go?" Kiara asked.

Rolling her eyes, Donna pulled a Dalmatian patterned scarf out of her black pea coat pocket. "I have had better Pap smear exams. I had three Rho's doing my interview. Cassandra, my freshman RA who wrote me up for breaking curfew. Cynthia, the Rho who wears what looks like every piece of makeup she owns every day to class, and some haint whose face was so twisted up I figured her drawers were cutting her in two. But like the Bible says, if someone doesn't make you feel welcome or pay attention to the words you are saying, you need to shake the dust off your feet and keep it moving."

Kiara was no Biblical scholar, but her recollection of that Bible passage differed from Donna's delivery. The two walked down the steps in silence and Kiara prepared to let this frustrated girl go her separate way. Something, however, in the back of her mind prompted her to reach out.

"Listen, you want to walk with me downtown to get a sub? I didn't get a chance to get dinner and I don't want to walk by myself. I would drive but I let my roommate borrow my car to go to work."

"Sure. Better yet, I will call my boyfriend so he can pick us up and give us a ride," Donna said, looking pleasantly surprised at Kiara's suggestion.

"Where does he live? I don't want him to make a trip just because I'm hungry."

"Peter doesn't mind coming from Martin. He will do anything for me. I mean, since the season is over coach doesn't have them under a curfew," Donna said walking toward the bank of six campus phones located in the student center lobby.

"He stays in the football dorm? Your boyfriend isn't Peter Darden, the center that people are talking about going pro?"

"The one and the same. We have been together since last year. I tutored him in English and we have been kicking it ever since," Donna said, picking up the phone and dialing his number. Kiara watched Donna's face change from expectation to resignation when the phone rang without an answer.

"I guess Peter must have run to get him something to eat or his roommate is on the phone. He never clicks over," Donna said hurriedly. "I will be glad to walk with you downtown."

"Kiara, Donna, wait up please," Gloria said, racing down the steps at such a pace that Donna and Kiara rushed to break her fall.

"So I guess your interview went well?" Kiara asked, smiling back at Gloria who looked joyous.

"Truly. Gwen Brantley, the chapter vice president, Keisha, who is in my Spanish class and Cassie Addams, a member of Tau Omicron Kappa, their local graduate chapter, did my interview. You know, it really wasn't that much of an interview. They asked some questions, I gave some answers and then we chatted."

"Lucky you having Gwen do your interview. She stayed on my hall last year. She is one of the few K-Rhos on the yard I think is alright. We were going to walk down to Famous Subs, do you want to go?" Donna asked.

"I'm all for exercise but I can drive us. My car is a little junky, but if you don't mind I don't," Gloria said.

Donna and Kiara surveyed the overflow of books, jackets and something resembling a plant occupying the passenger and back seats of the blue Toyota. They exchanged glances confirming their opinion about Gloria's definition of a little junky. Still, a free ride was a free ride.

"Damn girl, are you trying to blow out my ear drums?" Donna said responding to the syncopated rhythm of drums and cowbells of go-go blasting from the speaker behind her head. She shared the back seat with Gloria's leather knapsack.

Backing out of the parking spot Gloria said, "Apologies, I like to crank my music up and I was in a Chuck Brown frame of mind today."

"What is this we are listening to?" Kiara asked. Her shoulder and neck swayed to the rhythm of song. While she really couldn't make out the lyrics, the groove had her going.

"That my friend is the soundtrack of my youth, go-go. I spent most of my youth in D.C., and go-go is the district's unofficial theme music. Not too many people down here are into it," Gloria responded. "You remember the song "Da Butt" that was popular three years ago? Well the group who did that was E.U. and they are one of the biggest go-go bands there are."

The drive to the sub shop only took a few minutes but Kiara and Donna learned much more about Gloria than they requested.

"I was born in Baltimore, Charm City as we call it. My mom got a job during the last half of my junior year as one of the state's assistant attorney generals so she moved to Raleigh. I decided to go to school down here so I wouldn't have to drive so far when I need to go home to do my laundry or borrow money," Gloria said with rapid-fire delivery.

"I wanted to go to Howard or FAMU but I figured CRU would do, especially after I was awarded the P.A. Neal Scholarship. It covers my tuition and room and board until I graduate. Well, that's not the only reason I'm at CRU. I'm a big fan of Dr. Joffey who teaches in the Poli Sci Department. Did you know he used to work for the UN? I had a class with him last year and he is sooo brilliant."

Waiting for their sandwiches, the three discussed more about their backgrounds. Donna and Kiara grew up less than ninety minutes apart; Kiara in Wilmington, NC and Donna in Kenansville, NC.

"So Kiara, what do you want to do when you grow up?" Gloria asked, motioning the sub worker to add more black olives to her sub.

"Be employed," Kiara chuckled. "No, I'm trying to decide if I want to go to graduate school and become a therapist or work in some corporate human resources department."

"My goal is to get a job with the State Department after graduation. I had considered working stateside, but I would love to see the world and I figured if I can get the United States government to pay for it, even better," Gloria said. "Last summer, I spent three weeks in Haiti doing relief work with my church, Saint Joseph, and I grew so much. Did you know Haiti is the world's oldest black republic and it was the first independent nation in Latin America? You really should read *Tell My Horse* by Zora Neale Hurston. She went to Haiti and investigated the whole voodoo and political culture back in the 1930s. It is remarkable that what she wrote about in terms of their political process still applies today. I wrote a paper last semester and used her book as one of my sources and just blew my professor away by how a book written by an anthropologist/folklorist/fiction writer over sixty years ago is still relevant."

"Are you always such a know it all? If that is the case, I

may need you to become my roommate and help me with some of my courses," Donna said, monitoring her sandwich's construction. "I have this girl whose major seemed to be fucking fraternity members. Last semester, she screwed three Sigma Chi members. Now she is spending her days and nights at the Tau Kappa Epsilon house on East Tenth. Like my cousin Cheryl would say, girl is just giving out the goodness out of both draw legs."

"So Ms. Psych Major, what do you make of that kind of behavior?" Gloria asked, sitting on a yellow plastic chair waiting for the other girls to get their sandwiches.

"Well, I could say she has some daddy issues she is trying to resolve by seeking out inappropriate male attention. Or she could have low self esteem and is seeking to bolster it by engaging in a behavior that traditionally indicates a woman's worth, which is the ability to attract a mate," Kiara said, paying the worker for her turkey and Swiss. "Or girl just likes screwing."

Donna nodded her head and said, "I will take door number three for the win. I mean my roommate is good people. Don't get me wrong, I like having the room to myself most nights since she is out gallivanting, but I just hope she doesn't get hurt or get caught out there."

Getting into Gloria's car, Kiara replied, "Sounds nothing like my roommate. Ms. Freshman seems surgically attached to our room. She may venture down the hall to visit one of her high school friends, but other than that, she is either sitting in her bed eating cereal, in class or at work at Round-Up Ranch."

"She works at Round-Up Ranch? Man I love their fried chicken. It's not as good as my momma's, but it will do in a pinch," Donna said, licking her lips.

"It was cute the first two weeks she got the job when she would bring food home, but now both of us are so over their food she doesn't even bother to bring leftovers."

"Wow, I guess I'm lucky to have a room to myself. I got a private as part of my scholarship package," Gloria said. "It's great because I had a chance to put up a book case for all my books and my aquarium."

"You have fish in your room? The only fish that graces my room is usually fried with some tarter sauce and fries on the side," Donna said.

"Well just know, when you come to my dorm room, my tank is a no fry zone."

"Thank you for the ride, Gloria. It was good meeting you and Donna tonight," Kiara said when Gloria pulled in front of her dorm. The ten-story building sat on the east section of the sprawling campus set on the outskirts of North Carolina's tenth largest city. Donna and Gloria's dorm occupied the middle section of the university.

"Don't mention it. I had fun getting to know Donna and you tonight. I haven't had a chance to hang out with many black girls since I enrolled here. Tonight was cool," Gloria said. Donna looked at her with a somewhat bemused look on her face.

"Glad we could provide you with a cultural excursion. Now if you wouldn't mind, I would like to get to my room to catch the rest of *MacGyver*," Donna said.

"Oh, you're into *MacGyver*? I'm more of a *Murphy Brown* fan. Did you see the episode last week?" Gloria asked.

"Can't say I did," Donna said dryly.

"Oh well, I guess I will tell you about it on the drive," Gloria said.

Watching Gloria drive away, Kiara reflected on the connection she made with the Donna and Gloria. First impressions were often lasting impressions. Those two had certainly made an impression on her. The question was, she thought, 'did they make a lasting impression with the Kappa Alpha Rho sisters?'

CHAPTER TWO

Donna

FOR TWO WEEKS Kiara, Donna and Gloria haunted their mailboxes and hounded their roommates to take very detailed messages in case someone called when they were out. Finally, at 4:59 p.m. on the final Friday in February the call came.

"Donna Edwards?"

"Yes."

"The ladies of the Lambda Mu Chapter of Kappa Alpha Rho Sorority, Incorporated would like for you to be in the lobby of your dorm within the next hour," the voice on the line requested. "Your attire should be all black with no jewelry. A representative of our organization will arrive to transport you to a location where you will have the opportunity to continue to show your interest in our organization. Failure to be at the specified location within the stated period indicates a withdrawal of your interest in Kappa Alpha Rho Sorority. Do you understand?"

In a voice she hoped conveyed her appreciation of the gravity of the situation, Donna confirmed she knew what to do. Changing into one of the five black dresses she had in her closet, Donna headed downstairs to meet her destiny.

After the disaster of the interview, Donna felt she had no chance of becoming a swan. Still, she felt an attraction to the organization and the projects it sponsored. Her exposure to the group stemmed from her fifth-grade teacher who was a Kappa Alpha Rho sorority member. The plump plum colored woman had realized behind the exterior of a little girl with a quick temper was a shorter than average student searching for a way to stand out. Donna's teacher had often convinced the principal not to call Donna's parents in exchange for extra homework assignments, completed by Donna. Knowledge gained from the extra work earned her the rank of third in her graduating class and a series of scholarships. Donna knew her academic accomplishments weren't widely known on campus. She carried a 3.5 grade point average and spoke three languages. Instead, her tendencies to cause a scene concerning her boyfriend's alleged infidelities appeared to be her claim to fame. She knew her behavior didn't seem to fit the image of a graceful K-Rho woman. In fact, she knew the major reason she received an invitation was Dr. Vestina Samuels, the chapter's advisor. Dr. Samuels was her academic advisor and her favorite professor. Backed by Dr. Samuels' encouragement and her passing friendship with the chapter's vice-president, Donna completed the minimum of three Kappa Alpha Rho community service projects required for consideration of membership. On paper, she presented as the perfect candidate. Still, some people skipped reading a quality book because of the cover.

Reaching the lobby, Donna realized her freshman RA, Cassandra, was her designated sorority sister. Muttering "fuck" under her breath, she followed the black wearing sorority member to her car. After getting in, the two drove to Fairlane Farms Apartments to pick up another member of the organization. The three rode in silence until they reached the back parking lot of the Jenkins Fine Arts Center.

Watching the sorority members get out the car, Donna's mind raced about what was going to happen next. 'I hope for their sake they're not planning any sneaky shit or else I'll bust both of them up or go down trying,' she thought.

Cassandra opened her door and gestured for her to step out. Wind wiping through her hair, Donna waited, slightly nervous.

"Donna Eugenia Edwards, you are embarking on a journey toward life-long sisterhood," the winter white clad Kappa Alpha Rho member began, her New Jersey accent adding weight to her words. "Should you succeed, you will be welcomed with open arms and embraced by the thousands of sisters who make up Kappa Alpha Rho Sorority, Incorporated. The first steps on your path will be in darkness so you will begin to learn that in order to excel you need to rely on your sisters to guide your steps," Cassandra said, pulling out a purple, cotton scarf out of her large sorority bag.

Now blindfolded, Donna felt herself placed back into the car, only this time in the back seat. After getting over the weird feeling of traveling without seeing where she was going, Donna willed her ears to determine their destination. She could tell they were leaving the city because she heard fewer cars and felt the car pick up speed. After what seemed like hours, the car stopped. Sniffing the air, Donna registered the smells of smoke from fireplaces and wood burning stoves. Hearing her door open, the weight of the cold winter settled on her face.

Despite not knowing where she was going, Donna managed to move forward and climb four steps, guided by Cassandra and the other Kappa Alpha Rho member. Soon a feeling of heat washed over her. Feeling her blindfold removed, Donna's eyes adjusted quickly to a room lit by candles. Darting her eyes around, she realized she stood in a line with one person to her right and Kiara to her left. Gloria stood to Kiara's left along with three other girls. A little relieved at familiar faces, Donna noted Gwen with six women clad in deep purple robes standing behind a table. Donna thought, 'they look like the soprano section of my church choir.'

Gwen's mouth formed a quick smile when she met Donna's eyes. "My sisters of Kappa Alpha Rho Sorority, Incorporated, I present to you seven ladies who come with aspirations of achieving the levels of inspiration, dedication and reputation that makes Kappa Alpha Rho swans rise above the rest," Gwen said. She stood at the center of the table in between Ruth and Veronica.

"They have submitted written petitions, conquered oral interrogations, and traveled by faith, not by sight. My sisters, I stand before you in their stead, requesting permission for them to continue their journey. What say you?"

"Sisters of Kappa Alpha Rho Sorority, Incorporated, I offer acceptance of these seven and assistance while they travel their path," Ruth said in a low voice. "From this point on, you will shed the names of your mothers and fathers and assume the names chosen by your sisters. As I call your name, you will be inducted into the next step of the Kappa Alpha Rho Sorority, Incorporated selection process."

Seven Kappa Alpha Rho sisters who had been standing in the back of the room moved forward and stood in front of each girl. Ruth called each girl's birth name then followed with an assigned sorority name. One by one, the Kappa Alpha Rho sister pinned a purple ceramic 'C' on each applicant's chest. Maybe it was Donna's imagination; Cassandra seemed to prick her on purpose.

"The 'C,' which must always be worn on your left side, stands for cygnet or baby swan, which is how you will be known during this stage of the process," Gwen said. "The pin should be on your person at all times. My role is to oversee your process and sorority development. When you address me, it will be as Gracious Guide Brantley. During this process, I will convey my instructions and requests primarily to Gaia. She is the cygnet selected to occupy the first spot among you and will be your voice. When there is a request of your group, unless specified, she will answer and be responsible for your actions. You are now all each other have, so you must learn to trust and rely on each other. You must learn how to be sisters or else you will fail."

Gwen began listing the requirements of this stage of membership, which included a dress code. Monday, Wednesday, and Friday the attire would be a white button up shirt and black pants. Tuesday and Thursday, a white pullover shirt or sweater and black skirt. With the exception of work settings, classroom time, or family obligations, the seven were to limit their communication to their fellow cygnets and members of the organization.

"Whenever you greet a lady of Kappa Alpha Rho Sorority, Incorporated you are to address her as Big Sister followed by her sorority name or last name, depending on the situation," Gwen said. "Our sisters, our teachers, our family, and our friends address us by our given names. Since neither of you fit in either of those categories, a more formal address is required. The line starts with 1,000 points, each infraction incurred by a member results in a subtraction of a hundred points. An infraction could be something as simple as not knowing an answer when a sister asks you a question, not responding to a task requested in a required time, or simply because I felt like it," she said, smirking in a way Donna wasn't sure was mocking or menacing.

Along with knowing how to respond to the sorority members, the group would have educational sessions with Gwen and other members of the sorority up to four times a week to learn and confirm their knowledge of Kappa Alpha Rho Sorority, Incorporated information and protocols. Their first session would be at Gwen's house tomorrow night at 9:59 p.m.

"I would suggest you get together before tomorrow night so you can get to know each other better," Gwen said. "Your fellow cygnets can be your best asset. They will be the ones to support and strengthen you. The sooner you begin bonding, the better it can be."

Taking the hint, the group planned to meet at Gaia's house at noon. Kim Willis quickly provided everyone her address and promised to provide food and beverages. Donna volunteered to drive Kiara and Gloria. She thought to herself, 'I could probably fit half the girls in my Lincoln, but I don't know these heifers like that.'

The next day driving across Blueburg, Gloria struck up a conversation while Kiara looked at the scenery from the backseat window.

"I must say this is a rather large car for a sophomore to have," Gloria said looking around the interior of the 1987 black sedan Donna drove with practiced ease.

"Yeah, most people get a nice sporty car for their first vehicle, but me, I had to get one of the former fleet cars from my family's funeral home business. Man, you would not believe how much money I make from people on campus who need a ride to and from the store. I can get about three freshmen and their groceries in this. Five dollars a person three times a week adds up," Donna said gliding through a yellow light.

"I totally understand. My daddy owns a Cadillac dealership in Detroit, but my parents insisted I work and buy my own car. I spent three summers working as a Spanish translator for one of my mom's friend's law firms to earn enough to get Hilda the Honda, but it was well worth it," Gloria said. "How about you Kiara? Do you have a car on campus?"

"Yes," she answered simply. "It's a hand me down from my brother. He graduated two years ago from Shaw, so he gave it to me as a high school graduation present."

"Neat," Gloria said before pausing for a breath. "You know I just can't get over how interesting this situation with the three of us has already been. We meet each other at the interest meeting, have a conversation, hang out afterwards, then bam, not only do we get picked to go through the process, we ended up being lined up next to each other. It's as if the universe is saying this was the right way to go," Gloria said. "I mean, the girls with the twenty pearls had been at me and my mom is Zeta, but there's something about Kappa that speaks to me like Lionel Richie: 'Hello, is it me you're looking for?'"

Looking sideways with amusement at Gloria, Donna replied, "Yeah I guess. I hadn't thought about us meeting then ending up next to each other. That is some kind of coincidence."

"Truly. I mean, I felt a connection to the two of you from the moment I sat down, but I didn't want to say anything. I'm a big believer in signs and oracles, and this whole situation means nothing but good things for us and this process."

Pulling up to Gwen's apartment, Donna said, "From your

lips to God's ear. C'mon, let's get this show on the road. I have a report due Monday I'm trying to finish."

"What's it on?" Kiara asked walking to the door.

"Tracking the use of social services by migrant populations in Southeastern North Carolina for my Social Work Practices With Special Populations class; it's supposed to be twenty pages and I have seven more to go."

"Wow, sounds deep," Kiara said.

Donna responded, "It's not that bad. My Aunt Lizzie Mae works for the Brunswick County DSS, so I'm getting most of the figures from her. The hard part is making it flow, but I will make it through."

With the exception of Michelle Goodman, the #7 of the group and the current Miss Copper Road University, most of the girls selected for the process only knew each other by face or reputation. Digging into the snacks Kim provided, the girls discussed what seemed to be the most pressing issue from last night.

"What is up with these funky names?" Kiara asked sitting on the sage carpeted floor of the apartment. All of the girls except Gloria received Greek goddess names.

"I happen to like my name and I think your name is cool Kiara. I think naming you Iris after the messenger of the gods makes sense since you own the 400 and 800 meter on the track team," Kim said, sipping a ginger ale.

Grabbing a handful of chips from the bag on the coffee table, Gloria pouted, "Well at least when you look back, you will have had a dope name. Why I got to be just a mere wood nymph?"

"You have to admit, naming you Echo after someone who loved the sound of her own voice is cute. You do seem to talk a lot," Donna said, smiling at Gloria who stuck out her tongue and smiled back. "But check it, I get Karen's name of Artemis because she has a twin brother. Since Michelle is Miss CRU, I get the Aphrodite reference, and Kim's makes sense because she has a child. Why in the hell would you give me the name of a woman who tears up shit because her husband Zeus is always fucking around? Now she is the big man's wife, but still."

Her line sisters' faces reflected the answer.

"Now, Hera, all those times Public Safety had to break up fights after you had jumped on a girl for looking at Peter, please," Andrea Morrow said with a holier-than-thou attitude from her perch on the futon by the door.

"Well, if you had a boyfriend, you would understand wanting to fight for your man, Athena," Donna said using Andrea's assigned line name as she jerked her head around to face her.

Sneering at Donna, Andrea said, "James and I never had a type of relationship where I felt the need to fight for him. There is no man alive that would make me risk getting hurt in some kind of brawl. That is so common."

"Bitch, who are you calling common? I don't give a damn if you are my line sister, I will kick your motherfucking ass," Donna said, jumping up and crossing the room to confront Andrea, who stood up in alarm. Gloria and Kiara responded with alarmed eyes. Kiara thought to herself, 'dang, for a short girl with some weight on her, she moves fast.'

"Hey, hey. Y'all settle down now before somebody gets hurt," Kim said while Donna and Andrea stood eye to breastbone. "We have only been on line for two days and you are already at each other's throats. We are in this thing together, so we need to learn how to stick together and check our tempers."

"I'm sorry, Kim, no disrespect," Donna mumbled. Sitting down, she noticed only Gloria and Kiara made eye contact with her.

Donna's outburst put a damper on the getting-to-know-each-other session. Feeling the purpose of the meet up had been achieved, the girls decided to head their separate ways until their first education session at Gwen's that night.

Helping Kim clean up, Donna offered her apologies again. "My parents did not raise me to show my ass in someone else's house, but something about that girl just rubs me the wrong way."

"Don't worry about it. I knew going in there was bound to

be some tension," Kim said gathering the plates and bowls. "After all, most of us didn't know each other by name prior to last night and now we are expected to become sisters in a few short weeks."

Sitting on the taupe sofa Gloria asked, "Donna, I know we just met and everything, but are you always so quick to fly off the handle? I mean, Andrea was throwing shade like *Paris is Burning,* but did you have to go all Mike Tyson on the girl?"

Flushing with embarrassment Donna said, "I will admit I do overreact sometimes, but I do make an effort not to act a fool anytime something bothers me. I just have a low tolerance for bullshit or uppity acting people."

"I feel you on that, my sister. I wasn't going to say anything, but Ms. Lady did seem to be setting herself off like she was too good to mingle with the likes of us," Gloria said. "Coming in here carrying that fake Dooney and Bourke bag. She needs to quit it. The duck wasn't even facing the right direction. If you are going to be a knock off queen, make sure your emblem is directionally correct."

Kiara was the first to catch the joke, followed Kim, and Donna who joined in the trio's laughter about the pretentious #5 in the group.

"See, you are laughing, that is a good thing. A laughing #2 is a happy #2 and that makes this #4 pleased," Gloria continued. "No disrespect to Kim, but you, Kiara and I are the only sophomores on this line. I want us all to make it to the next level. I don't want to lose you for cold cocking somebody. Therefore, my mission impossible, like Peter Graves, and I choose to accept, is to keep you from going shell. I have seen a pissed off Donna and a calm Donna, and I very much like the calm one."

"I appreciate the thought," Donna said grabbing car keys out of her purse. "Contrary to what some people may think, I'm the sweetest person you ever want to meet, but my momma and daddy didn't raise a push over. Like the Bible says, judge not lest you be judged or don't start none won't be none. If I kicked a bitch's ass in Sunday School for trying to steal my solo in the church choir, then I won't hesitate to check someone for getting above herself when it comes to my affairs."

"How do you mix religion and fighting in the same sentence?" Gloria asked.

"Try growing up with a mom who reads the Bible for fun and is the head deaconess at Calvary Rock Baptist and a daddy who is a Marine and see how you turn out," Donna said. "Speaking of which, I got to usher tomorrow at church so I hope we aren't out that late."

"Truly, I have early morning Mass so I hope tonight is short and sweet," Gloria said. "Kiara, do you follow a particular religious path?"

"I'm more of a bedside Baptist. I try to make it to a service every now and again," she said. "My mother is one of the trustees at home, so when I'm under her roof I have no say about how I spend my Sunday mornings. So whenever I get the chance to be a bit rebellious I take it."

"Well if you are ever in need of a church home, my church here, Martin Street Missionary, Pastor Walter T. Gossett presiding, would love to have you. But enough about saving souls, I'm trying to get me something to eat. I appreciate the snacks you provided Kim, but if I'm going to have to deal with Andrea again tonight, I'm going to need something in my stomach to hold me."

CHAPTER THREE
Gloria

ARRIVING AT GWEN'S that night, Donna, Kiara, and Gloria received individual packets. Ruth directed them to find a seat around one of two purple covered card tables positioned in the center of a purple and platinum themed living room. Gloria noted, it seemed half of the chapter's twenty members were there staring at the group with blank expressions.

"Greetings. What you have in your hands is an agreement between Kappa Alpha Rho Sorority, Incorporated and each of you. It outlines the requirements which must be completed during this stage of your process," Gwen said at exactly one minute to 10:00 p.m. Gloria confirmed the time by discretely checking her digital watch. "Please make sure you read through it and understand what you are signing. If you have questions or concerns, speak up. Once your signature is on the dotted line, the terms are binding."

While the others quickly signed, dated and handed the forms back, Donna, on the other hand, raised three questions per page. By the ninth question, a sense of frustration floated among the sisters and cygnets.

"No disrespect, but I'm not signing my name on anything I haven't read and understood completely. Y'all may just sign your asses away on a humble, but I'm not the one," she said.

"Hera, please curb your tongue. We are not in an alley

shooting craps. We are about the business of Kappa and that requires some decorum," Cassandra said sharply.

In a syrupy sweet voice Donna replied, "My apologies, Big Sister Williams. Your sister, our gracious guide, said if we have questions or concerns, speak up. I'm just doing what my gracious guide asked me to do. You wouldn't want me not to do what our gracious guide asked, now would you?"

Something about the way Donna appeared to mock Cassandra amused Gloria. While she usually cut people down with her words, Gloria liked the way Donna handled herself.

"Soror, I would appreciate if you let me be the gracious guide and address anything out of order the cygnets do," Gwen said with a slightly perturbed look on her face. "Hera, please govern the way you talk while we are in sessions."

Gloria noticed Cassandra expected more of a reaction from Gwen, and not getting one glared at the line of girls. Once the girls completed the paperwork, Gwen told them to exit the room and re-enter five minutes later in numerical order.

"Tonight cygnets, we are going to cover how you greet your Big Sisters," Gwen started while Ruth handed each girl a purple notebook and two pens. "Greeting some of my sisters requires a little bit more than just saying their names. For instance, Poetic License requires each person greeting her to recite a line of poetry after you greet her," Gwen said, gesturing toward Cassandra. "It could be Shakespeare, the Song of Solomon, or Sonia Sanchez."

Wearing a confused look, Gloria raised her hand. "Gracious Guide Brantley, if we are to recite a line of poetry when we greet Big Sister Poetic License and there are seven of us, doesn't that mean she is going to be hearing seven lines of poetry all at the same time?"

Cassandra clarified in the cases when the group of girls addressed her, they would say "Greetings Big Sister Poetic License" in unison, then one by one recite a line of poetry. When individual potentials greeted her, they would say her name then the line of poetry.

"Thank you Big Sister Poetic License. *I was born in the Congo and I built the Sphinx,*" Gloria said.

"Aw snap, how you know "Ego Tripping" is my favorite poem?" Cassandra asked beaming broadly. "The line gets fifty points. Since my sister told you my line name, it is only right I share hers. Your gracious guide is known as Big Sister I.L.T.S, otherwise known as I Love To Singa."

Unable to contain her outburst Gloria blurted, "Like the Cab Calloway song from the cartoon?"

"Oh, #4, you know you are not supposed to speak unless a sister asks you to. Now I have to subtract the points you just got," Cassandra tsk, tsked.

"Don't worry, I'm giving the line one hundred points for knowing where my name came from," Gwen said. "I'm a vocal performance major and my glorious guide Big Sister RhoMantic loves cartoons. Just like Poetic License, my greeting requires a little extra. The line says, "Greetings Big Sister I.L.T.S. Then #3 sings the first three lines of the song from the cartoon. Soror Infinite Grace, would you be so kind to demonstrate?"

Slowly rising from the couch, Ruth repeated the initial greeting, then in a crisp soprano voice belted in operatic fashion, "I love to sing-a, about the moon-a and the June-a and the spring-a, I love to sing-a."

"You know #3, you may have wanted to write the lyrics down so you will know the next time. But then again, maybe you really don't want to be my sister," Gwen said dryly. "Soror, will you just say the words this time so they can get it?"

This time Kiara's pen rushed across the page. Gwen also provided the names of the rest of the sisters of the chapter and the founders of the Lambda Mu Chapter. In total, thirty names, which included references to flowers, cartoon characters, and acts of nature.

Sitting on the empty couch, Gwen crossed her legs and said, "You are expected to have this information memorized by next Friday. In addition, each Tuesday, I will call Gaia with a question that has to be answered at 4:59 p.m. by one of you. The question will relate to our chapter history or one of my sisters. I will tell Gaia whose responsibility it is to answer the question. One of my sisters will have the answer to the question. Your goal is to find the right sister, who I have also called and asked to be your resource. Only one sister will have the correct answer. If that means you have to speak to all twenty of my sisters, so be it. If the answer relates to the chapter, then you have to find me and give me the answer. If it relates to one of my sisters, then you have to find her and give her the answer."

Behind Donna's head, Ruth purred out, "When my sister says 4:59 p.m., she means just that. Not 5:00, not 4:58, but 4:59."

"Number three, what is the significance of 4:59 p.m.?" Cassandra whipped out while standing in front of Kiara.

The answer burned in Gloria's chest like a three-day-old enchilada meal. Since her sophomore year in high school, Gloria had researched, compared, and aspired for membership in Kappa Alpha Rho Sorority, Incorporated. Though her mother became a member of Zeta Phi Beta Sorority, Incorporated while attending law school, her heart beat for the prestigious purple and poised platinum. Any information available for public consumption, she knew. Every opportunity to volunteer for any community service project, she was there. Her attraction to the organization stemmed from their support of causes near to her heart: diabetes awareness, financial literacy and child abuse prevention. They were in the trenches making life better for women and children impacted by society's ills, something Gloria unfortunately knew from life experience.

"Big Sister Poetic License, *spring is like a perhaps hand*, 4:59 p.m. is the time Kappa Alpha Rho Sorority was incorporated on October 16, 1924. The reason for the time is because the original members didn't get to the incorporation office until one minute before they were set to close for the day," Gloria blurted out in spite of herself. "Because of this, all significant Kappa Alpha Rho programs start at one minute to the hour."

"Two things, because that is the right answer, the line gets three hundred points. Second thing, because Echo answered when she wasn't supposed to, the line gets two hundred points taken away. My sister clearly asked Iris for the answer," Gwen said and sighed. "Echo, how do you know that information when your #3, who grew up in the organization, didn't know it?" Gwen challenged.

"I don't know how I know it, I just do," Gloria said, sounding a little squelched. Sometimes her ocean of knowledge was too much of a deluge for people to stand and she realized this was one of those times.

Exasperated, Cassandra stood hands on hip in front of Gloria. "What is wrong with you? Nobody was talking to you, but yet again, you have the right answers. Since you and I share the same number, I'm going to give you a Rho reminder: it's good to be smart and know things, but sometimes the best thing to know is when to keep quiet."

Gloria's first reaction was to correct Cassandra's comment that no one was talking to her by pointing out Gwen had asked her a question. Therefore, Gwen was talking to her. Then Gloria realized one of the first rules of intake: the cygnet is usually never right.

For the rest of the ninety-minute session, Gloria kept her mouth closed. She had met the 18-year-old cut off for consideration for membership by only two weeks. She didn't want to mess it up for herself or the line by having more points subtracted.

"Gloria, did you have to answer every fucking question?" Donna asked, turning on the heat in Kiara's 1987 Ford Escort. The three were heading home after the session ended at one minute till midnight.

"Like the Bible says, my people are destroyed for lack of knowledge, but shouldn't be wise in their own eyes. What I take that to mean is just because you got it don't mean you have to flaunt it."

Dejection seeping through her voice Gloria replied, "I'm

sorry. I just know things and I was trying to be helpful."

"Gloria, don't worry about it," Kiara said, looking up in the rearview mirror. "Nobody's mad at you. I'm sure we all will have a chance to strut our stuff. You were just in the spotlight tonight. Trust me; we will all get our chance."

"Thank you Key. I wasn't trying to be a show-off, but sometimes I have trouble holding back if I know something. My intention was not to step on your toes or get you in trouble," Gloria said smiling at Kiara. Catching the sight in her rearview mirror, Kiara smiled back.

"Well if nothing else came out of tonight, at least you know who your ism is. They can either be your best friend or your worst enemy," Kiara said.

"What in the hell is an ism?" Donna said scrunching her face in confusion.

"An ism is the sorority sister who shares your number," Kiara said. "Cassandra must have been the #4 on her line and Gloria is the #4 for ours."

"That makes sense. I'm glad Cassandra is a four and not a two. If she were mine, I would have a problem because that heifer has no love for me and I damn sure don't have any for her. But hell, it could be worse. I just hope my ism isn't Patricia. You know I heard she is a dyke."

Kiara positioned her mouth to say something about the use of dyke, but Gloria responded first. "Donna, you should be ashamed of yourself for using such a derogatory word for a woman who happened to have found love with another woman. It is rude and mean spirited. We African American women have a tendency to slur each other with harsh terms because someone isn't like us. Trust me, after all the stuff I have been through in my short life, Oreo doesn't have a place on my menu. If someone learns, likes, or loves differently, we should respect them. If she does do girls, then call her a lesbian. Dykes keep waters from flooding the Netherlands and Patricia looks far from being Dutch to me."

"My apologies, I heard Patricia is a lesbian." Donna drew

out the word. "Supposedly, her roommate caught her and Gabrielle from the tennis team going at it last semester. Word along the grapevine was Patricia's ass was in the air when the girl walked into the room. I heard it shot her nerves so bad, her roommate couldn't come back this year."

Kiara interjected, "Girl, I heard that same story, so I went right to the source to get the details. Said roommate was Claudine who used to date Tony who went to high school with me. He told me Claudine got her walking papers because of cheating. Patricia turned her in after she stole one of her papers. Claudine spread that rumor about Patricia being a lesbian out of spite. Patricia is happily dating a Sigma who goes to Winston Salem State. He was all she could talk about when we volunteered together for the Kappa's Hug-A-Thon last year."

"Hey, all this rumor busting has made me hungry. Do you want to come up to my room and order a pizza? I know this guy who works at Naples who will give us a discount," Gloria said once Kiara pulled in front of her dorm.

Never ones to turn down free food, Donna and Kiara agreed. Entering Gloria's room, Donna and Kiara's eyes didn't know what to look at first.

True to Gloria's description, a twelve-foot aquarium filled with a rainbow fleet of fish occupied the back wall. Prints of works by Frieda Kahlo, Van Gough, and Cynthia St. James decorated the walls. Books occupied a metal bookcase while a plush multi-colored rug embraced their stocking feet. Gloria had motioned them to remove their shoes and stacked them on a wooden rack beside the closet door. Instead of the standard dorm bed, Gloria had a full metal frame bed covered with a green and gold striped duvet. Kiara and Donna's lust over their line sister's sleeping arrangement competed with their confusion about the piece of art in the back of the room.

"What the hell?" Donna asked walking toward the four-foot high metal sculpture of the female torso. Complete with two perky breasts, rounded belly and upper thighs, the sculpture consisted of spare nuts, washers, and bolts glued together.

"This guy I went to high school with is a visual artist and gave it to me for graduation. He called it "Totally Screwed," Gloria said, chuckling at the look on their faces.

"Wow, very eclectic," Donna said, sitting down on a blue leather footstool.

"I know, but you never know. That piece may be worth something down the line when Anderson becomes famous. That bucket of bolts may end up being the way I pay for my retirement."

"Wow, nothing like thinking ahead," Donna said, opening the bottle of apple juice Gloria handed her. "Here I am worried about next semester's tuition and you thinking about stocks and bonds and shit."

While Gloria and Donna chatted, Kiara perused some of the titles on the bookshelf. The offerings were diverse and grouped according to theme. There was the international section with Gabriel Garcia Marquez, Chinua Achebe, and Pablo Coelho. The Harlem Renaissance section with Dorothy West, Wallace Thurman, and Zora Neale Hurston intermingled with a womanist section with bell hooks, Angela Davis, Audre Lorde, and Barbara Smith. She even had a religious section with *Siddhartha* sandwiched in between the *Catholic Bible* and *Tao of Pooh*. What caught Kiara's eye and heart was the supernatural section. Gloria had the complete works of Octavia Butler, Anne Rice and Edgar Allan Poe.

"Nice to meet a fellow avid reader," Kiara said. "I'm a big fan of James Baldwin, Alice Walker, and Toni Morrison, but I see some things I may like to borrow, like one of the Anne Rice books."

"Anytime you want to borrow a book, just let me know. I'm really into the whole vampire literature thing. I started with the classic Bram Stroker's *Dracula* then moved on to other works like *I am Legend, The Lair of the White Worm*, and *Salem's Lot*. In fact, I read somewhere that vampire literature is so popular because it allows the writer to write about sexual themes in an undercover way. When you think about it, the whole notion of a vampire, being suave and charming who wants to get you on your back and have his way with you, is similar to the process of getting freaky-deaky with someone."

"You really have a unique way of looking at things," Kiara said.

"Yeah, I get that a lot. I just have a different way of looking at things. I got it from my mom. She was always encouraging me to try different things and if I didn't like it, I didn't have to keep doing it," Gloria said shrugging her shoulders. "What do you guys want on your pizza?"

Kiara voted for sausage and extra cheese. Gloria, who had given up meat for Lent, voted for green peppers and mushrooms, while Donna wanted black olives and ham. They decided on a large with black olives on one side and sausage on the other.

"So Kiara, are you living the single girl's life or you got some man missing you?" Gloria asked after she called in their order.

"No, there is no man counting down the days, hours, minutes, and seconds until I'm free," she said, feeling a tug of guilt about lying about her love life.

"Good to know I'm not the only single lady. I dated a guy who lived in Cameron Hall, but it didn't work out. I think the fact I was black and he was Chinese was too hard for him. Que sera, sera."

"You dated an Asian guy? Wow, you really do have diverse interest. So is it true what they say?" Donna said.

Smiling, Gloria replied, "Unfortunately not, I ended up tutoring him in math. As far as his ancient Chinese secret goes, he could have kept it to himself. Still he was sweet and I enjoyed spending time with him. But the stares we got when we went places and the comments we heard from both sides just got to him."

"Being in a relationship can be a pain in the ass sometimes. I love Peter but sometimes he irritates the flying fuck out of me. Still, my mom always told me, only one man was ever born perfect. He is currently sitting on the right hand of the Father and he is known as the Lamb of Judah, not Peter Avalon Darden. So, I take Peter for what he is, a man."

"I'm happy for Peter and you, but I'm somewhat glad to be single this time in my life. Even though I got the P.A. Neal Scholarship, I have to keep my grades up to keep it. A boyfriend or girlfriend can be such a distraction," Gloria said, her eyes briefly meeting Kiara's. "I mean the classes I took at Enloe were tough, but this is next level stuff. I thought having Mrs. Gill for trig was hard."

"True, and did you hear how much we have to learn by next week? Man, if I knew it was going to be like this, I may have waited," Kiara said, seizing the opportunity to talk about something other than relationships. "Some of the stuff I know already because of my mom and my aunt are K-Rhos. Still, along with schoolwork and track practice, it seems like a lot to absorb. Which reminds me, how exactly did you know about 4:59 p.m.?"

Before she could respond, the phone buzzed letting Gloria know she had a visitor downstairs. Slipping on a pair of furry slippers Gloria simply said, "A lady never reveals her secrets so soon in the process. But I will say, an unasked question never gets answered."

"I will have to remember that," Donna said.

Hitting the stereo on her way out the door, Gloria left them with the sounds of Billie Holliday requesting a pig's foot and a bottle of beer.

"Wow, your #4 is into a lot of stuff. Dating Asian men, jazz music, and whatever you call that thing in the corner. But, she seems like good people. She may be heavy handed with the movie and song references but at least she has good conversation," Donna said inspecting the pictures of Gloria sitting on her bedside table. One that caught her eye featured Gloria in what looked like a wedding dress with a veil attached to a wreath of flowers. Her line sister looked to be around six or seven and clutched a white Bible. Donna read the writing on the bottom of the frame, *Gloria's First Communion*. Even then, Gloria had a wide-eyed smile, which to

Donna, drew you in and put you at ease.

"And, did you hear how she just turned eighteen on the tenth of this month and is already a sophomore? I turn nineteen next month and your birthday is when, October? How old will you be?"

"I will be twenty since I missed a year in school because I was born after the October cutoff date to attend kindergarten," Kiara said feeling old.

"This girl just now is able to vote and she dropping knowledge and using SAT words like it's nothing special. Like my cousin Ricky from Waycross says, she is just an 'iologist. You know, someone that knows something about everything. Geologist, sociologist, psychologist. I certainly hope this process isn't too much for her," Donna said reclining in the desk chair while Kiara sank down into a purple beanbag.

"If she went to the trouble of finding out such a random fact like 4:59 p.m., she is going to be in it to win it. Even I had to think about the answer," Kiara said.

Hearing Gloria's footsteps approaching the door, Donna responded, "But you know what they say, book smarts don't always mean you have common sense. Let's hope she is working with a little bit of both."

Gloria, Kiara, and Donna sat eating, talking and laughing close to two in the morning about family, future plans, and favorite things to do. Kiara felt herself loosening up. She didn't feel secure enough to come out with every detail about her life, but the two were growing on her.

"You know I think it is so cool we have an only child, me, the oldest of six, Donna and the middle of three, Kiara," Gloria said sitting crossed legged on the carpet. "Then, you add in the fact I'm an Aquarius. You know we are known to always pursue knowledge, which is me to a tee. Donna, since your birthday is March 23rd, you are an Aries, one of the signs highly compatible with mine. Then you have Kiara born on October 19. They say friendship between Aquarius and Libra is one of the best zodiac pairs. Even the stars agree this is going to be a good thing."

Finishing off the last piece of pizza, Donna replied, "I know, you said it earlier today in the car. I mean, Kiara and you seem like good people, so I guess I will agree things appear to have worked out well."

"Groovy. Listen, since we have a gang load of information to learn, why don't we get together tomorrow to start studying," Gloria said. "I know Donna has her paper to finish so let's say around 5:00 p.m."

Kiara agreed and suggested moving the get-together to 2:00 p.m. That way, she explained, her roommate could fix a box for them and have it ready.

"Wow, free food two nights in a row. This Kappa Alpha Rho thing is going to work out just fine," Donna said, smiling broadly.

CHAPTER FOUR

Kiara/Donna

GLORIA'S PERCEPTION OF the bond between the trio proved correct. Even though one of the goals of the process was to nurture a sense of sisterhood among the seven, Kiara, Gloria and Donna seemed to click more. The sisters didn't require the girls to spend extra time together beyond community service projects and education sessions, but the three choose to eat lunch together, study together and in Donna's case, make love connections.

"You know Key, if you are interested, after this is over I could introduce you to some of Peter's teammates. You know I think you and Scott would make a cute couple. He may be small but his ass looks like something good in those red pants," Donna said. The three had decided to camp out in Donna's room following tonight's educational session. While she cooked pork cutlets for the girl's midnight meal, Kiara and Gloria worked on homework.

"No thanks. I'm not looking to get hooked up with anyone right now. Just want to get through this process and keep my grades up. My mother is fond of saying how she kept a near perfect grade point average all while being active in Kappa Alpha Rho, volunteering in the community, and attending church every Sunday. It's a bitch sometimes being the daughter of Ms. Perfect," Kiara said, a touch of resentment in her voice. "From the time I could remember, my mom has groomed me in her image. She always wanted to take piano lessons when she was little, so of course I had to take piano lessons. She wanted to take ballet lessons when she was little, but there was no one in Lincoln County to teach little black girls. So guess where my tutu-ed ass spent most Saturdays before the age of ten?"

"Well at least you spent the weekends getting some culture. My weekends were spent helping the bereaved. It sucked being the eldest child of the only black funeral home owners in Duplin County. But hell, it provides for me and my brother and sisters."

"I thought you got a full ride to Copper Road?" Gloria asked.

"I did in a way. I got scholarships to cover my tuition and room and board, but as far as the important things, like a meal plan to help me keep this gorgeous figure of mine, my parents are paying for that. But I'm not trying to talk about who is paying for what. I'm trying to get you matched up. I never hear you talk about a boyfriend or anything so I guess you are single. You sure I can't convince you to give him a chance? He's cute and I hear his people make a good living doing whatever they do in Greenville. Not trying to be nosy or anything, but when was your last relationship?"

Realizing she would not be totally lying she answered, "The last time I had a boyfriend was high school. We met in eleventh grade and dated until graduation. He got a scholarship to Tuskegee and I got my track scholarship here. We didn't want to do a long-distance thing so we broke up."

Donna looked incredulous at Kiara. "You mean to tell me the last time you got broke off was two years ago?" she asked.

"I didn't say the last time I got laid was two years ago. I said the last time I had a boyfriend was two years ago," Kiara replied and smiled.

"So maybe the better question would be who was the last person you kicked it with?" Donna asked.

Feeling pressured Kiara murmured, "No one you would know."

Looking up from her textbook Gloria interjected, "Donna,

everyone in the world doesn't want to be hemmed up with a man. Can you put away your matchmaking magic wand for one night?"

"I'm sorry but I just think Kiara is too good of a catch to be single. She got a nice shape on her. She is smart, funny and has a good heart. I'm just surprised she doesn't have dudes banging down her door," Donna said shrugging her shoulders.

"I appreciate you thinking about me but I'm fine," Kiara said, then hoping to steer the conversation away from her brought up Donna's favorite topic. "So have you had a chance to talk to Peter this week?"

Smiling, Donna confirmed she had managed to arrange a secret rendezvous with her boyfriend. Despite the cygnets being forbidden to see significant others, everyone snuck around. It was part of the fun. Even Kiara had managed to steal a few moments with Chris. Since she wasn't ready to share her secret, she just told her sisters she was running extra laps or volunteering at the local mental health center.

During the weeks of their process, Kiara always managed to sidestep the relationship questions when posed by her line sisters. Prior to this process, she and Chris rarely spent time on campus together. The majority of their classes for their respective majors kept them at opposites sides of campus. When the couple socialized, it was with Chris' friends off campus or out of town. Since she had never crossed paths with her line sisters before their induction, she assumed she was safe from suspicion. Still, she wondered if any of the Kappa Alpha Rho sisters knew about Chris. While Copper Road had about five thousand students, someone who stood six-foot tall with flame colored hair and emerald eyes tended to stick out. Each day of her process, Kiara waited for a comment, question or accusation. Six weeks into the process, she received her answer.

"Oh man, I can't believe Gwen set me up like this," Veronica said. She was the answer to the 4:59 p.m. question. "How did you figure out I was the sister known for her butter burgers?"

"Big Sister Saving Grace gave me the answer, Big Sister

Amazing Grace," Kiara responded.

Shaking her head, Veronica smiled, "You managed to track down Symone? Damn, I am giving the line 300 points. My line sister seems to live and breathe in the chemistry building. She rarely comes to sorority functions. I'm not mad with her though. Sister has her eyes set on med school and can't be distracted. For that, my cygnet, you have earned a home cooked meal."

Taken aback by the offer, Kiara mutely followed Veronica to her car. Usually, the sisters did not interact with the potentials beyond sessions or when they encountered them on campus. To have a sister treat her like an individual instead of #3 should have made her suspicious. Instead, Kiara felt relaxed— a welcomed sensation from the stress of the past two months.

Walking up the gravel driveway to her rented home, Veronica said, "Kiara, I'm so glad you decided to go through the process. I know I may not have made the best first impression. I was cramping and the medications weren't working. I will confess, I was afraid you were going to get on line and rest on your laurels since you are a legacy. But from what I see and hear from my sisters and your fellow cygnets, you are the glue keeping things together."

Receiving the praise and checking out Veronica's house, Kiara relaxed even more until Veronica asked. "Did you know Chris and I went to high school together?"

Kiara's mouth felt full of sawdust. Her potential sisters finding out about her relationship with Chris was one of her biggest fears going into the process. Black girls at Copper Road University were supposed to date black boys. Chris was no black boy and Kiara feared that fact would damage her chance of becoming a member. She knew Gloria's dating card concerned some members after she "accidentally" overhead a phone conversation Gwen and Ruth had last week. She had worked so hard to keep their relationship under wraps. She knew Chris had attended Hunter Huss High in Gastonia and Veronica grew up in Bessemer City. Chris never mentioned Veronica, and Kiara damn sure wasn't going to ask Veronica if they knew each other.

Walking into the kitchen Veronica took out a box of frozen lasagna and placed it in the oven. Kiara followed her silently and sat down at the wooden kitchen table. Mentally she berated herself. 'How long did I think I could keep that part of my life hidden?' Kiara imagined all the hard work of going through the process going down the drain, probably along with whatever reputation she had on campus. 'Damn, I knew I should have waited to join the sorority after graduation,' she thought. Her stomach suddenly turned sour.

Veronica poured herself and Kiara glasses of iced tea. "Yep, we were on the debate team. Chris is an excellent speaker who is persuasive enough to talk a nun out her drawers. Took the team to state championship our junior year and we almost won, except an opposing team member coincidentally had written a senior essay on our topic and just killed us. Still, Chris made an impression," Veronica said looking at Kiara who avoided her eyes. "We lost touch once we got here. You could probably guess we don't run in the same circles. I mean, we would wave to each other if we bumped into each other on the yard, but that's it. I didn't make the connection between y'all until about a week ago. Gayle, Chris' ex, is in my Spanish class. She noticed you on campus in your black and white and asked if you were a cygnet. When I didn't answer, she told me all about how Chris and she broke up and how the two of you got together soon thereafter."

Veronica looked silently at Kiara appearing to be waiting for Kiara to speak. Instead, the phone rang.

"Oh hey Mommy, how are you? School is fine. I'm just sitting here talking with one of my girls…Yes, I will be home this weekend for Danny's ceremony…I'm proud of him too…I know, I wish Daddy was here to see him," Veronica paused, her voice catching a little. Kiara saw her big sister's carefree face contort from suppressed grief.

"Yes, Daddy would be proud of him, but you and I both know he is looking down on all of us. Listen Mommy, I will call you back later. I'm making lasagna and I think it's almost ready to come out the oven. Love you."

Hanging up the phone, Kiara could detect tears forming in her big sister's eyes. Grabbing a napkin, Veronica attempted to wipe them away.

"How long has it been since your dad passed?" Kiara asked quietly.

"Three months. Car crash on the way home from a fishing trip," Veronica said. "He and my mom had been saving up to go on this trip to Memphis. He had always worked two jobs to make sure our family had, and he was this close to retiring. Some son of bitch trying to pass a truck hit him dead on."

"My dad died when I was sixteen. He was the football coach at my high school. One day during practice, he had a massive heart attack. All of a sudden, he was gone," Kiara said, eyes welling up. "I had stayed after school to work on a biology project. I planned to catch a ride home with Daddy because my mom had taken my car for some reason or another. She is always on my ass for something. Daddy always had my back when stuff really went down. To him, I was his princess."

Kiara told Veronica at first when she heard her name over the intercom she didn't think much about it. Sometimes her father ended practice early and had the office page Kiara instead of walking the length of the school. Walking into the office and seeing the burly assistant coach's grim face, Kiara realized something was wrong.

"Don't worry Veronica, it's hard losing a parent, but as long as you carry the love you feel for him in your heart, he is never gone. Just focus on the good memories because it helps you deal with him not being here. It doesn't get easier but it does get better," Kiara said, patting Veronica's hand. She meant her words not just for Veronica's ears but for her heart as well. After three years, her heart still hurt from not having her father.

The timer interrupted the tender moment. Smiling and blinking back tears, Veronica fixed their plates and thanked Kiara for her words. Soon laughter and discussion about other students and TV shows passed between the two.

"Kiara, I'm glad I had a chance to get to know you better. Knowing Gayle and how she gets down and now getting to know you, I feel much better about Chris and you dating," Veronica said clearing the table. Kiara looked suspiciously at the smiling big sister. "You don't have to worry about me blabbing about the two of you to my sisters. Your love life is your business. I love my black brothers something fierce, but I don't sweat those who like a different flavor. If the two of you are happy together, then I am happy."

"Thank you Big Sister Amazing Grace. You are officially now my favorite Kappa Alpha Rho swan," Kiara said hugging Veronica. "Well, not considering my mom or my aunts."

"No worries. Anyway, you are a legacy. You can almost shit in front of Elder Swan Samuels and still become a sister," Veronica said smiling. "Speaking of the process, I know Gwen mentioned session is scheduled for 8:59 tonight and it's almost seven. I will take you back to campus so you can meet up with your line sisters."

Walking into the lobby of her dorm, Kiara felt a little bit of the burden she carried when it came to hiding her relationship had been lifted. She trusted Veronica to keep her secret. Denying her relationship made her feel sad, but nothing was going to stand in her way to crossing those sands to sisterhood.

Soon she would share Chris with her line and sorority. Gloria was open-minded and seemed to have no problems with people coloring outside the lines when it came to relationships. 'Maybe she will be the first one I tell,' Kiara thought riding in the elevator. Definitely not Donna. Even though Peter was known to be highly unfaithful, Donna always held up the black woman with the black man as the ideal relationship. She could never understand the love Chris and she shared. Still, sisterhood sometimes had to adjust.

"Hey you, we were starting to get worried you weren't going to make it," Donna said when Kiara rushed up to the table where the rest of the members of the line sat. The purpose of the time in the library was for the girls to study their scholastic work in order to keep up their grades. Since the girls were often running in different directions during the day, they typically spent the time studying sorority information.

"Sorry I'm late. I had the 4:59 question and it was about Veronica so I spent the evening with her. She cooked dinner and everything," Kiara said.

"What she cook? I hope it wasn't that dried ass meatloaf she brought to the potluck dinner last month at Elder Sister Samuels. My piece was as tough as leather and no amount of ketchup could hide that," Donna said.

"No, she made frozen lasagna. Did you know her dad died the first of the year? Car crash, I feel so bad for her. I could tell they were close like my dad and I were. Losing a parent is a hurtful thing, I'm here to tell you."

Shaking her head as she reflected over her big sister's loss, Donna said, "Damn, that's some sad shit right there, no disrespect Kiara. I know you lost your dad not too long ago. George and Ruby Jean may worry the living fuck out of me, but I can't imagine life without them."

Seeking an opportunity to switch the focus from her and poke around her line sister's past, Donna decided to direct the topic of parental background to Gloria.

"You know Gloria, you don't really talk about your family much. I know your last name is Allen and your mom's last name is McCloud. You said your dad owns his own car dealership, Campbell's Cadillac in Detroit. What's up with all the last names?"

"My mom and my dad never got married," Gloria responded looking up from her textbook. "They met when she was a junior in high school. My dad's younger sister and my mom were best friends so mom was always hanging out at their house. To hear my dad tell it, he had never looked at my mom all those years she was at their house. To him, she was just another one of the pigtailed pains in the ass that hung around his younger sister. One night, when he was coming in the house and she was heading out, he looked at her. I mean, like really looked at her. My mom's nickname growing up was Penny because she is reddish brown and looks like new money when she puts her mind to it."

Gloria explained her father asked her mom out for ice cream. Movies and concerts soon followed. Her father, a dead ringer for Malcolm X, with the reddish brown hair and glasses, wrote sonnets praising her mother. Her mother, flattered by all the attention, soon relented on the vow to save it for marriage.

"I don't know if you know this or not, but the Catholic Church isn't big on birth control, sex before marriage or basically anything a women does with her body other than pop out kids for her husband. My mom didn't have the best resources when it came to protection. They had been kicking it for about four months when she discovered she was pregnant."

Gloria explained her grandmother's response was to "suggest" her mother live down South for nine months with relatives then return home sans baby and resume her life. Carolyn Allen had a different plan in mind. She decided to move in with her best friend and finish out school. She managed to hide her pregnancy under increasing larger and larger Catholic school uniforms until the blessed event in February.

"My dad's mom saw that my mom had potential. She talked to some people who knew some people at Morgan State and got my mom in so she could attend college. Due to the pregnancy, my mom never really officially graduated from high school. Thanks to them and my mom having a good head on her shoulders, she graduated from college on time. When I was in middle school, she enrolled at Howard Law and graduated in three years," Gloria said beaming.

"I guess the smart apple don't fall far from the tree. So if your mom is a McCloud, I guess she ended up getting married. Is she and your step dad still together?"

"No, they divorced when I was seven. I heard he lives in Jersey. They were only married for about five years, which to me was five years too long. All I can say is fuck him and his entire family," Gloria said with a strange look on her face.

Donna looked at Kiara with a puzzled look on her face. Something about how Gloria's energy shifted when she talked about that period caused Donna to feel it was something the open book and open mouth Gloria wasn't sharing.

Kim's computer watch beeped notifying them it was time to gather their gear to head to Gwen's for their nightly "educational" session. Gloria, keeping her secrets, gathered up her books and prepared to leave with the rest of the girls, leaving Kiara wondering if she wasn't the only cygnet with secrets.

CHAPTER FIVE

Kiara/Gloria/Donna

"DAMN GIRL, I didn't know you could sing like that. You sang the exit song like it was altar call during Sunday service. Made me feel like I wanted to make a donation to the building fund," Donna said. Kiara had ended the night's study session by singing the first and fourth verse of the sorority's hymn. It was two weeks after Veronica's dinner with Kiara.

"I know right. You held that note like it was for ransom," Gloria said, offering Kiara and Donna salt and vinegar potato chips from her backpack. "You know, sometimes I wish I wasn't Catholic because we don't have choirs who sing traditional spirituals. There are only so many ways you can sing Mass."

Stopping at a stoplight, Kiara said into the rearview mirror to Gloria, "Trust me, growing up Baptist isn't all that it's cracked up to be. Imagine having to go to Bible study on Wednesday, choir rehearsal on Thursday, usher board meeting on Saturday morning, Sunday School, church, and some program on Sunday and you realize growing up in the church isn't for the faint of heart."

"Or soft of ass. My church service would start at eleven, but depending on if Sister Carolyn or Brother Matthews had a bad workweek and felt like shouting out their worries, we could be in church until two. Sometimes the spirit runs high and you have to wait until it moves through people."

"I have often wondered about the running music the pianist always played before people started shouting. I mean, it is always the same beat. I wonder do they teach them how to play it? Like is there sheet music somewhere for it?" Kiara asked.

"Running music, what is that?" Gloria asked.

Bouncing over the speed bumps at the entrance to campus, Kiara responded, "Well, you have heard of shouting right? People professing their love of the Lord in a very loud manner; it can involve people crying, speaking in tongues or passing out from the sheer exhaustion of believing so strongly in the power of God you can't remain upright."

"Preach," Donna said, waving her hand.

"Well, sometimes people are moved to break off and run around the church or stand in one place and jump up and down," Kiara said. "Usually when this happens, the church pianist— or in some churches the drummer, keyboardist and guitar player— play a rhythm that whips up the spirit. In my church, we had a trustee that would just break out and run around the church when he got the spirit, full tilt with his eyes closed. He never ran into anyone and would turn at every corner."

"Oh," Gloria said.

"Yes, I do admit we do things differently in the Baptist church, but really how weird is it? You Catholics go in a box to confess to a man. The Bible says if you confess with your mouth Jesus is Lord and believe in your heart, you will be saved. To me, that means it's a one-time deal. You don't have to repeat it on a weekly basis. Plus that thing with the ashes on the forehead for Lent, that's just weird," Donna said, rolling her window down to enjoy the April air.

"Donna, I would have never pictured you to be that intolerant. You aren't talking about some random person. You are talking about me, the girl who proofreads and types your papers. The fish on Friday chick that covers for your ass saying you were with me when you were with Peter. The person who loaned you my last twenty dollars to fill that tank you drive," Gloria said.

Kiara joined in, "Yeah D, that was somewhat foul. I know you, and I grew up where black folks were either Baptist or AME Zion, but Gloria is our girl. So what if we come from different religious backgrounds? We are cygnets, and to borrow your phrase, 'God willing and the creeks don't rise' we are going to be sisters. I mean, look at our backgrounds. Your parents own a funeral home, my folks are teachers, and Gloria's mom is a state attorney general and her dad owns a car dealership in Detroit. Gloria listens to The Cure, I listen to Color Me Badd, and you listen to Shirley Caesar. If it wasn't for us being on line we probably would have never connected."

Kiara had pulled up in front of Gloria's dorm but no one felt the need to move. Feeling inspired, she continued.

"Yet, with all our differences we have clicked. Gloria was right with saying how the stars seemed to have aligned for us to go through the process together. The first people I talked to at the interest meeting were Gloria and you. Gloria just made the age requirement, otherwise she would have had to wait for fall. Donna, you know Gwen damn near had a stroke during session when Cassandra told you if it hadn't been for one sister's vote, you wouldn't have been selected. Girls, we are meant to be on line together so we need to keep each other strong and not tear each other apart."

Silence filled the car. Kiara had never spoken so many words at one time, but she had been carrying around these thoughts in her heart for a while. This seemed the right time to share.

"Damn girl, you going to start me to crying and you know I don't like to cry. Gloria, I'm sorry if you felt like I was picking on you. You have been a cleft in the rock for me when I was out there doing things I shouldn't be doing, like socializing. I know you have spoken your peace about me fucking around with Peter since he has been known to stray, but you always had my back when I made moves to see him," Donna said. "Come up to the room and I will fix you a sandwich to make it up to you. I know you are not still full from that salad we had for lunch. Hell, I heard your stomach growling during sessions."

"Since I gave up meat for Lent, a sandwich is not going to cut it. However, if you are willing to warm up some of that macaroni and cheese, yams, and collards you brought back when you went home during the weekend, I think I could find a way to forgive."

Tensions resolved, Gloria and Donna got out the car and Kiara headed to her dorm. Riding in the elevator, Kiara reflected on the bond she felt with Donna and Kiara. It bothered her slightly she had not been honest with them. Soon, she would tell them about Chris. The time just had to be right.

"Surprise," Chris' velvet voice greeted Kiara's shocked stare.

With a fake broad smile Kiara responded, "Hey baby. I wasn't expecting to see you tonight. Have you been waiting long?"

"Not long. I ran into your roommate downstairs. She said I could wait in the room since she was going to stay at her boyfriend's tonight. I figured we could sneak in a quickie then I can hit the road. I set my alarm for 4:00 a.m. so I could be up and out before anyone sees me."

"Baby I wish I could, but I'm on my period. You know how I get about doing stuff when I'm bleeding."

"We can put a towel down. You know I don't mind."

"Honey, no."

"How about you do me? That way you don't have to take off your clothes."

Kiara's tired eyes answered in the negative. She realized give and take was part of any good relationship, but tonight she had no plans to put anything in her mouth she couldn't swallow.

"Honeybunches, can we just hold each other tonight? I have had a busy day with track practice, classes, and sessions. I just want to lie down and get some rest."

"Kiara this is some bullshit," Chris erupted. "I told you not to pledge but you are so busy trying to please your mother you don't care anything about your relationship. I can't talk to you on campus. I got to sneak around at night and now you can't even give me any?"

"Keep your voice down. You know it's after curfew and you are not supposed to be in my room on top of that," Kiara shushed. "Everyone on this hall knows I'm on line and just wanting to have something to run back and tell. Speaking of which, did you know Gayle told Veronica about us?"

"So you are more worried about what my ex has to say to one of your potential sisters than what I'm feeling. Man, that sorority shit got you all twisted in the head," Chris said.

"When we met I told you I planned to join K-Rho when I got the chance and you didn't seem to have a problem. Hell, you gave me the money I needed to get my clothes. What is your problem now?"

Chris stood silent then took Kiara's hand. "I know some of those Rhos got ideas about their sisters dating people that look like me. I just don't want you to get hurt. I love you and I want to be with you. But I can't keep waiting around. Sororities are just about buying friendships. I thought you were better than that. So busy trying to be something you're not."

The words felt like bee stings to Kiara's soul. Feeling tears come to her eyes, Kiara crossed the room to stand at the window.

"Baby, I'm sorry. I didn't come here tonight to start a fight. It's just I miss you and I want it to be just us again," Chris quickly apologized. "This is my last year and who knows where I'm going to get a job. I want to spend as much time together as I can."

Kiara murmured acceptance of the apology. Turning her around and kissing her pouting lips, Chris smiled and suggested they go the bed. "Come on, let me do that thing with my tongue you like. It always makes you feel better."

Kiara pursed her lips. Chris always pulled that trick out when she was upset or mad, still the effect of feeling Chris' tongue tracing the crock of her elbow always made Kiara's spine turned to jelly. Before she knew what hit her, Kiara was laying on her back, topless while Chris kissed, nibbled and nuzzled her lips, earlobes and neck. Kiara may have been menstruating but her lover's actions still caused her clit to pulsate with desire. Kiara was tempted go ahead and 'kiss it' as the couple liked to refer to it when Kiara performed oral sex. Still, she had said she wasn't going to do it and she didn't want to give Chris the satisfaction of knowing how easily she could be swayed by her lover's touch. Finally, after what seemed like hours of the sweet pain of holding back from experiencing total sexual release, the two fell asleep.

A door slamming in the hall snatched Kiara from her sleep. Checking the alarm clock, the green digits displayed 3:50. She turned to look at Chris' features, relaxed and regal, and reflected on their earlier conversation. She knew what her lover had said was right. Kappa Alpha Rho's relationships tended to look different from hers. But even if she didn't feel like she could be open about her relationship, her loyalty to Chris wasn't enough for her to abandon the goal she had pursued since coming to CRU. She realized Chris and she would probably end their relationship eventually. Some states, including this one, actually had laws on the books banning their relationship. Sisterhood, however, promised to be forever. The sounds of bird chirping interrupted her train of thought.

"Baby, your alarm is going off. Time for you to be up and out," Kiara whispered. Smoothly, Chris silenced the watch alarm, was dressed and left Kiara's room with a kiss and a promise to see her soon. Since she was already up, Kiara decided to do a little bit of studying for her major instead of the sorority.

Her high school business teacher gave her the idea of a double major. During her sophomore year, he gave a lecture on how people who flip out and kill people often exhibit signs they are under a lot of stress before they finally snap. He proposed to the class being able to recognize mental health triggers could lower work place violence. The Morehouse College alumnus was her favorite teacher and always challenged her to do her best. Not only was he responsible for helping Kiara choose her major, he was the key to her getting a way to pay for school. He was cousin to the CRU track coach, and he called the coach constantly to urge him to come see Kiara run. His persistence paid off with a four-year scholarship that required that she maintained a B average. Thumbing through all the psychology chapters she skimmed through, in light of learning all K-Rho history, she realized keeping the average was going to be harder than she thought. The ringing phone broke Kiara's sudden burst of studying and she jumped as the loud noise broke her concentration.

"Greetings most noble sister of Kappa Alpha Rho Sorority, Incorporated," Kiara automatically responded. After all, she thought, who else would be calling at six in the morning.

"Greetings most honorable cygnet. My, how long I have waited to say that to my daughter. Sweetie did I wake you?" Kiara's mother said brightly.

"Actually, no ma'am, you didn't wake me. I was up studying. You are up early, however," Kiara said.

"I know, I have a breakfast meeting at school at seven. I just wanted to call and see how the process was going."

Kiara rolled her eyes. In the two years of her attending CRU, her mother had called less than ten times. Since she started the process, her mother had called six times.

"It's going along, just learning information, reciting information, and doing community service. No one has called us out our names, put their hands on us, or made us doing anything we don't want to do."

"Good," her mother said firmly. "I know our national process mandates all cygnets are to be treated with respect and there are strict guidelines of what that entails. I know you and the other girls are not going to let anything happen that shouldn't. I want to just let you know if those girls make you or your line sisters feel disrespected or in danger you tell them no and you call and tell me. I want you to be a swan, but I don't want you to be put in harm's way to get to the other side."

"I know, Momma, I know. I told you about my line sister Donna. If any of those girls even thought about coming out of their way at her, she would tell them where to go and how to get there and send them on their way with a Bible verse," Kiara said chuckling about the deuce of their line. "And if that doesn't work, Gloria would pull out some random analogy to confuse them so they would forget what they planned to do."

"Yes, I remember what it was like going through the process. You know we had twenty-five girls on my process. We started out with forty but those others didn't have what it took to complete the process," Dorothy said.

Kiara, accustomed to hearing the next words her mom would say repeatedly during her years being around the organization, mouthed the rest of her mother's conversation.

"A Kappa Alpha Rho swan is successful, wise, accomplished, and noble. She succeeds, serves, and speaks succinctly. A woman of Kappa Alpha Rho Sorority, Incorporated is a credit to her community and gives back while moving forward," Dorothy said. "But I didn't call you to tell you what I'm sure you are already learning. I just want to let you know I'm proud of you and I would still be glad to be your mother if you decided not to pursue membership."

'Why are you lying so early in the morning?' Kiara thought closing her textbook and sighing deeply. She knew even if her mother wouldn't ever admit it, she valued Kiara being named the top Rho Rose in high school more than she appreciated her winning state track titles.

"Kiara, you aren't just going through the process for me are you?" Dorothy asked. "I know I have always promoted being a member of an organization as being important, but I hope I didn't force you into doing this process."

"Honestly Momma, when I started it I was doing it more so for you. Now that I have gotten to know the girls better, especially Donna and Gloria, I'm starting to understand all the stuff you and Aunt Vita talked about. This process has given me a feeling of support and understanding. I'm no longer angry with you for giving me two knucklehead boys as siblings."

Laughing, her mother responded she was happy her sins of

only having one girl had been forgiven. "Sounds like the process is going fine for you. Well, baby I am going to let you go back to studying. I just wanted to check on you and let you know I love you."

"I love you too and I will talk to you soon," Kiara said hanging up. Sighing, she turned back to her books. She thought, 'Yep it has been a bitch not being able to spend time with my friends and Chris, but having Donna and Gloria as substitutes has been worth it.'

CHAPTER SIX

Donna/Gloria/Kiara

A WEEK AFTER Kiara's conversation with her mother, a surprise greeted the line when they arrived at their Wednesday night session.

"Good evening cygnets. I know we haven't seen a lot of each other during the process, but know I have been following your progress," Vestina Samuels said. "You have undergone a lot and hopefully have learned more about yourself and our organization. Kappa Alpha Rho Sorority requires its members to be dedicated to our goals and to our mission. We have no tolerance or desire for those pursuing this for the wrong reasons. You should come to our sisterhood not to rest on our reputation and good works but to create your own legacy. To allow you to weigh your willingness to carry on with this process, for the next forty-eight hours you are allowed to return back to your lives as Copper Road University students without being potentials of Kappa Alpha Rho Sorority."

Fourteen eyebrows rose in amazement. Even Kiara was surprised. She never knew this was part of the process. Sure, she noticed, during her time on campus, some of the girls appearing to be going through the intake process would appear wearing street clothes after their black and white. She assumed it meant they had crossed over and was just bidding their time until their debut show announcing their membership.

Gloria was the first to break the silence. "So we are free to talk to whoever we want, dress in whatever we want, and not have to do what the ladies ask us to do?"

Gwen nodded yes. "For the next two days, you are free to go back to doing what you did prior to starting this process. Those who wish to continue should arrive here at 6:59 Friday night. If your decision is not to continue, then we wish you well in your journey," she said with a serious look of her face. "But, I will tell you, if you don't show up by one minute to seven, we will take that disinterest in our organization. In that event, the organization will return half of the money you paid. Kappa doesn't need to profit from your indecision. Now, if each of you will remove the 'C' you have worn for the past six weeks. You are free to return to your dorms to prepare for your first day in a while of being able to wear your own clothing."

Vestina spoke next. "One last thing, during the next forty eight hours, the members of Kappa Alpha Rho Sorority, Incorporated will not have contact with you. Unless we have a class with you, you should not attempt to have contact with us. We will also be using the time to decide on whom we want to continue with the process. Don't think just because you show up two days from now, your place is assured."

The next day, Gloria awoke with a song in her heart and strode out her dorm wearing her favorite blue jeans, and screen-printed t-shirt featuring Mag Wildwood from *Breakfast at Tiffany's*. Walking to class, she received looks from most people accustomed to seeing her in black and white. She was so grateful to have use of her voice she felt compelled to use it with strangers and classmates alike. Still, with all the connections she made and re-established after six weeks of silence, she missed her girls.

"Hey Donna, it's me Gloria. What are you doing?" she asked holding the phone with one hand and rapidly assessing her TV viewing choices by maneuvering her remote control.

"Working on my biology homework that was actually due

last week. Dr. Morgan is an Iota so he is cutting me some slack since he knows I'm going through the process. You know for a balding fifty-year-old, whose breath smells like two dogs fucking some mornings, he's not that bad."

Settling on a documentary on UNC TV, Gloria replied, "I'm surprised you're not hugged up with Peter."

Taking a big sip of her soda before answering, Donna replied, "I would have been, but it seems since I have been going through the process Peter has found someone else to occupy his time."

"Oh," Gloria said. 'I guess he finally found the cojones to fess up about all those other girls he has been screwing on the side,' she thought. "Sister, I am sending you all my strength, love, and support to help you deal with what must be a horrible betrayal."

"Well…Peter has decided to be a mentor to a middle school kid. He tutors the kid Wednesday and Thursday from three to five so he doesn't miss curfew or team meetings."

"My, how noble it sounds," Gloria said. Then shifting the topic of conversation, she asked, "Can you believe they are giving us this break? I'm still in shock. I can't wait to see who comes back Friday and who stays on line."

"Exactly, my money is on Kiara for sure, Kim, Karen and maybe Michelle. You, of course, and you know Andrea would rather have her credit cards cut up than not be a Rho."

"Wait, Donna, you didn't say you were coming back."

Silence.

"Donna, you didn't say you were coming back. Are you coming back?" Gloria asked with urgency.

Silence, then a peal of laughter on the other end of the line.

"Girl, you know I'm going to be there. I have spent too much money and put up with too much bullshit not to come back. I had you going didn't I?"

In a tone that didn't even convince her, Gloria replied, "I knew you were playing."

"Yeah, and I'm the Queen of Sheba. Listen, since we are back in circulation I was wondering if you and Kiara wanted to go out tonight. One of the guys from my biology class has a band and they are playing at S&B. When he saw I was back among the living, he offered to put me on the list and said I could bring some friends."

"Wouldn't Peter mind?"

"Shit, my parents are in Kenansville. I's grown. Be ready in thirty minutes. I will call Kiara and see if she can make it out."

"I think Kiara is going to take a pass. I ran into her at the cafeteria and she said she has a paper to knock out so she was going to stick close to her room."

"I hear that. Let me get up and put some clothes on. Since I'm getting us into the club, do you mind driving?"

"No worries. What's the name of this band anyway?"

"Tragic Mulattos. Everybody in the band is biracial so they thought it would be a neat name to call the band."

"Do they know the history of that term? I mean the idea of calling yourself after a stereotypical fictional character that stems back to the 1840s who is assumed to be sad because they don't fit in the white world or black world is very odd."

"Gloria, it's music not literature. Put on some clothes and meet me downstairs in my lobby in twenty minutes."

"I can think of worse ways to spend a Wednesday. See you in fifteen."

The next day Gloria caught Kiara up on the lack-luster night she missed while the two waited for Donna to join them in Kiara's car. Without consulting each other, each of the three knew they were going to continue on with the process. All they had to decide was who was going to drive to Gwen's.

"Oh my God, the club stank, the sound sucked, and half-way through the set, a fight broke out and they had to end their set. If I had paid to get in I would be have been like the hatter in *Alice in Wonderland*, mad."

"I'm sorry the party wasn't good, but at least D and you

got a chance to get out and socialize. Me, I was stuck in the room finishing up a paper about Maslow's hierarchy of needs. Right now, I'm thinking with this process I'm on the third level working toward my fourth," Kiara said.

"You and me both, honey bunches of o's. I think the fourth level, self-esteem, confidence, respect of and by others is such a difficult level to obtain. Most of us fail to achieve that, utilizing such desperate methods such as plastic surgery, living above our means and falling prey to what the media feeds us as being socially acceptable goals of bigger house, bigger car, and bigger bank account. In order to achieve that fourth level, you have to be content with accepting who and what you are. It's no crystal stair, but at least it lets you reach a higher level of being," Gloria said, seemingly not taking a breath.

"Wow, sometimes I forget how next level you are. But I love it," Kiara said smiling. "If anyone had to be the balance point of our line, I'm glad it was you."

"That is right, we do have seven people. You know in Chinese culture, seven is a lucky number. It means togetherness, which is truly how I feel about this process, especially when it comes to Donna and you," Gloria said. "And you being #3 is a good thing because three is a lucky number. It usually stands for something that is solid and real. You have really been the rock of this line, nothing seemed to have fazed you, and I for one really appreciate that."

"Let me co-sign that. Thanks to you, I have been able to refrain from punching your #5 in her smart-ass mouth. Andrea just makes my ass itch every time she opens her mouth," Donna said getting into the car. "Since Kiara is a rock as the #3, what am I?"

"You, my deuce, symbolize the most feminine and underestimated. Your number is a symbolic representation of the ultimate survivor and an extremely resilient force. You've been through a lot or will go through a lot, but like Maya says, *and still you rise*."

"Yes, I am phenomenal, but it's getting close to that time so let's bounce and get to Gwen's."

Arriving with a minute to spare, the trio was pleased to see all their line sisters waiting for them. Gwen informed them they would be traveling to Raleigh for their comprehensive Rho review. The written and oral exam would test their knowledge and dedication to the organization. Gloria, Donna and Kiara rode to Raleigh in separate cars and faced different panels for their reviews. On the way back, seating arrangements changed so the three ended up in the same car driven by Ruth. Sitting in the front seat, Kiara was the first to notice the car heading in a different direction than the way they had come. She turned around to meet her sisters' concerned eyes about where they were going. A few minutes later, the girls received the answer to their unspoken question when they pulled into a paved driveway in front of a green and white painted home.

"Oh my God, I can't believe they are bringing us here," Kiara whispered to Gloria and Donna after Ruth had exited the car. "This is Eternal Emerald Martha Maddox's home. This was the first headquarters for Kappa Alpha Rho Sorority, Incorporated. I had forgotten it was here."

Ruth opened the car door and motioned for them to get out and line up one after another, based on their line number. The home's wrap around porch appeared to be a sea of purple and platinum. Kiara, noticing her mother's beaming face among the women, smiled and inwardly sighed with relief. 'I guess I passed the test,' she thought looking at the back of Donna's head.

"Cygnets, you are standing on the grounds of history," a petite grey haired woman standing on the purple painted steps said. "This basket I hold contains the final tasks each of you must complete to make the end of your journey. As I call your name, please come and select your envelope. Do not open them until I tell you."

One by one, they approached the porch. With nervous hands, they stood waiting for the signal. When it came, the girls acted as if one.

For a minute, the girls stood silent. Then, Kiara's voice soared with the first two verses of the sorority's national hymn.

Michelle chimed in with the final two verses as the other girls hummed. Their rich alto and soprano voices intertwined in the air like a vocal rope pulling the girls together and through their trials. For Kiara, who had grown up hearing the song sang at ceremonies, weddings, and funerals, singing it in the yard surrounded by the women who had stood by her side, and in front of the women who had gone through a similar process, it made her heart swell with pride.

"Sisters, oh Sisters of Mine, we come before you today to request acceptance into your ranks as members of Kappa Alpha Rho Sorority, Incorporated. My sisters and I have journeyed weeks, days, hours, minutes and seconds. We have forsaken lovers, friends, and follies to reach our goal of uniting in sisterhood," Kim said as the last notes floated out of Kiara and Michelle's mouths.

"Daughter, oh Daughters of Ours, we open our arms and hearts to you. But tell us why you are worthy?" the petite woman asked.

"We are worthy because we have committed our bodies through hours of service to others. We have given our minds toward mastering our academic studies and acquiring the information given to us. We have devoted our spirit to portraying the intention of sisterhood through our actions," Donna replied in a voice clear like the blue sky.

"Sisters oh Sisters of Mine, we come before you because we are ready to swim as swans, portraits of grace, beauty, and strength. We are here to form a permanent bond that once formed will never be broken," Andrea said. Stepping out of line, she took Donna's hand and began walking the hall's entrance. Michelle and Kim followed, then Kiara and Karen. Gloria walked solo behind the three pairs. Reaching the bottom of the steps, the stout, baritone voiced Vestina Samuels stopped them.

"Before you can gain admission to the halls of Kappa Alpha Rho Sorority, Incorporated, one of you must serve as the bearer of good news and announce your arrival."

With a smile, Gloria belted out, "To the Sisters of Kappa

Alpha Rho Sorority, Incorporated my fellow sisters of the Gamma Delta Line of the Lambda Mu Chapter, and to the universe who bears witness to the evolution of these seven cygnets to swans, I present to you the Goddess of Greatness, the spring 1991 class of Kappa Alpha Rho Sorority, Incorporated."

CHAPTER SEVEN
Kiara/Donna

KIARA, GLORIA, AND DONNA spent the remaining two months of their sophomore year practicing their sorority calls, posing for multiple pictures, and performing community service. They went their separate ways for the summer. Kiara headed north to Delaware for an internship. Gloria spent her summer studying and sunning in Puerto Rico, while Donna headed back to Duplin County to work for the family funeral business.

There were opportunities for Kiara to come clean about Chris and her after she became a K-Rho. Gloria and Kiara met Chris during graduation, but for some reason, the time didn't seem right. Kiara trusted Gloria and Donna, but she had kept Chris a secret for so long that she found it hard to break free. When Chris received a job offer two hours away, Kiara found it easier to keep her secret in the closet. Since Chris was an out of sight, out of mind situation, Kiara didn't worry about having to share her relationship with her sorority sisters.

Kiara and Donna kept in touch and made plans to rent an off-campus apartment for junior year. In the back of her mind, Kiara was worried about living in close quarters with her sorority sister. But after two weeks of home cooked Southern meals like smothered chicken and collards with homemade dumplings, Kiara's misgivings melted away like butter on Donna's biscuits. Life soon settled down to a routine of studying, sorority, and secrets.

"Key, if my mother calls tonight, tell her I'm going to be in the library studying late and I will call her tomorrow. If Dawn calls, tell her to send me the forty dollars she owes me for buying her that Gamma Sigma bracelet. If Peter calls, tell him I'm on my way to his room and he better be there when I get there," Donna said, hoisting her backpack on her shoulders. "And Kiara, why is this thermostat on hell? Do you have to have it so warm in here?"

Fall had come to Blueburg almost a month after the calendar marked its arrival. Even though the days were still pleasantly warm, the nights tended to be chilly. Tonight the forecast called for lows in the 50s.

"Donna, I turned the thermostat up because I was in the shower and I didn't want to have icicles form on my body while I was drying off," Kiara said walking into the kitchen dressed in a Copper Road sweat suit and purple house slippers. "Don't worry, I'm going to turn it down since we don't want the light bill to be sky high."

"Thank you," Donna said. "I will probably see you on campus tomorrow. Peter's roommate is out of town so I plan to stay in his room tonight."

Putting the kettle on to make her nightly mug of almond tea, Kiara replied, "I don't know why you pay rent here? You're always over Peter's."

"Well, I need somewhere to lay my head when he has football games and I can't stay in his room. I don't know why you are sweating having the house to yourself. You should take advantage of it and have a guy over."

"I would if I could find time. Pledging brought my GPA down to a 2.9. Only reason I kept my scholarship is that I placed second in the 400 when the team went to the state meet. I need to concentrate and bring my studies up."

"Well, we all need to get our groove on now and then. What's the saying? All work and no play make Kiara a hard bitch to deal with."

"Ha-ha, very funny. You get fucked all the time and you are still a bitch."

"Well at least I'm consistent. See you later," Donna said and walked out the door.

Taking a sip of her tea, Kiara went back into her bedroom and settled down to study. While her eyes focused on the page, she listened to the most popular show on the campus' radio station, *Cassandra's Confessions*. For four hours, people broke off relationships, called each other out for trifling behavior and announced their conquest by sending song dedications. For many on campus, the show also served as musical education. Cassandra's choices of songs to convey sentiments seemed endless.

"After all, anyone can let a singer tell someone how much they love them, but nothing lets someone know that you are done with them like a catchy chorus," Cassandra's raspy whisper delivered the show's tag line after she sent out "So Long Farewell," from Phoebe to Nelson.

After two hours of cramming, the one-two melody of the doorbell broke her concentration. Rolling her head to lessen the stiffness from sitting on her bed and studying, she walked to her front door. Her eyes widened when she looked through the peephole.

"Chris, what are you doing here?" Kiara said flinging open the door. She launched herself into her lover's arms and planted passionate kisses. Except for two weekends they spent together in D.C. during the summer, and a weekend spent in Atlanta during Labor Day, the two had only kept in touch through letters and phone calls.

Kiara wondered what Donna thought about the same tenor voice calling for her, but she never asked a question about whom it belonged to and Kiara never volunteered.

"You know I can't stay away from you for long. I told those people I would be coming in late tomorrow. I have gotten us a hotel room for the night so we have all evening to get reacquainted."

"Oh, you should have saved that money. Donna is gone for

the night so we can stay here. She even cooked dinner, which we can eat now. Or," Kiara said raising her left eyebrow mischievously, "we can eat later."

"I didn't drive two hours for whatever is in the kitchen. You know what I came here to eat," Chris responded.

Twenty steps later, the two stood in Kiara's bedroom. Watching Chris undress, Kiara's eyes feasted on her lover's washboard stomach, sinewy arms, and powerful thighs. Fittingly, the James to Nicole song dedication of "I Wanna Sex You Up" played in background.

Not wanting to leave her lover waiting, Kiara shed her clothing. Reclining on the bed, she waited for Chris to make the first move.

"Girl, you are making my mouth water. I spent all summer thinking about tasting you. I almost ran off the road a few times," Chris said. "It's been so long since I have seen you. I am going to have to re-introduce myself to all your perfect parts."

Purring, Kiara replied, "Well, don't talk about it, be about it."

Chris began the seduction from the bottom up, applying a skillful touch to one of Kiara's most sensitive parts.

"Oh my God baby, you know what that does to me when you do that," Kiara murmured while Chris began massaging her feet. Kiara's mind levitated in blissful separation from her body. Soon Chris began kissing a path up her body. The slight sensation of lips along Kiara's leg to her knees to her thighs made her quiver with nervous energy. She wanted Chris' lips on her lower lips so much that desire almost choked her. Chris was not taking the bait. Moving past the pot of gold between her tight thighs, Kiara received kisses on her hipbones and taut stomach. An electric current shot to the base of her spine while Chris lingered on her chest. She gasped in frustration. Squirming with anticipation Kiara thought, 'Damn, why is Chris taking so long?'

Appearing to read her mind, Chris murmured, "Patience is a virtue, my pet. You know I love your breasts and it wouldn't be right for me to leave them out."

"I know, but I'm not a patient woman."

While slowly sucking her breasts, Chris' thick fingers penetrated Kiara's wetness stroking her clit like a lap dog. She felt her bones dissolve with pleasure. Her vaginal muscles grabbed the two digits like a drowning woman to a life vest. Those Kegels came in handy.

After sucking and biting Kiara's nipples until they felt raw, Chris moved up, giving Kiara deep, probing, thrusting kisses. Kiara fell back in love, feeling their breaths tango. She could bench press two hundred pounds, but having the same amount of weight naked on top of her making her feel like incarnate pleasure was better. Shifting her hips, Kiara hoped her subtle signal would help Chris realize she was ready for the main course.

Pausing for a moment to look into her eyes, Kiara's lover sent a current of love and desire into her soul. Kiara mouthed the words "I love you." Chris smiled the smile that had inspired their relationship. Using both hands to spread Kiara's thighs, Chris sucked her clit like it held the antidote to all the world's ills. Kiara felt every nerve ending pulsate. Everything around her seemed to fade away. All brain activity focused on the sensation down below. The pleasure was maddening. She felt her head was going to explode. Her orgasm approached on angel's wings, softly, but with the force of creation behind it. For Kiara, reaching her climax was like an orchestra performance. Different instruments tuned up in anticipation of the conductor stepping up to wave his baton for the performance. There was a brief silence then with the right stroke, an awakening of brilliant sounds broke out and multiplied in the air sending cascades of aural pleasures.

Chris' tongue twirled like a baton in a Fourth of July parade. Riding the wave of pleasure, Kiara's body twitched while she moaned. Kiara felt secure allowing moans of pleasure bounce off the walls like sonic projectiles. Her loud outpour of appreciation masked the sound of the front door opening.

Donna's announcement of arrival halted on her lips. 'Old

girl getting laid. Hell I'm glad one of us is getting some tonight,' Donna thought, smiling to herself. Thankfully, Kiara's door was closed. Donna planned to go into the kitchen, grab a soda and head into her room. Hearing another voice call out praises to a higher authority halted Donna's steps.

'Either brother got a real high pitch voice or that is a woman Kiara is fucking,' Donna thought. Standing frozen in her tracks, hand on the refrigerator door, she processed what she was hearing and still couldn't believe it. Hearing Kiara's door open shocked her into action. Giving thanks to her petite size, Donna squeezed in the nook beside the stove so she could see into the hallway. Hoping to fade into the wallpaper, Donna saw a naked black woman with a short haircut walk to the bathroom. The naked black woman with a short hair wasn't her roommate.

Christina Annette Daniels went into the bathroom blissfully unaware her lover's roommate was about to die from surprise only twenty feet away. All she was concerned about was emptying her bladder and getting back to making love to her baby.

'Jesus on the motherfucking cross,' Donna thought. The last time she had seen Chris she was wearing a royal blue graduation gown. But Donna would recognize that copper-cropped cut anywhere. Kiara introduced Chris as her 'friend.' Now that she thought about it, Donna reflected, Chris did have a weird look on her face when she had said that. At that time, Donna chalked it up to the sun being in her eyes, making her squint. Suddenly everything made sense. Kiara's "I haven't had a boyfriend since high school" statement during their process. How whenever Gloria or she mentioned some cute guy, Kiara managed to change the subject. Kiara gave the impression she was single. Donna should have known something when she introduced Kiara to her gay cousin when they moved into the apartment two months ago. Looking at Kiara, he raised his arched eyebrows, shook his mane of freshly permed hair, and told her to be careful around Kiara. All this time she thought he was hinting she might make a move on Peter. 'Well that was a train bound for nowhere,' Donna thought.

Punching her pillow to help cushion her conflicting thoughts, Donna's mind veered between feelings of betrayal and sadness. Why didn't Kiara trust her enough to share something like this? 'All the times I have shared my feelings about Peter and his two-timing ways and she didn't think to bring up she was a coochie eater,' she thought drifting off to sleep. 'Damn, I thought we were closer than that.'

An hour before the sunrise, Kiara's door cracked open and two the lesbian lovers walked out, exhausted from a night of love-making. Satisfied with a goodbye kiss and promises from Kiara to return the favor soon, Chris left the apartment beaming. Walking back to her bedroom, Kiara noticed Donna's closed bedroom door. She could have sworn Donna left it open when she left. Kiara managed to get thirty minutes of rest until her eyes shot open. Hearing Donna showering, panic coursed through her body. 'Did she just come home or did she come home last night? If she came home last night, what time did she come home?' Sitting straight up in bed, Kiara's mind cycled. 'If she came home last night, did she hear Chris and me,' Kiara thought. 'Shit, I knew I would have to tell Donna eventually about Chris, but I didn't think it was going to be today.'

Kiara had always known she was gay, but arriving at college, she didn't want everyone to know her as "that lesbian." There had been a few public appearances with guys now and again to keep folks around her from suspecting. If her dates expressed desires of getting more than a hug, she explained her church background taught her to save it for marriage. Kiara soon became that girl who was cool to hang out with but wasn't putting out. Going through the process, Kiara provided enough vague answers or switched topics to avoid sharing her truth. Kiara wanted her sorority sisters and everyone to get to know her first, before they found out about her preference. She felt bad about keeping her secret, especially from Donna and Gloria. Still, her fear of being judged had kept her mute.

Kiara did worry about her love of women coming out

when she met Donna's cousin in August. She could tell in his eyes he knew. To borrow her older brother's favorite phrase at the moment, 'game recognize game' or in her case, it took a gay person to recognize another gay person. 'Oh well,' she thought walking down the hallway toward the kitchen. 'May as well get it on and over with.'

"Morning sunshine," Donna chirped between bites of her liver pudding and grits after Kiara walked into the kitchen.

"Morning. I didn't expect to see you this morning," Kiara responded, heading straight for the coffee maker. She was not ready to make eye contact or conversation.

"Yeah I know. I planned to stay the night with Peter but I ended up coming home early this morning. It seems Peter and I have a difference of opinion about girls not named Donna Eugenia Edwards popping up at his room after curfew."

"Did you know the girl?" Kiara sighed behind Donna's head. Preparing her breakfast, she anticipated hearing a repeat of the same old song.

"Yeah, that trash Kimberly Hines who stays in Gibson. She said she was coming by for some notes but I think she was coming to get it on with Peter."

Sitting down at the table with her oatmeal, Kiara asked, "Why you say that?"

"Do you carry a backpack to somebody's room when you live across the street just to get some notes?"

"I would if I was coming from a night class."

"Well, me and her got into it and then me and Peter got into it."

"And he kicked you out?"

"And I came home."

"Oh," Kiara said eating her breakfast. When it came to Donna's continued support of a relationship with a cheating boyfriend, Kiara often refused to comment. She felt Donna should cut her loses and move on. But, since she had issues with being out about her relationship, she felt she had no place to criticize how someone else lived their life.

Donna and Kiara sat in silence for about ten minutes. Kiara prayed silently her previous night activities wouldn't come up.

"It seems to me you took my advice about getting some last night. The way you were calling the hogs last night made me think of how it was when Peter and I started dating. That boy had me climbing the wall. Who is the lucky person?" Donna asked.

Kiara realized Donna's words opened the door for her to walk through and come out. Her mind stalled. She muttered, "No one you know. C'mon, let's get ready to go to class. You riding with me?" Kiara got up from the table.

Exhaling in frustration, Donna grabbed her backpack from the back of the kitchen chair.

All during the day Kiara's mind burned with how to deal with the night before. Unable to concentrate in her Business Communication class, she weighed her options. 'Donna is my sorority sister, roommate, and closest friend,' Kiara thought taking notes. 'If I have to pick someone to be the first person at Copper Road to come out to, she would be the best choice. After all, she has already seen half my ass when I got that sorority brand on my upper thigh.' Walking to her final class, Kiara's internal debate continued. 'Donna has never said anything too homophobic around me. She and her cousin seem close. It's not like she doesn't like gay people. I should just go home and tell her the truth.'

Driving home, all the positive pumping up from the day ebbed away. Switching gears, Kiara fretted to herself, 'My name is on the lease too so it's not like she could put me out. Then again, I don't want to live in a situation where I feel like I am being judged every time I turn around. Donna doesn't seem like one of those judgmental Christians, but she does seem to have a Bible verse for every situation.'

"Fuck. We should have just gone to the hotel last night," Kiara said aloud, pulling into the apartment's parking lot.

Usually running helped Kiara clear her thoughts. Today, she decided a different way to refocus her mind.

"I'm home. Damn something smells good," Donna announced, walking into the kitchen.

"Hey, I'm cooking spaghetti for us since you cooked last night."

"Thank you. After the day I have had, a little comfort food will go a long way," Donna said, plopping her books on the table. "I'm so tired of school, especially Dr. Morris. That strumpet can kiss my entire Duplin County ass. You know ever since she realized I was a K-Rho, she has been riding my ass like I got a fucking saddle on it."

"I'm sure she doesn't have it out for you because of your letters. Did she bust out with another surprise pop quiz?" Kiara asked, stirring the meat around in the frying pan.

"Yes another blasted pop quiz and on the one chapter in the book I didn't study last night. I tell you some days it doesn't pay to be a social work major."

Leaning against the kitchen counter, Donna opened her mouth, but before she could form her question, the phone rang.

"Hello, oh hey you," Kiara blushed. "Hold on, let me get the phone in my room."

Fighting to hide a smile, Kiara walked down the hall. Grabbing a beer from the refrigerator, Donna began making a salad for dinner. Halfway through peeling the cucumbers she felt Kiara behind her.

"What the hell is wrong with you? Your face is tore up like you were back there cutting up onions," Donna asked. "That must have been one hell of a phone conversation."

"Yeah, it was," Kiara said, sitting down with a scowl.

"What, you and old girl have a lover's quarrel?" Donna asked with her back to Kiara.

"What the hell do you mean lover's quarrel?"

"I know from experience few people can get your blood boiling quicker than your momma or your man. Since it doesn't seem Ms. Dorothy picks your nerve like Ruby Jean does mine, I figured it wasn't her. Plus, I saw Chris coming out your room last night naked as a jaybird, so my money is on her. I recognized her from graduation."

For five minutes, the only sound in the room was boiling water from the pot as the spaghetti cooked. Donna and Kiara looked at each other waiting to see who would have the first word in this new conversation.

"So, what do you have to say for yourself? Am I wrong to assume you and Chris are funny?" Donna asked.

"We prefer the word lesbian."

"So now that we have established that y'all are 'lesbians,' what was y'all's fight about?"

"She started off the conversation like she had called just to say hi then snuck in the fact her friend Gayle was in town for a job interview. The two planned to go out to grab a bite and catch up."

"So does she always call you ahead of time and tell you her dinner plans?" Donna said, draining the spaghetti.

"Gayle is her ex. She tried to get back in the picture when Chris and I started dating and wasn't too happy when Chris turned her down. I bet she told me Gayle was in town so I would get in a jealous fit and drive up to Rocky Mount to stake my claim."

Shaking her head, Donna said, "Well I guess that just proves that even women can be assholes in relationships. C'mon let's dig in before the food gets cold. Nothing's worse than being pissed off on an empty stomach."

The two ate in silence for a couple of minutes. Kiara searched for a way to broach the subject until finally deciding to go straight to the point. "So you aren't freaked out by me being gay?" she asked, fixing Donna with a skeptical gaze. She struggled to keep her voice level but she felt nervous. This was the first time she was having a conversation about her sexuality with someone not gay.

"Please. After some of the shit I have seen dressing bodies for the funeral home, very few things shock me. I will say I am confused. Why didn't you tell me you like girls before now? All the stuff we shared while we were going through the process and you didn't think to mention you like girls."

"I guess I was afraid of how you or anyone else on the line would react. Other than Chris and some of her friends, no one on the yard really knows that I'm gay. The lesbian community here is like an after-hours liquor house. You have to know someone to get in and once you get in, you don't talk about it to anyone who doesn't belong."

"So how long have you been, you know, funny?"

"I have always had an attraction to girls. Once, when I was in high school one of my teammates was goofing off and showing off some of her gymnast's moves. You know, handstands and flips. She did this one move where she did a handstand and then a split in the air. The first thought that popped in my head was damn, I bet she would be fun to have sex with."

"Damn girl, you are nasty as hell. I had no idea," Donna chuckled. "I mean I would never look at you and think you were into that kind of thing. Now Chris, on the other hand, looks like she may be into girls. No disrespect, but your girl looks like she could play beside Peter. She must be the man in the relationship. You, on the other hand, got a pretty face and a nice shape. You wear dresses and makeup. Why don't you like men? Did something happen to you when you were younger?"

"Donna, there are so many backward sounding things in what you just said I don't know where to start," Kiara said, fighting not to appear too pissed. She didn't want the conversation to spin too far out of control. "Chris is not the man in the relationship. First off, the point of being a lesbian is that we are both women. I never said I didn't like men and nothing happened to me when I was younger. I had a boyfriend in high school and we had fun together. I lost my virginity to him April Fool's Day and I had a good time. It's just I like being with women."

"So have you been with a lot of girls? I mean, maybe you're not really a lesbian. Maybe you just are exploring your options," Donna said shrugging her shoulders.

"There is no magic number of women you have to sleep

with to be a lesbian. And to answer your question, Chris is the third woman I slept with. I messed around with a friend in high school and I hooked up with this girl from Bennett when I did an overnight campus tour."

"So you have been doing this for a while? Well hell, I'm close to being speechless," Donna said, putting her plate in the sink. "So you mean to tell me I'm the first straight person you have told you were gay?"

"Technically, you are the first person I have said I'm a lesbian to that wasn't gay. You remember that night when I had dinner with Veronica? She told me Chris' ex blabbed about Chris and me dating, but I didn't say anything, yay or nay."

"See, now I really want to whoop that trick's ass and I don't even know her. Broad sounds like she is just messy. But you really haven't told anyone else? I would have thought for sure you would have told I love-everyone-peace-love-and-hair-grease Gloria. Damn, I really feel special."

Hugging her roommate, Kiara reassured her, while she carried love in her heart for Gloria, her favorite Kappa Alpha Rho was #2.

"Hey hey, don't get any ideas. I said I am cool with you doing girls, but I'm all about that thang that swings," Donna said, pulling away and giving Kiara a sideways glance.

"Donna, contrary to popular belief, every lesbian don't want to screw every woman they see," Kiara said, eyes narrowing with irritation. "All I was doing was giving you a hug like I have done before. You are cute, but I don't want to have sex with you."

"I wasn't saying that I think you wanted to have sex with me. I just want to make sure we are clear. I don't get down like that. Damn girl, you can't just come out your mouth with something like what you just said and expect someone not to get a little freaked out when you start feeling on them," Donna asked. "Anyway, why wouldn't you want to have sex with me? You don't think I'm pretty?" Her face was a mixture of embarrassment and indignation.

"Donna, please, don't flatter yourself. You are straight, and

I don't date straight girls. Listen, I don't want you to be walking around here scared I'm going to hem you up if I happen to get too close to you. Maybe I should see about finding somewhere else to live," Kiara said, storming out the room.

Sitting on her bed, Kiara began feeling sick to her stomach with hurt and regret. She had hoped Donna would not have a problem with her being gay. She expected some questions but didn't anticipate Donna to recoil from her hug. It felt like a blade in her spine, crippling and sharp. 'If coming out is this painful,' she thought,' no wonder people stay in the closet.'

"Knock-knock," Donna said after thirty minutes had passed. Walking into the room, she sat on the bed beside Kiara and hugged her line sister.

"Girl, you are not going anywhere. My mouth, once again, seemed to have gotten my ass in trouble. I don't have a problem living with you," Donna said. "I had a little talk with Jesus and I realized I was wrong for the way I acted. Since we have met, you and I have been cool. You have been a good sorority sister and friend. You have never come at me when I didn't know you liked women, and now that I have had time to think about it, I realize I was being ignorant thinking you were trying to goose me. I hope we can put this behind us. Sometimes my mouth moves before my brain reacts."

Accepting the hug and the remorseful words, Kiara smiled. Assured all was forgiven, Donna continued. "Now I know some Christians are quick to run out with Leviticus and Romans about how man shouldn't lie with man and stupid shit like that. The Bible also says you shouldn't eat shrimp or wear clothes of mixed fabric. Well, I tell you what. I have no problems eating me a fried popcorn shrimp plate in my cotton and nylon blend outfit. I'm not going to come at you with some hellfire and brimstone mess. We are swans and swans swim together. If anyone comes at you with some ying-yang about you, they are going to have to come through me."

"So we are cool?" Kiara said.

"Yeah we're straight. Well, I am," Donna said smiling.

CHAPTER EIGHT
Donna/Gloria/Kiara

EVEN THOUGH IT killed her not being able to discuss Kiara's sexuality with Gloria, Donna kept quiet. Kiara had not asked her to keep her lesbian identity secret, but Donna felt a sense of protection for her sister's privacy. Plus, a small part of her cherished knowing something no one else did. During the two weeks that had passed since the great reveal, Donna and Kiara talked more about Chris. Donna shared with Kiara, during one of their talks, she enjoyed having someone to swap relationship stories. They both agreed it would be great if their line sister could join the conversation.

"Oh my God, if I could have reached into the sky and pulled down a thunderbolt like Zeus, I would have struck Trevor down for embarrassing me like that. The nerve," Gloria fumed, leaving Cleveland Auditorium with Donna.

It was homecoming week and the day after Halloween. Along with what seemed to be half of CRU's population, they had spent the past three hours enjoying the annual Air Guitar Show. Each year, students usually limited to singing in the shower, got up the nerve and the ten-dollar entrance fee to perform for their classmates in a lip sync contest. The winner, voted by a panel of student and faculty judges, walked away with a cash prize of $150 and $100 credit at the student bookstore. Donna, Gloria, and Kiara considered entering but Kiara had a night class and couldn't participate.

Knowing he had no chance of winning, Trevor Riggs decided he would spice up his performance of Peter Gabriel's "Sledgehammer" by leaving the stage and gyrating in front of Gloria. Quoting the song, the freshman offered to be her bumper car, among other things.

"If the floor could have opened up and swallowed me I wouldn't have been happier," she said. "I still can't get the spectacle of his pasty, white, skinny, sweating chest just shaking in front of my face."

Walking beside Gloria toward her dorm, Donna said, "I know one thing. That boy won't soon be forgotten on the yard after that performance. You need to go out with him at least once. I don't even like that song and I was entertained."

"Girl, you know if he got a piece of this yum-yum, I wouldn't be able to get rid of him. My stuff is so good it should be in clinical trials for a replacement for aspirin. It makes all your pain go away. His white bread ass wouldn't know what to do with me."

"You do seem to attract those of paler persuasions," Donna said considering Gloria's dating card resembled the makeup of the United Nations Security Council.

"Black guys don't seem to approach me. I don't know why," Gloria said. Donna fixed her with a disbelieving look. "Maybe I intimidate them or I don't look like the usual round the way girl, with the door knocker earrings or the bone straight perm. Not that there is anything wrong with getting your no-lye on or sporting bamboo earrings, but that is not me. I like my cigarette pants and shell earrings."

Entering Gloria's dorm, the two continued their conversation while waiting for the elevator.

"You say none of the brothers on the yard are clocking for you? I'm fixing to prove you wrong. How about Tracy? Brother is the president of the Phi Beta Sigma Chapter, on the dean's list every semester and has the prettiest white teeth. Every time I see him on the yard he is asking about you," Donna said.

"Naw, I heard he was dating somebody going to school to be an esthetician. I have been meaning to ask him to get me the hook up. My skin can do for some tightening up."

Sighing with exasperation, Donna tried again. "Fine, Tracy's out. How about Akil Semaj that lives in Belk? He is from Jamaica and transferred from Florida International. Accent just makes you want to grab a Red Stripe and some jerk chicken. And you know what they say about them island men."

"Yeah, and no. Brother got too much stuff going on, always volunteering with this group and that group. His Volvo stays in the wind like leaves. I need a man who can make time for me."

"Damn, you are bound and determined not to play along. How about K.C.? You know the Kappa and the president of the Social Work Honor Society? He is friends with Capri and Kristen."

Gloria replied she didn't think Aaron Donahue from the Omega Tau would like Donna hooking his boyfriend up.

"Damn, is everyone at this school gay and I just don't know it? Sometimes I feel like Jesus could come back and say I am the new and risen Christ and I would be the last to know," Donna said shaking her head. Reclining on Gloria's bed, she chuckled at Gloria's exasperated facial expression.

"What are you talking about? I'm not gay and you are not gay, so obviously not everyone at this school is gay. Anyway, Donna, I appreciate the effort but it just comes down to two things. I tend to date people that approach me, or I date someone with whom I have a shared interest. Most of the guys in the classes I take or the clubs I belong to are either white or Asians," Gloria said walking to her refrigerator.

"Gloria, when it comes down to it, I want you to be happy. I'm not your momma. Whoever you choose to date is your right. Just as long as you don't mess with my man, we are fine."

"Trust me, when it comes to Peter, you have nothing to worry about from me. I wish I could say the same for some of the other girls on campus," Gloria said dryly.

The two sisters stared at each other, their glances filled with memories of previous conversations about Peter's widely known infidelity.

"Like I've said before, you are my sister and a black woman with a good head on your shoulders. I respect and honor the choices you make, and—"

Cutting her off, Donna retorted, "But you can't understand why I stay with Peter when he seems to have trouble keeping his dick in his pants. Yes, Gloria I know some people just don't get it. I love Peter and he loves me too. The tramps he screws around with don't mean anything to him. They see some football player and feel like if he screws them, they got him. Peter isn't going anywhere. He knows he has a good thing."

"I wish you could see that is not fair to you, hanging on to a man who can't honor his commitment to you," Gloria said gently. "Just because you have keys to a candy store don't mean you have to lick every lollipop around you. Peter may have the moves on the field that gets the girls gushing like fountains, but he needs to limit his Xs and Os to just you."

"Well thank you for your relationship advice, but I'm keeping my man. Anyway, who takes relationship advice from a woman who hasn't had a single relationship in the time I have known her?" Donna said.

"Don't worry about who I date. As you can tell, I have men willing to make asses of themselves in public to get with me. In fact, I have an invitation to go to a frat party tomorrow at the Kappa Sigma house with Thomas. You want to come with?"

"No, I will pass," Donna said checking her watch. Kiara would be getting out of class soon and she was going to pick her up from campus. But Donna had let Peter borrow her car since his was in the shop. "You know I try to limit my party experience to like hued people. I'm saving my moves for the Wheel party Saturday night after the game."

For the previous ten years, the male and female track teams held a joint homecoming party at the American Legion building on the outskirts of town. Based on her status as an upperclassman, Kiara had the power to admit someone free to Wheel parties. Knowing their sister planned to work the door from 10:00 p.m. to 11:00 p.m., Donna and Gloria timed their arrival that Saturday for 10:45.

"K-Rho!" Gloria shrieked seeing Kiara's smiling face.

"K-Rho," Kiara said, stamping each of the girl's hands with a red stamp marking they'd paid. "Sorry I didn't get a chance to make it to the game. After I finished working on my class project, I went over to Kim's house to see how she was doing and got caught babysitting her daughter. By the time I got home to change clothes, you had already left."

"Yeah, Gloria and I went out for dinner with some of the old school sorors who came through Lambda Mu back in the day," Donna said while Gloria went ahead into the party. "Anyway, you didn't miss much. Winston stomped our ass, so don't expect the entire team to show up tonight. They had an eleven-point lead going into fourth quarter and ended up losing twenty-eight to twenty-seven. Alex was too busy trying to look like John Elway."

"Nice to know we have such strong support D," Alex, Copper Road's quarterback said walking through the doorway. Flanked by Peter and two of the other members of the offense team, the blonde senior smiled at Donna. Observing his look of appreciation for her sorority sister, Kiara wondered about the motivation behind it. Since Donna dated the other star football player at Copper Road, Kiara assumed she would be friendly with Alex. Still, something in his glance struck her as off. She noted how his sapphire colored eyes clouded and his jaw tightened when Peter enveloped Donna in a hug. Word along the grapevine was Alex liked all things chocolate. Could that include her roommate? A wave of folks at the door, who had probably been waiting in their cars until members of the team arrived, turned Kiara's attention away from her roommate's possible love triangle.

Everything was going fine until Kiara looked up from stamping hands to meet Chris' playful eyes.

"Hey Kiara. I drove down to surprise you," she said standing in front of a dropped-jaw Kiara. "I guess I did."

"Soror, Ike sent me up here to ask if you could work until Udon gets here," Gloria said interrupting their reunion.

"I guess I can. You remember my friend Chris?" Kiara said, gesturing toward her girlfriend. Out of the corner of her eye, Kiara noticed her lover's nose flare slightly.

"Oh hey again, I remember you. We met during graduation. I was a marshal. How are you doing?"

"I'm good. You are looking well in your purple and platinum. Here I thought Kiara owned every sorority shirt ever made. I don't think I have seen this one," she said, admiring the baby tee with a platinum colored swan square in the center.

Uncomfortable with how Chris was looking at Gloria, Kiara interjected, "Soror, tell Ike I can work the door until Udon gets here but he needs to remember this when we have our Thanksgiving food drive next week. I'm expecting a big donation from the track team."

"Bet. Well let me head back inside. Donovan has been after me to dance so I had better get it in before the DJ starts playing house music. I don't want one of the few white boys in the spot to be embarrassed by trying to keep up."

Chris managed to sit outside with Kiara for about the length of time it took the DJ to play "Now That We Found Love." Then she ventured inside the room to mingle.

Udon didn't show up until midnight, but Kiara's ire about being kept away from getting her party on was lessened by the two drinks she drank while stamping hands and collecting Lincolns. Released from her duties, Kiara headed straight to the bathroom. Seeing a line outside the girl's bathroom, she cursed under her breath. Armed with the knowledge that the boy's bathroom had a lock on the door, she took a chance and knocked. Unoccupied, she rushed in to experience sweet relief.

Sneaking out of the bathroom, Kiara met the surprised eyes of two guys waiting for their turn with a smile. She headed toward the party. Intent on dancing and strolling with her sorority sisters, she looked past the 6' 3" mocha junior with a carefully trimmed goatee and olive framed glasses walking toward her.

"Oh excuse me," he said after Kiara bumped into him.

"You are fine. I wasn't looking where I was going," Kiara apologized. Assessing the milk chocolate eyes, the shy smile, and the well-defined chest, embraced by a navy short sleeve shirt, she realized "fine" truly fit.

"I'm Malcolm, nice to meet you."

"I'm Kiara," she said shaking the hand with nicely trimmed nails offered to her. The thump, thump of the bass from the party faded away as the pressure of his grasp shot currents down her legs to her purple painted toes.

"Some party they have going on. Ike told me track team parties were a big deal, but I wasn't expecting anything like this. I guess I'm going to have to get used to this kind of thing. I just transferred here from Boone and we didn't have enough black folks there to do anything like this."

"So you're Malcolm Miller? Ike told me about you, and you are just what they need to get to regionals. I run the anchor on the girl's four by eight hundred, so I know being an anchor is no joke."

"Oh, a fellow runner, no wonder your legs look so good in those jeans," he said, trying to sound smooth and debonair.

The intention wasn't lost on Kiara. She felt strangely thrilled by the compliment. Graced with a shape sometimes compared to a soda bottle, sweet words from men had poured in and out of Kiara's ears since puberty. Typically, their words registered as white noise. This time, for some reason, she felt excited. Her desire to get to the dance floor was replaced with a sense of wanting to know more about Malcolm. The two stood and chatted for about fifteen minutes, until Kiara saw a pissed off looking Chris coming toward them.

"Kiara, I have been looking all over for you. Can I see you outside?" Chris said tensely.

"Malcolm this is my friend Chris, Chris this is Malcolm. He just transferred from Appalachian and he's on the track team,"

Kiara said.

Chris looked like she gave less than a damn about knowing Malcolm's name. Looking from Kiara to Chris, Malcolm exited the situation. Gesturing for Kiara to follow, Chris walked outside.

Walking toward Chris' truck, Kiara could hear the faint thump of the music. Her mind lingered on Malcolm while she anticipated the conversation with her girlfriend.

"Didn't you see me looking for you? Who the fuck was that you were talking to in there?" Chris asked sharply once they reached her truck.

"I just introduced the two of you. His name is Malcolm and he is on the track team."

"Oh yeah I forgot. I'm your friend. I have been your friend all fucking night," Chris said, eyes blazing. "I drive all the way up here to see you and you grinning up in some dude's face. I can't leave you alone for a minute."

"What is your problem? I was just talking to someone who is on the track team. I bumped into him when I came out of the bathroom and we struck up a conversation. It is no big deal. What, you don't trust your girlfriend now to be able to come and go from the bathroom?"

"So now you're my 'girlfriend,'" Chris sarcastically replied. "You could have fooled me. Ever since you became a duck, goose, or swan, whatever you guys call yourself, I have been your 'friend.' I know you told me your sister Donna knows about us, but I get the impression no one else knows. I'm not going to keep being a little secret you keep from your friends. I went along with that shit when I went here because I knew you didn't want everyone in your business. You got your precious letters now. You need to start being yourself. And I will not let you disrespect me and our fucking relationship in front of me."

Eyes ablaze with indignation, Kiara said, "What do you mean disrespect our relationship? I was just talking to him. You act like we were going at it in the hallway."

"I saw how close you were standing to him and don't you

raise your voice at me."

Tilting her head back and forth, Kiara responded, "Who the fuck are you to tell me how to talk? I pitch my voice where I please."

Before Chris could reply, Donna stepped in between the two.

"Key, is everything all right here?" she asked. Gloria stood slightly behind Kiara watching the three over the rim of a red plastic cup.

"Yeah. I'm fine. Y'all go back to the party and I will see you later."

"Gloria and I came out here to get you so we can get our stroll on, so I guess 'we' are going back to the party," Donna said giving Chris a challenging look. During the course of the party, Donna had seen Chris drink three cups of the "Purple Passion" the track team was selling for five dollars. She knew it was grain alcohol mixed with fruit, and was potent stuff. Purple colored alcohol plus the green tinge of jealousy was a color palate Donna had painted in too many times before. Waiting in line for the bathroom, Donna had seen the exchange between Kiara, Malcolm, and Chris. She was glad she'd decided to pull Gloria away from her dance partner to come outside with her, in case she had to prevent an argument from veering into a physical altercation.

"So now you got your sorority sisters in our business? She comes out here and tells you, my girlfriend, what you are going to do. Fuck this! I'm going home. Enjoy the party with your new friends. I'll call you when I think about it," Chris said getting in her truck.

As the truck lights headed down the road away from the party, Kiara's face crumpled in tears. "Can y'all just leave me alone for a minute?"

"Hell no, we are not leaving you alone. Especially since I don't know what just happened," Gloria said. "I mean I have an idea of what just happened, but I'm not into being Kermit tonight and jumping like a frog to conclusions."

Donna and Kiara looked at each other, then at Gloria who stood with her arms crossed and an expectant look on her face.

"Why don't we go get a bite to eat and I will explain the whole thing," Kiara said.

"Good, I think DeShawn the Kappa was going to get into it with Winston the Omega over Cassie the Zeta. I don't know why they want to fight over her when she has been sneaking around with Charles the Iota," Gloria said, waiting to see who was driving.

"Dang, I didn't think Cassie had it like that. She isn't even that cute in the face," Donna said walking toward her car.

"I just hope DeShawn's frat calms him down before he gets himself into some trouble. You know they are on probation for that hazing incident. What kind of duck heads, knowing you have someone on your line with a pre-existing medical condition, are going to intentionally make it worse? So very arsine," Gloria said.

Using half of her mind to process Gloria's conversation, Kiara's mind whirled with trying to understand what had just happened. Everything happened so fast. Did she and Chris just have an argument about her talking to some guy? Did her girlfriend just storm off in a huff about an innocent conversation? Was the conversation innocent?

"Huh, did you just say something to me D?" Kiara said meeting Donna's questioning eyes.

"I asked you if you want to ride with us in my car or follow us to the restaurant. Judging that it took you five minutes to answer the question, I'm going to make the call for you. Get in, and before you say it Gloria, buckle your seatbelt. Because trust me, I can tell it's going to be a bumpy night."

CHAPTER NINE

Kiara/Donna/Gloria

FORTIFIED BY A chicken cheesesteak and steak fries, Kiara told Gloria and Donna the reason for her argument with Chris. Her girlfriend was upset about her talking to a guy. After receiving clarification that meant Kiara was a lesbian, Gloria shrugged her shoulders.

"Oh, is that all? I thought sister was crazy. If y'all are together, she doesn't need to sweat who you talk to. It is who you are laying down with she needs to focus on. As long as it's her, she doesn't need to worry," she said, pouring ketchup on her eggs. Kiara and Donna stared wordlessly at her.

"What? Why are y'all looking at me? I knew you were gay, Kiara, when we went on line. I must be the only straight girl with dead-on gaydar."

"So why didn't you share this information with us while we were pledging? Hell, you could have at least told me. I didn't find out until a few weeks ago when her and old girl was getting down or going down or whatever they were doing in the room," Donna said.

"You country bumpkins, no disrespect, would have flipped out and I didn't feel like dealing with anymore drama than what was already going to be there," Gloria said.

Acknowledging the server bringing her order, Donna replied, "Thank you for doing your part to ease the tension."

"Anytime, my sister. It's a hard job spreading peace and tranquility across the land, but alas, someone must do it."

"So it doesn't bother you?" Kiara asked.

"Not at all. I know it's cliché, but some of my best buds are gay. We used to sneak in gay clubs all the time in D.C. My mom's best friend is a lesbian. I'm cool with whatever you do and whom you do it with. You are my sister and I am confident enough in my sexuality not to sweat whom you choose to fuck. It is none of my business," Gloria said.

"Thank you for understanding. You know Donna, and now you, are the only people I have told about me being gay. It's not like I'm ashamed that I like girls. I just don't want people to judge me before getting to know me," Kiara said. She exhaled partly from relief and partly in response to the jalapenos mixed in with her sandwich.

"I feel you on that sister," Gloria said and sipped her soda. "It sucks when people form opinions about you based on how you dress or the company you keep. Now I will say, half of me wants to ask the stereotypical questions about how long you have known you were gay. But when it comes down to it, it doesn't matter. The only thing that matters is that you are comfortable in your own skin. But I will ask how did you and Chris meet?"

Donna, who neglected to ask the question herself, leaned forward anticipating the answer.

"Don't tell anybody, but during my first semester here, I posed nude for a figure drawing class. It paid fifty dollars for a two hour class and I needed some spending money," Kiara explained. "She was in that class but never said anything to me. Flash-forward to the next semester, I'm walking to my dorm room and she is coming up the hall toward me. She asked me if I posed for Dr. Richmond's class last year. When I said yes, she said, 'I thought you looked familiar. You look different with your clothes on.'"

"Damn player, that's a line for your ass," Donna said.

"So I asked her, 'well, what do you think looks better, on or off?' She asked me if I wanted to have coffee with her at Selma's downtown the next day and I said yes. We have been kicking it ever since. Well, I hope we are still kicking it after tonight."

"If Chris is like most dudes, her ego is probably hurt Kiara wasn't grinning up in her face the entire night. She will probably call you tomorrow all apologetic," Donna said, motioning the server to fill up her glass. "Don't let it bother you girl. Let her sleep it off. Now, let's talk about something else besides Kiara's crazy girlfriend. Did you see that dress Egypt had on? That thing was way too small for that ass of hers."

Kiara agreed, and the trio turned their conversation to other matters. Chatting with Donna and Gloria, Kiara inwardly sent up a prayer of thanks for having understanding sisters. Even if they avidly appreciated men, their sense of loyalty to her seemed to trump any uncomfortable feelings.

The next morning, when Kiara awoke, the house was quiet and Donna's door was open. She served as a member of her church's usher board, so Kiara figured it was her Sunday to be a woman in white, seating the faithful. Fixing eggs and corned beef hash, she considered calling Chris to apologize. Then again, she wasn't the one who was rude. Instead, she turned on the TV and caught the last hour of *CBS Sunday Morning*. As the final nature shot filled the screen, she flicked off the TV and headed toward the shower to wash up. While in the shower, she heard the phone ring.

"Hi, you have reached the purple and platinum domicile of the soul-stepping sisters Kiara and Donna," the answering machine announced. "Leave your message for the sister of your choice and we will get back to you. K-Rho."

"Hi, Kiara. It's Malcolm from last night. Your sorority sister Veronica said you left the party early. I know your friend was a little heated, so I wanted to make sure things are all right." He recited is number then finished his message. "I'm going to be around for a while, so give me a call."

By the end of the message, a dripping and conflicted Kiara

stood in her bedroom listening. As soon as the message ended, she played it back to write down the number Malcolm had left. Staring at the seven digits, Kiara pondered calling Malcolm. Would that be cheating? 'No, I would just be being polite. After all, he called to check on how I was doing. I can't leave him hanging.'

"Hello?"

"Hi, it's Kiara. Did I catch you at a bad time?"

"No I was just sitting here staring at my drafting book, thinking I should do some work."

"Oh, what's your major?"

"Chemistry."

"That's interesting."

"I guess, if you like having an instructor who tells stories about folks having their ass blown to kingdom come because they mixed the wrong chemicals together because they weren't paying attention."

Kiara laughed and Malcolm thought it was the most beautiful sound he had ever heard. Prior to him walking into her, he had checked her out at the party, looking cool in her tight jeans and t-shirt. The way the lights hit the auburn highlights in her hair dazzled him. He had been scoping her out for weeks after he saw her running laps at practice. Her intense gaze struck him as she sprinted up and down the straightaway. He had asked around about her on the yard and found out she was a psych and business major and lived off campus. Most importantly, he had found out she didn't have a boyfriend. Sure, he had heard the rumors about her, but he didn't believe it. As good as she looked, must have been a lie.

"What are you doing for dinner? Why don't we go to Applebee's for a bite, say at six," Malcolm asked.

Without hesitation, Kiara answered she would be thrilled. As she hung up, she did a little two-step then caught herself. 'Oh, dinner with a dude; this is definitely dangerous territory.'

Seeking to distract herself from what she planned to do later, she headed out to do laundry and pick up some items from the grocery store. When she returned, she found Donna and Peter curled up on the couch watching football. Rather, Peter was watching TV and Donna was reading one of her textbooks with highlighter in hand.

"Hey you, Peter and I stopped by Parker's after service. I picked up a BBQ dinner with greens and mac and cheese for you in case you're hungry. It's in the fridge," Donna said, looking over her shoulder as Kiara came in, three bags in each hand. Hoisting the grocery bags on the counter, Kiara expressed her appreciation of Donna's thoughtfulness but responded she actually had plans for dinner.

Smiling and assuming Chris was the other party, Donna asked, "What time are you heading back out?"

Bending down to put away the canned goods, Kiara said, "I'm meeting Malcolm around six at Applebee's."

The corners of Donna's mouth dropped down. "Kiara, can I have a word with you in my bedroom?" Donna asked getting up and walking toward the back.

Closing the door and facing a meek looking Kiara, she said, "I'm confused. Last month you came out to me that you are into girls. Now you are going out on a date with some guy? Does this mean you are whatchacallit, bi?"

"No, it means that I'm hungry."

"Is this the same guy from last night? If it is, I don't know what to say. Something in my spirit is telling me this is not going to end well. Honey, I'm not Elder Swan Dorothy, otherwise known as your mother, so I can't tell you what to do and who to do it with. Just be sure you don't get hurt or hurt someone in the process."

Shaking her head, Kiara replied she just planned to get a bite to eat, not get married.

At Applebee's, Malcolm's brown eyes and conversation captivated Kiara. She thought, 'it's so refreshing to be able to be out with someone I enjoy talking to without worrying about who is looking.' It was a feeling she didn't have when going out with Chris. When Malcolm asked about the situation between her and the girl from the night before, she dismissed it by saying it was just a misunderstanding between friends. Feeling guilty, but not wanting to tip her hand too soon about her sexuality, Kiara steered the conversation away to getting to know her dining partner better.

Kiara discovered they had so much in common. Malcolm was the middle child as well, but his bookends were a sister and a brother to Kiara's two brothers. Both pulled for the Bulls in basketball and the Redskins in football. They even shared the same favorite fair food.

"It's nice to know I'm not the only person who lived for corn dog day at school when it came to lunch," Kiara said, smiling over her steak. When she placed her order, Kiara noticed Malcolm eyes sparked. He told her it was nice she wasn't a frail salad-eating girl, too afraid of her waistline to enjoy a good meal.

"I know. I used to beg my mom to make some for dinner but she wasn't having it. So other than Kappa and track, what else are you into?"

"Not too much else, really. Donna and I usually try to catch a movie at the student center on Fridays. If she and Peter are together, I will go with one of my sorors or some of the girls on the team," Kiara replied. "I like to read and watch sports. My dad was a big baseball fan so we used to catch all the Braves games. Since he passed, it doesn't feel the same. Another thing I like, and you have to promise not to laugh, is crochet."

Malcolm folded his lips inward in an attempt to prevent himself from laughing. Kiara started giggling in response. In the back of her mind, she thought, 'he looks so cute.' She nodded her head giving him permission to let it out.

"Wow, I have never met anyone our age that does that. So what kind of stuff do you usually make?" Malcolm asked, taking a French fry from Kiara's plate.

She answered scarfs and hats, but right now her major projects were a purple blanket with K-Rho stitched in platinum thread for Donna, and a purple and platinum purse for Gloria. She planned to give them to her sisters for Christmas.

"So you don't have a man to show you off on campus?

I figured you didn't since you are here with me, but just want to check to make sure."

Kiara felt her mouth involuntarily twitch. She needed to come clean. No need to lead Malcolm along thinking he had a chance when he didn't. She was a lesbian. She had a girlfriend. She was in a committed relationship.

"No, you are cool. I don't have a boyfriend," Kiara said.

Relieved, Malcolm nodded his head and grinned. "I'm glad to hear that. I mean, I'm not trying to crowd you or anything. I just want to make sure we cool."

Kiara beamed with amusement. "We cool."

The two sat talking for close to an hour. At the end of the night, when Malcolm walked her to her car, she could sense he wanted a good-bye kiss. Instead, he got a warm hug and thanks for a lovely night.

Kiara walked back into the apartment with a broad smile of her face. She felt like singing, but her heart and mouth couldn't agree on a tune.

"Damn girl, you are coming in here looking like the children of Israel when Moses told them to pack their bags. That must have been one hell of a meal. You don't grin like that after eating my cooking," Donna said sitting at the kitchen table surrounded by books.

"Girl, after your cooking it's all I can do to stay awake. You make food that makes you want to fall asleep at the table it's so good. Malcolm and I had a good time chatting and finding out we have a lot in common."

"I bet I know one thing you didn't share with him that you two have in common. Both of you love the ladies," Donna said. Kiara's sheepish look confirmed Donna's assumption. "I shouldn't have to say it but I'm going to. You need to come clean with that boy. The Bible says anyone who knows the right thing they should do, but doesn't do it, is wrong. Sins of omission are just as bad as sins of commission. There isn't two ways about it. Now, it was wrong for you not to tell us about Chris when we were going through the process. I can excuse that because we weren't trying to get in your pants. This dude is probably plotting to get some. Did he pay for dinner or did y'all split the bill?"

Sitting down at the table Kiara said, "He paid."

"What did you order?"

"Steak, but it was small one."

"Oh hell no, brother took you out and you ordered a steak. Now I know he probably expects to hit the skins. Everyone is grown and knows what they need to do. Oh, and by the way, Chris called. I told her you were doing some K-Rho stuff," Donna said turning back to her books.

Kiara said thank you and walked into her room to call Chris back. Just like Donna predicted, her lover had called to apologize and said she hoped to be able to come down and see Kiara before she left for Thanksgiving break in three weeks.

Chris' words went unfulfilled. Her job and Kiara's sorority obligations kept them separate. Somehow, during the four weeks after they had meet, Malcolm kept popping up. At first, it was brief conversations if they bumped into each other at the athletic building. Then it was eating lunch in the cafeteria along with other track team members. Even with the noise of students talking, silverware rattling, and the sound of the campus radio station in the background, it seemed to Kiara they were the only ones there. Meals with the group soon turned into meeting for movies at the student center. She realized she should say something to him about Chris, but somehow other than the dinner at Applebee's, the subject of relationships didn't come up. Lying in bed following a two-hour conversation with Malcolm, Kiara felt forced to admit to herself, after hiding who she was on campus, it felt good to go out and have a good time with someone who was interested in her.

"Oh my God Gloria, this is killing me. I feel so conflicted. I love my girlfriend but I like this guy," Kiara said to Gloria.

The two were volunteering at a sorority sponsored bone marrow registry drive. Traffic had slowed down at the registration table so the two had ventured outside to sit in the December Saturday sunshine. In between directing those wanting to be added to the donor registry and keeping the snack table filled, Kiara filled Gloria in about her increasing feelings about Malcolm.

"You know I never doubted I was a lesbian. For me, it was just as much a part of me as the moles on my face. Now, I did sweat a little about it keeping me from being a Rho. Since I have my letters, and knowing you and Donna are in my corner, I thought about starting to be more open and telling more people. But then I bump into Malcolm over a month ago and everything seems like it has changed."

"So you met someone you enjoy talking to and spending time with. I don't see the problem," Gloria said.

"The problem is if I'm really a lesbian I shouldn't want to be around a guy so much. We can have the most mundane conversation and I find myself thinking about it hours later. He tells the corniest jokes and I fall over myself laughing. I mean, I have never felt this way about a guy before. Even my high school boyfriend didn't occupy so much of my brain space and I had known him since fifth grade."

"Golly, that is some Living Colour type action, "Cult of Personality." But my question is, in terms of you questioning your sexuality, would it be so terrible not to be a lesbian?"

"Ever since I was little I had wanted to be with girls. I mean, I had a boyfriend because that was expected of me," Kiara said. "Then I come here to CRU and meet Chris. She's smart, sexy, we have good conversation and she makes me feel safe and good about being with women. That's why I really can't understand this thing with Malcolm."

"Soror, you know I don't judge, contrary to what Donna may say when it comes to Peter and her. I feel there is nothing wrong with being attracted to someone, it's what you do with the attraction," Gloria said nudging Kiara, signaling it was time to go into the building. "Malcolm is a nice guy. He is in my Spanish class and I can see why you enjoy hanging out with him. To me, sexuality is fluid. You like what and whom you like. Yes, Chris and you are a couple. Yes, according to you, you have not been attracted to any men since your high school boyfriend. This is the time in our lives when we are discovering and firming up who we are. All I want to say is what matters is that you are honest with yourself and those who you love, not what letters you use to spell out your sexual preference. Love and lust are both four letter words that start with L, but they don't appear in the dictionary side by sid— so we shouldn't have to think they go hand in hand in life."

"Okay Glo, I think I understand your point," Kiara said. "You never fail to amaze me with your remarkable power of insight."

Gloria accepted the compliment with a wry grin. "I know, it's an awful curse I bear, but I manage somehow. But my services come at a price."

"What?"

"Can you run me to Raleigh Friday? My car needs breaks and I need to go to the federal building and fill out some papers."

"For what?" Kiara said sitting down at the registration table again.

"For my internship next summer with the State Department in D.C. It's unpaid, but I'm going to reach out to my Uncle Rufus, who runs a cleaning service in Silver Springs, to see if he can give me some hours. I'm going to stay with my grand in B'more so I don't have to worry about housing. So I should be good."

"Oh, I'm so proud of you; getting your career climb on."

"A girl has to do what a girl has to do. I'm trying to get in early so I can make a career of it. I get my chance to indulge in my love of Ethiopian restaurants. You can't swing an injera around in the District without falling into someone's wat. Those are staples of Ethiopian food by the way. Injera is the bread and wat is like a stew," Gloria explained.

"Thank you Julia Child for my culinary lesson. At any rate, I'm proud of you. You know this is going to look good on your resume. As if being on the dean's list the entire time you been in school and belonging to all these honor groups won't do it."

"Yeah, but you know how hard the job market is today. You have to have some actual life experience before people will look at hiring you," Gloria said.

"I'm sure when you graduate you are not going to have any trouble finding a job, Ms. Future Phi Beta Kappa and summa cum laude," Kiara said hugging Gloria who hugged her back.

Kiara felt grateful to have a sister friend she could talk to without judgment. Once again, Gloria proved true swans support even if they swim differently.

CHAPTER TEN
Donna/Kiara

KIARA HAD IT all planned out. She was going to invite Malcolm over to the house to tell him that she was gay. The start of Christmas break was three days away and she wanted to end the semester on an honest note. Kiara hoped after she told him, if there was no chance of being more than good friends, the two would still be cool. Unfortunately, the night she planned to come out, Donna's secret showed up on their doorstep.

"Alex, what a surprise," Kiara said, opening the front door. She shot a look at Donna who looked guilty. The two had been sitting at the kitchen table prior to the doorbell ringing. Kiara was studying and Donna was finishing the chapter's community service report. The deadline of December 15 was two days away and she wanted to make sure it was turned in on time to their chapter advisor.

"What's up Kiara? Sorry to drop by unannounced, but I took a chance Donna would be home, so I decided to stop through," Alex said, shaking the snow off his burgundy and cream Copper Road knit hat.

"Well as you can tell, I'm here. So what's going on?" Donna said.

Nervously, Alex looked at Kiara. Taking the hint, she headed to her room. Shutting her door, she turned on the radio to give the duo an extra level of privacy.

Even though every nerve ending in her body pulsated with wanting to know what was going on in her living room, she willed herself to keep her head in her books and her ear turned toward *Cassandra's Confession*.

Fighting back a yawn, Kiara looked at her bedside clock and noticed an hour had passed. Figuring it was safe for her to venture out, she got up to go into the kitchen to get her tea.

"Okay, my fellow Miners, this is Cassandra signing off with one last dedication. I had to dig in the crates for this one. Nevertheless, I have to give props for going with a classic. From Jeremiah to Eugenia, Marvin Gaye's "I Want You.""

Kiara whipped her neck around as if the confirmation of her thoughts about that last dedication would flash on the face of her radio. She just knew that dedication wasn't from whom she thought it was from, to whom she knew it shouldn't be to. Kiara thought, 'he can't be that stupid.'

"Donna, did Alex just send you a shout out on the radio? Is he nuts?" Kiara said walking into Donna's room. "Everyone knows his middle name, especially after that big production last week about him being named after his grandfather, who was his high school coach."

"True, but only a few people know my middle name, so a lot of people won't know who he is sending it out to."

"Peter will know," Kiara stressed.

Donna tucked her legs under herself and adjusted her body on her bed.

"You know it's one thing to know your man is cheating, but when one of his boys makes a special trip in the snow to tell you to your face how much he fucking around, you really feel like Boo-Boo the fool."

"Why this big show of concern for your love life?"

Pausing and taking a deep breath, Donna continued, "He wants me to break up with Peter and be with him. He told me he had thought long and hard about it and he would move heaven, earth and everything in between to make me happy. Peter has never said he would do anything to make me happy. He just assumed if he fucked me, took me out every now and again, and threw some piece of jewelry his sister picked out for me, I would be satisfied. I'm starting to think it's going to take more than that."

Kiara was speechless. She had no idea her roommate had so much going on in her love life. She thought her situation was complicated. At least her conflicts were in two different area codes. Donna's were on the same team.

"Damn girl."

"I know, I know. I don't know what to do. I mean, Alex came over here with this prepared speech about how he has always let me know how much he cared for me and how we have so much in common," Donna said. "Alex, not Peter, always remembers my birthday and makes sure I get an arrangement of daisies. Peter's dumb ass always assumed they were from my parents. When Alex went to Hawaii this past summer, he brought me back that gold leaf necklace Gloria and you always compliment me on when I wear it. Plus, he went half with me on that that tricked out jacket with my line name and sorority crest on the back I got for home-coming."

"Girl, you know I priced that jacket and that joint cost close to two hundred dollars. I knew he came from money, but dang, that is some serious infatuation. Hell, my sorority jacket isn't as fancy as yours and my momma is a Rho. You don't spend that kind of money unless you getting some from the person," Kiara's voiced trailed off.

Donna's silence answered the question.

"Donna!"

"I didn't mean for it to happen. Last month you had left early for class and I had overslept. When I got to campus, I had to park in what seemed like West Bumfuck, since all the parking was taken. On the way to class, I almost twisted my ankle rushing to get Dr. Gumbs' class. You know she locks the door ten minutes after class starts. That day I was twelve minutes late. I left my wallet in my car so I didn't have any money on me to eat lunch and when I got back to my car, someone had backed into it and broke the tail light. I just wanted someone to hold me and tell me it was going to be all better. I went to Peter's hoping he would wrap his arms around me, kiss me and make my bad day go away. When I went to his room, he didn't want to let me in and I could swear he had a girl in there with him. Kiara, after two years of his lies, I just didn't feel like fighting anymore. As I was walking down the hall trying not to cry, I saw Alex coming toward me. He took one look at me and offered to make me a drink. After I told him about my day, he gave me that hug I was looking for and then he started kissing me and I started kissing him and then he started touching me and I started touching him and…"

"And it happened."

"Yeah, it happened. I wanted to tell somebody but I was so ashamed. I know Peter is unfaithful to me, but two wrongs don't make a right. I shouldn't have cheated on him."

"If you know he is unfaithful, why do you stay with him? You are one of the smartest women I know, but you are letting him play you." Kiara's throat ached as she said the words. She hated asking a question that had no easy answer.

"I know it's hard to understand, but I know Peter loves me and I love him. His ego gets him into trouble, not his heart. Ever since he was in middle school, he has been a big football star. Sometimes he gets caught up in his own hype. I told Alex, as much as I would like to be his girlfriend, I can't leave Peter. I love him."

"Donna, you can't hold on to someone who doesn't respect you enough to be with just you. You are so much better than that."

Crying, Donna murmured, "Why love got to be so hard?"

Touched by the vulnerability her usual shit-talking, ass-kicking sister was showing, Kiara's eyes welled up also. While the struggles they faced dealt with different sexual orientations, holding her conflicted best friend, it felt the same.

The ringing phone startled them. Reaching for the phone on Donna's nightstand, Kiara answered on the second ring.

"Hey Kiara, it's me. Are we still on for tonight?"

"Oh hey Malcolm, can I get a rain check? Donna and I have some sorority stuff to work on. How about tomorrow night?" Kiara asked, watching Donna get up and head into her bathroom.

"Nah, that won't work. I have something I need to do that is probably going to take most of the night. I'm leaving Thursday after my final exam. Can I stop by then?"

"That works. Holla back."

Hanging up the phone, Kiara quickly dialed seven digits she knew by heart.

"Hola, como estas?"

"Gloria, I'm calling in a code K emergency. Are you able to accept?"

In a mock solemn tone Gloria replied, "I do, are we talking a level six or a level twelve?"

Kiara weighing the choices and the current situation responded, "A dozen isn't going to do the job. We are talking a dozen glazed and a dozen mixed."

Fighting the urge to giggle, Gloria responded, "I'm calling on the Hot Now gods to intervene in our favor so that when I make it to the shop with the double K's they are able to help me fulfill my mission. I will see y'all in fifteen minutes."

Donna, Gloria, and Kiara sat up until two in the morning, eating donuts and drinking cocoa, finally passing out on the living room couches. The next morning the three of them parted ways for the holiday break. Donna planned to leave after her exams and Gloria's flight time coincided with Kiara's final exam for the semester.

When Kiara extended the invitation for Malcolm to stop by, she didn't expect him to show up at 8:00 a.m. She had just walked out of her bedroom fully dressed when her doorbell rang.

"Hi Kiara," Malcolm said.

"Hey you, you are up early," Kiara said hugging him as she ushered him into the apartment.

"Yeah, I was up until three this morning finishing my paper. After catching a few hours of sleep I decided to get up and get it over to Dr. Eribo as soon as he got to his office."

"That's your Global Communication class right? Lisa from the track team is in that class and said he is a great teacher. Accent can get a little thick at times, but still you come out better than you went in."

Smiling as he checked out Kiara's frame in her jeans and purple and platinum t-shirt, Malcolm replied he didn't want to keep her from getting ready for her morning; he just wanted to drop off her Christmas present. Handing her a small wrapped present from his jacket pocket, he watched Kiara's eyes shine with glee. The track teams had played Secret Santa, and in what had to be coincidence, Kiara and Malcolm had pulled each other's name.

"Gosh, thank you. Hold on, let me get your present from my room," Kiara said walking down the hall. Coming back, she saw Malcolm had poured her and himself some coffee.

"I have a confession to make. I really didn't pull your name. I tracked down the girl that did and paid her to switch with me. When I saw that gift in the mall, I had to get it for you," Malcolm said, ducking his head and blushing. "Anyway, I saw you had taken the cups down so I figured you wouldn't mind. Two sugars, right?"

"You are so sweet, Malcolm," Kiara said taking the mug offered to her. Sitting on the couch, sipping and staring at each other over their steaming cups of dark roast, Kiara felt the words about her sexuality dancing behind her lips. It was just a matter of her opening her mouth to say, "Malcolm I'm gay. I have a girl-friend." For some reason, she couldn't get her mouth to move. Kiara thought, 'what is wrong with me? Why can't I be honest with Malcolm?' Her thoughts then shifted to noticing how good he smelled.

"Malcolm, I'm loving that cologne you have on," she said, leaning closer to him and sniffing his neck.

Pleasantly startled, Malcolm told her the name. Ironically, it was the same one Chris wore when she felt like being sexy.

"Small world, one of my friends wears that same brand.

But I have to say you wear it much better," Kiara said smiling, then catching herself, excused herself to take the cups into the kitchen.

'Pull it together Kiara,' she said to herself. 'You acting like some chickenhead all on his tip. You are a lesbian. We don't get geeked out about some dude.'

"Well Kiara, I'm going to head back to campus," Malcolm said, interrupting Kiara's internal pep talk. "I'm riding with Demetrius back home and we should be pulling out around one. I'm going to catch me a few Zzz then I'm going to pack up."

Walking Malcolm to the door, Kiara's mind raced. It's now or never. Her speech was ready. She parted her lips slightly and—kissed Malcolm. Kiara, confused and aroused at the feeling swirling and pulsating throughout her body, felt lost. What in the hell was she doing? She had planned to tell him she was gay. All they could be was just friends. She had a girlfriend she kept thinking to herself. 'If that was the case,' she thought, 'why am I pulling him closer to me so his bulge is pressing assertively into my sacred spot?'

"Key, are you sure about this?" Malcolm said, as they broke apart for a breath.

Gloria had once said sexuality is fluid. Right now Kiara felt like a pulsating stream of desire. It had been two months since she had been intimate and she wanted Malcolm. Everything in the moment, the smell of his cologne, that hazelnut taste of the coffee on his lips, and the way his body seemed to curve into hers made her swoon. Grabbing Malcolm's hand, Kiara led him to her bedroom. Undressing, she rationalized: 'I never said I didn't like men. It's just I like women more. I mean, I'm sure vegetarians eat a burger every now and again when no one is looking.'

Malcolm taking the hint pulled off his jacket and almost ripped off his shirt pulling it up and over his head.

Moving to him and rubbing her hands across his chest, Kiara shuddered. She wanted Malcolm so bad; she could taste it in the back of her mouth. Kissing his chest and rubbing her tongue across his nipples, her breath eluded her like it had warrants.

Kiara's mouth explored Malcolm's torso. Her teeth nibbled at his neck as he wrapped his arms around her waist. 'What the fuck am I doing?' Kiara thought as she guided Malcolm down on her bed and leaned him back. She felt repulsion about betraying her girlfriend, but arousal at the thought of doing something unexpected. Kiara always prided herself on acting logically, weighing her options before committing to an action. She pulled down Malcolm's jeans and boxers, realizing she couldn't blame her actions on alcohol or betrayal from a lover. She was doing this because she wanted to. It was just that simple.

No words had been spoken since the living room. Malcolm broke the silence, raising his hand to halt Kiara.

"Wait a minute, I want this too, but I want to make sure we use protection. I mean, I'm not trying to say you have anything and I'm sure you may be on the pill or something, but I don't get down like that."

Rocking back on her heels, Kiara paused as she remembered straight people do use condoms. She was so used to dental dams; she forgot how the other half lived.

The two looked at each other intently while Malcolm sheathed his penis. Kiara knew she had the power of no. She could tell Malcolm she had changed her mind, this was a mistake. The moistness between her thighs and the hardness of her nipples from excitement confirmed her intention about the situation.

"Damn girl, you are tight. I'm not going to rush it because I don't want to hurt you," Malcolm said, inserting more and more of him inside her.

Kiara felt a sense of pressure she had not experienced since her last pelvic exam. Only this was much more agreeable to her senses. She felt full and pleasured. Moving her hips to adjust to Malcolm's pace, she thought to herself, 'he must have had dance lessons before, because he is really moving it all around."

If making love to Chris was an orchestra, Malcolm was a rap concert. The thump of the bass represented by the tapping of his balls against Kiara's lower inches. The twists and the turns of the artist's tongue symbolized by the shifting of Malcolm's motion. Lifting her legs up and resting them on his shoulder, Malcolm penetrated Kiara at an angle that made her spontaneously curse, "Damn boy, what are you doing to me?" Pausing mid stroke, Malcolm looked down in concern.

"Why are you stopping?" Kiara shrieked, feeling her vaginal muscles mambo with pleasure. "Don't stop."

Malcolm owned the stage that was Kiara's body. Kiara had never felt like this before. Even her high school boyfriend— who she had tried out so many different sexual positions with, she lost count— didn't make her feel like this. Even with the heat in the apartment on low, she found herself sweating.

Kiara felt aroused watching Malcolm's expression change from total concentration to satisfaction while he increased his pace. Kiara threw her head back and prepared to give praises for his performance.

"Oh, baby, this is it. This is it, oh baby," Malcolm said moving faster and faster and faster. "Oh baby, this feels so good. Oh, ooh, ooh. Uh-oh," Malcolm said as he withdrew from Kiara.

"What's uh-oh?" Kiara said.

"This is uh-oh," he said showing her the broken condom.

"Uh-oh," Kiara said, looking at Malcolm with a stricken look in her eyes.

"Don't worry, I don't have anything that is catching," Malcolm said sitting beside her on the bed.

"Well I'm clean too, so you don't have to worry about that. What else is there to worry about?" Kiara said with a half-smile.

The two sat silently for a few minutes then Malcolm began getting dressed.

"Um Kiara, I'm really sorry that it ended the way it did, but I'm glad we had a chance to you know, do it," Malcolm said. "If you don't mind, I'd like to call you during the winter break or maybe you can call me."

"Yeah, that would be nice," Kiara said grabbing a piece of paper from her desk. "Here is my number. I should be leaving tomorrow to go home so whenever you want to call me, it will be cool."

Putting on a robe, Kiara walked Malcolm to the door. The two hugged and Kiara turned her thoughts to getting ready for her final exam. Kiara replayed the morning's events back in her mind while she took her shower. Having sex with Malcolm felt so good. But as she weighed the feelings she got from his touch beside the sensations sparked by Chris, she realized the grass was truly not greener on the other side.

CHAPTER ELEVEN
January 1992
Kiara/Donna

"OH MY GOD, I'm still gagging about Malcolm and you doing it. Most times, you hear about straight girls having a same-sex fling in college just to say they did it. I have never heard about it going the other way around," Gloria said to Kiara and Donna over Chinese takeout.

The three were sitting at Donna and Kiara's kitchen table catching up after their winter break. During a two-hour, three-way conversation, two days before Christmas, she filled the girls in with all the juicy details. Still, once they connected the day before spring semester started, Kiara had to repeat the story, complete with facial expressions and physical reenactments.

"It wasn't my plan to have sex with him. I guess I was thinking with the wrong head," Kiara said, twirling her fork in her lo mein.

"If it makes you feel any better, I still consider you a lesbian," Gloria said, using her chopsticks to lift a piece of shrimp to her mouth. "As long as the ratio of women to men tilts toward women, I consider you a gay girl."

"Thank you. Donna is of the opinion, now that I have slept with Malcolm, I'm going to be banging guys left and right on campus, which I totally disagree with. It was a one-time thing and I don't plan to make it a hobby."

Shaking her head, Donna bit into her egg roll. "I didn't say you were going be humping around. All I said was now that you have had a taste of what most of us go crazy for, you are going to start wanting to be with dudes."

"Well it's not like I have a girlfriend anymore standing in my way. Can you believe the nerve of that bitch? Breaking up with me on New Year's Day because she wanted a new start," Kiara said rolling her eyes. "I mean, she comes down on Christmas Eve and has a lovely time with my family. My brother Nelson couldn't chew his food for looking at her. Then a week later, she hits me with the whole so bye-bye-bye routine."

"How did that manage to happen? I thought you said your family didn't know you like girls?" Donna said.

"They don't. She called me on Christmas Eve saying her folks had driven down to see her grandmother who lives in Southport and she wanted to come by and say hello. Southport is just over the bridge from Wilmington and I couldn't think of the word no quick enough to keep her from coming over," Kiara said. "I introduced her as my girlfriend and my family just assumed I meant girlfriend like friend girl. I didn't bother to correct them. That really irked her. But hell, what did she expect? I have never talked about being gay with my family. I didn't think it was appropriate to come out to my family around the dinner table during a holiday. I mean, really? Who does that? Just takes all the fun out the holiday."

"I know your mouth is saying fuck her and the horse she rode in on, but how do you really feel about her breaking up with you?" Donna said.

"Real talk, I am sort of sad we didn't make it. She was my first real girlfriend and I had hoped we would last longer. But she was there and I was here so I figured it would happen eventually," Kiara said, taking the last swallow of her iced tea. "But it's just the way she did it that chaps my hide. My mom and I had gone to Watch Night service and didn't get back home until three in the morning. I just had gone to sleep good when she ups and calls me six hours later. I mean dang, if you are going to kick someone to the curb at least wait until the afternoon."

"Well soror, it would seem the universe is suggesting you go a different way," Gloria said. "First you hook up with Malcolm then your girlfriend dumps you. Perhaps, you may need to rethink how you fill in your dating schedule."

"No, I am attracted to women. I love women. I am a lesbian. What happened with Malcolm was a mistake. I let my loins think for me and I don't plan to go down that path again," Kiara said vigorously. "It was just something about him I felt was attractive. Now that I have gotten that out of my system, I don't plan to go back to men."

"Sounds like you are trying to convince yourself more than you are trying to convince us," Gloria said looking out the corner of her eye at Donna. "Regardless of how you decide to identify yourself, you are going to always be my #3 and I love and honor you. Whatever you decided to do about Malcolm or whoever, I support you."

"And if you decide you going back to being with men, Scott from the football team is still available," Donna said. "I can still put a good word in for you."

"Why is it that a straight girl can have a one night romp with a girl and people just chalk it up to being open minded and trying something new? Her sexuality doesn't get called into play. But I sleep with a guy one time and you are ready to throw away the fact I have come out as a lesbian to both of you and just ended a lesbian relationship," Kiara said, her voice rising with indignation.

"Calm the fuck down Kiara. Gloria and I are just saying if you happened to discover you like getting stuck instead of being licked, we are cool with that," Donna said, her voice rising as well.

"Hey, hey my sweet sorors, let us take it down a thousand. We love each other and don't need to sweat who we choose to date. Sisterhood should supersede sexuality," Gloria said, waving her hands downward in an attempt to lower tempers. The two roommates looked at each other, both waiting for the other to say something. "Hey, did I show you guys my new tattoo," she said extending her wrist in hopes of breaking the icy stares between Kiara and Donna.

Donna was the first to drop her eyes to admire the word *Echo* in purple cursive.

"Damn Glo, how many is that, seven, ten?" Donna asked.

Kiara looked down at the tattoo and said, "Nice work."

"Ha-ha, this is just my third one. You know I have the swan on my hip and the sun on my shoulder. Neither one is big and you can't really see them unless I'm wearing something to show it off. Since the tattoo is on the underside of my wrist, it can't really be seen unless I show you."

The three turned back to their food until Donna offered an auditory olive branch. In a calmer voice she said, "Damn Kiara, I have never heard you get crunk like that before. I guess fucking Malcolm got you thinking you got balls enough to loud talk me. Homey don't play that. But on the Kappa crest, Gloria is right. I'm not sweating you and who you decide to date. I mean, really I have gotten used to living with a lesbian. I don't have to worry about no sweaty rusty butt Negro using up all the hot water or stinking up the place when he takes off his shoes. I have Peter for that."

"Thank you for that D. I know you weren't trying to be funny. This semester, I'm actually planning to spend being a single girl. You know we have a full semester ahead of us with intake, plus I'm getting knee deep in my major. This year I plan to enjoy not having to worry about soothing someone's ego. This semester is going to be about Kiara being Kiara."

"K-Rho to that," Gloria said raising her glass of ginger ale. "So, what are you going to do to mark this new age of independence?"

"I don't know exactly, but I know one thing for certain. I'm going to have to tell Malcolm not to expect a repeat because I actually like girls. What happened was just a one time thing," Kiara said putting her food container in the trash.

"How do you think he is going to react?" Donna said.

"You know I really don't know. I mean, he seems like the laid-back type who won't act the ass, but you never can tell by looking at people. Just in case, I plan to tell him in a public place. If he starts acting foolish I have plenty of witnesses."

"Well if you need me to come along, just let me know. I was ready to whoop Chris' ass when she was loud talking you at the track team party last year. And let it be known, I'm an equal opportunity K-Rho defender," Donna said.

Kiara didn't have to tap into that resource when she finally spoke to Malcolm about what happened. Sitting down across from him at the library three days later, Malcolm brought the subject up first.

"Kiara, I really like you and I don't want whatever happens between us to be just about hooking up," he said. "My dad instilled in me a man shouldn't be in a hurry to get into a woman's pants before he gets into her heart."

"Your dad sounds like a good man. I really appreciate you wanting to get to know me better," Kiara said. "I have a confession to make Malcolm. I wasn't totally honest with you. Last semester when we were hanging out and getting to know each other better, I was actually sort of dating somebody."

Malcolm's face froze. Kiara strained to read the message his eyes were giving. Taking the fact he remained seated as a good sign, she continued.

"Her name is Christina and she and I had been together for about year. The night we met, the girl that stepped up to us when we were talking, that was her. We had a big fight that night and even though we tried to work through things, we never really got back to where we were. We actually broke up about a week ago. I'm sorry I didn't tell you this before."

Released of the words she had been carrying around for months, Kiara felt relieved and worried. She was glad she had come clean with Malcolm, but the fact he had not said a word caused the hairs on the back of her neck to stand up. Maybe she should have had Donna come with her, just in case.

"Well I wasn't expecting to hear that you had a girlfriend. I suspected you were seeing someone else, but I didn't expect that," Malcolm said leaning back in his chair. "So if you are into girls, what was what happened at the house all about?"

Dropping her head Kiara murmured, "I don't know exactly. I guess I was curious what it would be like to be with you. It was nice and fun but I don't want to use you."

Malcolm's mouth twisted in a half smile. "There are worse ways to be used, but I feel you. You are a good person who I really do enjoy spending time with. I guess we will truly just be friends from now on."

Kiara felt so relieved Malcolm didn't freak out about her coming out that she insisted they go out to dinner, her treat. She picked their favorite restaurant and ordered her usual.

She woke up the next morning with a queasy stomach. Brushing off her morning nausea, Kiara grabbed a ginger ale when she got to campus and got on with her day.

While Kiara and Malcolm no longer spent so much time together, they seemed to be proceeding along with forming a good friendship. If they happened to meet up in front of the student store, they might stop and chat for a while. Running into each other at the athletic building, they asked about how each other's classes were coming along. Everything between them seemed normal for Kiara. If only she could say the same about her sorority sisters. Kiara noticed if she encountered some of them around campus, they seemed to avert their eyes. Maybe it was her imagination, but she could have sworn she heard two of them whisper when she passed them on campus, "Yeah, that's her. Can you believe she is like that?" Kiara found out the reason for the whispers during a sorority meeting on Groundhog Day.

"Swans, before we start our chapter meeting, I need to bring to the floor a concern that has been raised about our spring intake process. I know we discussed having Sister Swan Michaels serve as the assistant gracious guide, but there has been a request she be removed from that position," Gwen said. The senior and now chapter president looked uncomfortably at Kiara. "It seems some of you have concerns about her ability to interact with the cygnets in an appropriate manner."

Puzzled, Kiara looked toward Gloria who returned the look with questioning eyebrows. Donna looked across the table at Andrea.

"I don't understand what you are talking about Sister Swan Brantley. I don't have a beef with any of the girls we have selected. True, I nominated three of the potentials, but another member seconded each of them. I promise you there would be no bias toward any of them on my part," Kiara said.

"Sister Swan Michaels, the issue isn't if you would be biased toward the girls. The issue is some of our sisters, myself included, don't think you should be in a position where you may feel you can make our cygnets do something they wouldn't feel comfortable in doing," Andrea said.

Kiara furrowed her brow in confusion. She thought being close friends with Gloria enabled her to understand long-winded sentences, but this went beyond her. Donna, on the other hand, seemed to get a quick handle of the situation.

"Are you saying some of the girls have a problem with Kiara supposedly being a lesbian? I know word has been spreading fast on campus about the Rho that does girls," Donna said while Kiara wore a shocked expression. "One of the football players told Peter he heard it was Kiara because he heard it from one of the track team members. I didn't say anything because I don't believe in trafficking rumors. I happen to know what side my line sister's bread is buttered, but if I didn't I would ask her directly. I hadn't said anything to Kiara about it because I thought it was idle chit-chat. I had no idea it would come up in a sorority meeting."

It seemed to Kiara all eyes turned toward her. She hesitated for a moment then squared her shoulders and stated, "For those who care, I am gay. I'm also a K-Rho, which means I'm your sorority sister. I'm not interested in dating any of you or anyone that would be considered a cygnet. Just like I have done since I crossed, I will conduct myself in the manner of a K-Rho swan, with wisdom and elegance. I don't judge any of you for who you date and you need to extend me the same courtesy. Now if you will excuse me, I'm going to step out of the room so I can collect my thoughts."

Kiara's feeling of frustration and anger about her sorority sisters judging her based on rumors peaked just as her bladder signaled it was go time. Rushing to the bathroom, she made it just in time. Pulling up her pants, Kiara thought to herself, 'Damn, this is the fourth time today I had to pee. I usually can go all day without having to run to the bathroom. Must be that new energy drink coach has us drinking. Then again, it's not doing me any favors. Practice has been kicking my ass lately."

"Key, you in here?" Gloria's voice echoed in the bathroom. "Since I didn't see you in the hall, and I hoped you didn't leave, I figured you came in here."

Walking out the stall Kiara saw Gloria leaning against the sink.

"Girl, you just missed it. I had to momma arm Donna to keep her from going at Andrea," Gloria said, demonstrating the arm gesture parents sometimes use when stopping a car suddenly with a child in the front seat. "Gwen had to jump in too to keep Donna from swinging on Andrea. Girl must have balls like a Chicago Bull because she was talking about feeling violated having you as a line sister. She said she is going to report you to nationals for withholding information in order to get on line."

Kiara felt a sliver of ice shoot down her spine. Could she really do that? What would her mother say? Reading the concern on her face, Gloria told her no sorority laws had been broken according to Gwen. Her sexuality wouldn't affect her sorority membership.

"C'mon. Gwen gave everyone a fifteen-minute break to get it together," Gloria said putting her arm around Kiara's shoulder. "Don't worry about Andrea and whoever else is hating. You are going to be the assistant gracious guide and all the upcoming cygnets are going to love you."

"No. I'm going to tell Gwen I changed my mind. If there is some tension in the chapter, I don't want it impacting new girls coming in," Kiara said. Her heart and mind was a cauldron of sadness and anger. She felt let down by the actions of some of the members of the sisterhood she had chosen along with anger about the way it was expressed. "I have a lifetime to be a K-Rho, I don't have to waste my time, talent, or treasure with sisters that can't appreciate that."

Gloria's face crumpled in disagreement. "I don't think you need to let anyone bully you out of being the best K-Rho you can be. My opinion is you should carry on with the plan. Ruth picked you to be her assistant. If Ms. Third Generation K-Rho has faith in you, screw what everyone else thinks."

"Thanks for the vote of confidence, but no, I'm going to step down. Andrea was lusting after that position so I say let her have it. Wait till I see Malcolm, I'm going to give him what for. He said he wasn't going to put me on blast and now this. Donna said the word came from a member of the track team and I'm betting I know which one."

CHAPTER TWELVE

Kiara/Donna

AT FIRST, MALCOLM denied he was the culprit the next day when she saw him. Facing Kiara's doubting stare, he soon recanted and admitted he had complained about Kiara not telling him the truth to one of his teammates.

"But I swear Kiara, I'm not hating on you. We are still cool," he said, pleading with a crossed armed Kiara outside the athletic building. "I mean, sure I was pissed when I got back to my room and thought about it. Then I figured hell, why not stay friends with Kiara? Maybe she could give me some tips on how to please the ladies since she knows both sides of the story, or I can watch and see for myself."

Chuckling at his own joke Malcolm looked at Kiara, who looked less than amused.

"Ha-ha, very funny. Boy, don't be spreading my business around campus. If I want people to know something about me, I will tell them myself."

Driving back to her apartment following the confrontation, she thought dealing with the shock of being outed would be the biggest problem she would have to face this semester. She was wrong.

"I'm pregnant?" Kiara exclaimed to the slightly hunched Student Health Center doctor.

Concerned about her increasing need to pee and fatigue, Kiara had made an appointment to be tested for diabetes. It ran in her family, so after sharing her symptoms with her pre-med teammate, she assumed that was the reason. Her teammate actually suggested something else could be the culprit, but Kiara quickly dismissed it. 'I guess I lost that bet,' she thought, staring at the gray-haired woman who looked sad but not surprised. 'This is so not how I planned to spend my Valentine's Day.'

"Ms. Michaels, you are about seven weeks and…" Kiara tuned out the rest of what the doctor was saying. Her mind ricocheted between emotions. Fear, shock, then back to fear again. How could this happen to her? She just had sex with Malcolm one time and they used a condom. What was she going to do? 'Damn my lack of impulse control,' she thought. 'The one time I let go and this is what happens.'

Walking into the waiting room, she jerked her head at Donna to follow her outside.

"So what's the story? Am I going to have to lock up all the sweets in the house from now on? I can't be responsible for nobody's sugar being high from my cooking," Donna said. Then looking at Kiara's face, stopped her and said, "What's wrong?"

"I will tell you once we get to the car," Kiara said walking briskly toward the parking lot on the side of the building. Donna followed and once they got into Donna's vehicle, Kiara spilled her news.

"What the fuck? Are you serious? You are pregnant and you didn't suspect anything? I know you don't usually do boys, but I would think you would keep up with your cycle," Donna said, turning to face Kiara.

"Every so often, I go more than twenty-eight days when I start training hard so I thought that was the case," Kiara said, tears of confusion flowing from her eyes. "I mean, how could this happen?"

"You screwed Malcolm and the condom broke. That's what happened. Man, don't this beat all? You haven't had sex with a guy in forever and you get pregnant. Who says God don't have a sense of humor? C'mon, let's go get something to eat. I can't handle news like this on an empty stomach."

Sitting at the restaurant, Kiara felt overwhelmed with emotions. She felt pissed at Malcolm for the condom breaking and terrified about the choice she had to make because of it. This was so not part of her plans for the semester. She felt paralyzed. If a magic wand existed to wipe away that December day, Kiara felt like she would have mortgaged her soul to use it.

"I know you just found out you are pregnant and you are probably still in shock. Hell, I'm still in shock. Do you have any idea what you want to do?" Donna said.

"Donna, I just found out I'm pregnant less than an hour ago. No, I don't know what I'm going to do," Kiara responded.

"Well excuse the fuck out of me," Donna said dragging her fries through the pool of ketchup on the tray. "I don't know what else to say. Hell, I figured if one of us was to get pregnant it would be me since I have a boyfriend. Thank God for the pill. Of course, my mother doesn't know I'm on the pill. I found some empty bottle at the house that I put all my pills in and just tell her it's medicine to help me stop smoking."

"Donna, I'm sorry, can we focus on me for a second? I have a lot going on right now and hearing about how you are pulling the wool over your momma's eyes isn't helping," Kiara said angrily, taking a bite of her sandwich.

Donna raised her eyebrows. Deciding it would be better to sit and chew silently, Donna focused on her food.

"Well, I know I'm not having an abortion. I support a woman's right to choose, but I don't want to carry that around for the rest of my life. I have a cousin that had one and she hasn't been right since. Don't get me wrong, plenty women have them and go on to live productive lives, but I just can't see myself doing that."

"Look, I'm Baptist-born and bred, but I'm also a realist. You are a college junior who just a few months ago was down with going down. I'm sure being an unwed mother wasn't on your to do list. I'm just saying, give it some thought and whatever you decide, I'm here to support you. Have you thought about how and when you are going to tell your mom, Malcolm and your coach?"

"I guess there's no need to delay it. I'm going to tell my coach today at practice. Since today is Tuesday the guys are in the weight room. I will stick around and catch Malcolm. I'm sure he is going to love hearing this. Oh my God, I'm going to have to tell my momma," Kiara said choking up. "This is going to kill her."

"Shit happens. You are not the first college girl to get pregnant and you won't be the last. I'm sure this is not going to kill your mother. Disappoint the hell out of her, yes. Cause her to keel over, I hope not. Listen, let's just worry about one thing at a time. It's almost two. You have track practice and I have to meet my professor about my social issues project, so let's head back to campus. And Kiara, just remember, like the Bible says, weeping may endure for the night but joy cometh in the morning. It's going to be okay."

Cranking up her car, Donna couldn't help but try one last time to lighten the mood. "And you know this is going to kill Andrea. Here she was gunning for you to be kicked out of K-Rho for being gay. Now you up and get pregnant. You are just a big bundle of sexual deviance wrapped up in purple and platinum."

Kiara just shook her head and fastened her seatbelt.

Waiting for Malcolm after practice seemed to be the longest fifteen minutes Kiara had ever experienced. Finally, she saw him walking toward his car where she stood.

"Malcolm, I'm pregnant," she blurted when he reached the driver's side.

"Wow, hello to you too Kiara. How was practice?"

"Good, did you hear what I just said?"

Getting into his car, Malcolm stared at his steering wheel as Kiara stood impatiently outside. "I did. You just said you are pregnant and it's probably my baby. You are probably carrying my baby and I just met you," he said.

Kiara felt heat rising up in her chest watching Malcolm's lips move. He still had not opened the door for her to get in. Half of her wanted to throw him the finger and get in her car and go home. Half of her wanted to stand and wait for him to get himself together so they could talk about this like intelligent human beings.

Malcolm made her choice easier when he put his car in reverse, backed out of the parking lot and drove away with her still standing there.

'Did that limp dick, son of a bitch, motherfucker just leave me standing here like some low rate chicken head? Fuck, I really should have stuck with women. Chicks don't knock you up and leave you hanging,' Kiara thought getting in her car. 'This is what I get for being open-minded.'

Cursing Malcolm's name as she pulled in her apartment parking lot, Kiara saw the vanity license plate of her second least favorite CRU athlete parked in her parking space.

Walking up to his car window, she rapped sharply with her knuckles. Startled, Peter rolled his down window to face an irritated Kiara.

"What are you doing here?" she asked through gritted teeth.

"I needed to talk to Donna, but since she isn't here I can come back later," Peter stammered. Kiara usually looked so relaxed and stress free. He didn't know how to react to this person looking down at him as if she could bite his head off.

"No need for you to sit out in your car waiting for her since I'm home now," Kiara said walking toward the front door.

"Donna had a meeting on campus so she should be getting here soon. Make yourself at home. It's not like you are never always over here anyway."

Peter followed her inside warily and settled his bulk across the sofa. He watched Kiara jerk open the refrigerator, snatch a soda, stomp down the hallway and slam her door behind her.

'Shit,' Peter thought, 'I thought I was dating the K-Rho quick to kick off in someone's ass. Looks like her roommate might be coming for her crown.'

"Hey baby, what brings you over here?" Donna asked as

she walked in twenty minutes later.

"A man can't see his lady when he wants to? He has to have a reason?" he said giving her a big hug. He even turned off the TV in the middle of the six o'clock sports segment, a first for him. Donna's suspicious sense started tingling. Peter loved some Darren Kershaw who did the sports for WCTV. Something serious must have gone down.

Joining Peter on the green and white striped couch, Donna asked, "Peter, I was born on a Monday but it wasn't last week. Why are you here?"

"I have been doing some thinking. You are a real catch Donna and I haven't treated you like I should have. It came to me, if I didn't step up and act right, I might lose you. I wanted to come over and tell you from this point forward, I am going to do better. No more other girls, no more not supporting you, no more assuming you are happy just being with me."

'Humph,' Donna thought to herself, 'I wonder if this declaration of fidelity is genuine?' Or did Alex follow through with his intent to tell Peter about his feelings for her?

"As much I want to believe what you are saying to me right now, this is not the first time we have had this conversation. Almost from the time we got together, we have had to deal with other girls taking up your time. I step to you and tell you I'm tired of all these girls being in your face. Every time, you would promise you were going to shut them down. Then, next thing I know, I'm walking to my class and I hear a whole lot of whispers behind my back about you being with this one and that one," Donna said looking unconvinced.

"I know baby, but this time is different. I have been doing some thinking and I realize I can't keep doing that type of stuff. You know Alex and me had a long conversation and he gave me some good advice. He told me when you find a good woman, you have to do everything to keep her or else you would end up by yourself. He helped me realize I have a good woman. I mean you fine as hell, smart, and you aren't with me just because I'm a beast on the field. You get along with my mom, I can take you around the fellas and you don't try to juice me to get you everything under the sun."

"Wow, it took Alex to help you realize I'm a catch? All the shit I put up with for the past three years didn't hip you to that?" Donna said smiling while she fussed. "See that's the problem with you black people. You don't think anything is the truth until the white man tells you."

Pulling Donna close to him, Peter said he always knew the truth; he just hadn't let her know that he knew.

"Whatever man. So what brought this little heart to heart on with Alex?"

"I ran into him in the weight room and he was telling me about this honey he had been crushing on since he got to CRU. He finally stepped to her last month and she told him no go. I was like man, that must have hurt like a motherfucker."

Feeling her stomach contort, Donna asked if Alex volunteered a name.

"Naw, but I'm thinking it was that girl Dominique that lived in Slay last year. You know her, dark skinned, her sister's an AKA. She works for *Expressions* as their features editor."

"Yeah, I know her. They would have made a cute couple," Donna said, sighing with regret and relief.

Pulling Donna toward him, Peter said, "You're right, but hell, everyone can't be in love like us. Can they baby?"

"Truly, college love is not for the faint of heart by no means," Donna said, resting her head on Peter's chest. In her mind, Donna doubted the sincerity of Peter's words. It was the same thing he had said at least three times before. But this was a new year. Things were bound to be different. She sighed while Peter kissed her forehead and turned the television to his favorite game show.

CHAPTER THIRTEEN
Kiara/Gloria

"SO EVAN, TELL me more about what it was like growing up as a military brat," Gloria said over a plate of humus. After ogling the brunette sophomore for the past two months, she made her move and asked him out. Dining at the Persian restaurant around the corner from the city's newspaper building, she stared intently into his greenish brown eyes.

"A lot of moving, that's for sure," he said, appearing slightly bored.

"So where was your favorite place to live? I remember you mentioned your dad had been stationed in California, Korea, and Washington State before getting stationed in Jacksonville."

"I would say California because I like to surf, and even though Wilmington isn't that far away, I don't like having to drive so far to catch a wave."

"I totally understand," Gloria said smiling. "So you're an accounting major, how did you pick that?"

Gloria knew sometimes when she was nervous she asked questions to have something to say without sounding as if she was talking a lot. After all, most people's favorite topic was themselves.

Usually, most people would get tired of being the subject, turn around, and ask questions in return. Evan was the exception.

For the entire hour-long dinner, Evan talked about himself, starting from him winning the fourth grade math bee to how he thought electronic calculators were the best invention.

Driving back to campus, Gloria chastised herself for running after someone just because he had cute eyes and a tight ass. Maybe Donna was right; she needed to expand her dating pool. At least if she decided to date someone black, they would suggest somewhere with food that would stick to her ribs.

Walking into her room, Gloria grabbed her cordless phone. Hearing the staccato beeping, she hit the number key to retrieve messages. One from Kiara, one from Donna, one from Donna and Kiara, and most surprisingly, one from Malcolm. Deciding it was better to return two messages with one phone call, Gloria called her sorority sisters.

"Are you serious?" Gloria shrieked when Kiara and Donna told her about their afternoon. "I just can't believe Malcolm is acting the ass about you being pregnant. And Donna, you know I believe Peter about as far as I can throw him, but that's your boyfriend. Gosh, I should have hung out with y'all today instead of going out with dude from class. He was boring and the food wasn't even good. I don't know which is worse. How about I pick up a pizza and head over there so we can discuss everything face to face?" Gloria said, pulling off her sexy slacks and pulling on her purple jeans.

Pulling on her sweatshirt, Gloria considered calling Malcolm back. Her phone ringing again halted her decision.

"Hello."

"Gloria? It's me Malcolm."

"Boy, you have some nerve calling me. I just finished talking to Kiara and she told me what happened today. You are such a dirty so and so."

"I know I flipped out and shouldn't have left, but that was too much for me to take in at once. Kiara is pregnant and she thinks it's mine. Man, she isn't even my girlfriend."

"Why are you calling me?" Gloria said sitting on her bed.

"Shouldn't you be apologizing to Kiara, the mother of your child?"

"I tried calling her with no luck. Every time her or Donna heard my voice they would hang up. I would go over there but I don't want to be hemmed up. I have heard about Donna's reputation and I hear she can throw some blows."

"First of all, Donna is a lady of Kappa Alpha Rho Sorority, Incorporated. We don't throw blows. What you may have heard about Donna reflects a time before she was a member. What she did before is no indication of how she is now. Anyway, you don't need to be worried about Donna. Your concern should be Kiara."

"I know, but I don't know what to say. I mean I'm too young to be a father. I just transferred to this school, trying to fit in with the track team and figure out how to handle coach. You know I was considering going Beta next year. I just came from their smoker."

"You're thinking about Beta Nu Phi? I didn't know that. I'm tight with Eduardo their secretary. He is in my Spanish literature class, so maybe if you play your cards right, I will give you a recommendation. That depends, however, on how you deal with the current situation."

"Gloria, I called you because we got along good in class last semester and you and Kiara are so close. I want to do the right thing by her, but I don't want to be screwed in the process. I mean hell, she wasn't even honest with me about her dating girls and then she up and tells me that she is pregnant."

Gloria shook her head in understanding. She loved her sister, but she had to admit to herself she had been a little bit scattered since meeting Malcolm.

"I carry Kiara in my heart not only as my sorority sister but as my sister. I have only known her for a few months longer than you, but she is truly a good spirit," she said. "She told me before she met you she hadn't thought about being with a man, but something about you made her decide to try something different. Look where it got her. The least you can do is be there for her. I'm not telling you what you should do. Well, I am telling you what you should do. But you have to be willing to be a man and do it."

"You know that is asking a lot."

"If you were man enough to lay down with her, then you should be man enough to stand up with her and face the consequences. I am on my way over to Kiara's. If you want to ride with me, I will be glad to pick you up so you are not walking in by yourself. You can be a stand-up guy and do what is right, or you can be a putz. Like Black Sheep says, this or that. The choice is yours."

Sighing, Malcolm said he would be ready in fifteen minutes. He even agreed to front the cost of the pizza Gloria promised her sisters.

Opening the door, Donna's eyes smiled when she saw her sister carrying the red, white and blue pizza box, then squinted with disdain when she saw the person standing beside her. "What the fuck are you doing here?" she asked with arms crossed after letting Gloria enter.

Malcolm, looking at the obstacle blocking his path to redemption, uttered, "I need to apologize for the way I acted today and hope Kiara will talk with me about what is going on."

Donna glared at him for about a minute then moved out of the doorway. Jerking her head toward the back of the apartment, she said, "Hell, you're here already so come on in. She's in the tub, but she should be out in a minute."

Nodding with gratitude, Malcolm said thank you. Coming in, he shrugged off his coat and walked toward the bathroom. What he had to say couldn't wait until Kiara dried off. He knocked gently on the door and asked for permission to come in. As soon as the door closed behind him, Gloria and Donna walked down the hall and stood outside hoping to hear the conversation.

"You got some nerve showing up here," Kiara fumed while attempting to cover her upper half with the washcloth. Struggling to mask her nakedness, she felt the absurdity of trying to cover the naked black body carrying this man's child with a piece of square red terry cloth.

"First of all, let me say I'm sorry about what happened

this afternoon. This pregnancy caught me off guard as it did you and I acted badly. I'm here to say that I'm going to be here for you in whatever way you need," Malcolm said, standing rather stiffly. Even though he was there on a serious mission, the sight of Kiara's sleek and glistening breasts, coupled with the steamy atmosphere of the bathroom, was making him a little bit excited.

"Well, sorry isn't going to cut it. Let me tell you right now. I don't need your half-assed attempt to be a father. You are going to need to step up to the plate and be there for me, for us. Or you can just step off," Kiara said, starting to cry. During the afternoon, she had resolved she was going to carry and keep the baby. After the unlikely chain of events leading to the child's conception, Kiara felt she deserved to give it a chance. But, she was so scared of what it would mean. Her tears came from a place of fear of the unknown. Sitting in the tub looking up at Malcolm, Kiara thought back to Donna's biblical saying about weeping. Morning definitely couldn't come quick enough.

Hearing Kiara's heated words, Gloria and Donna inhaled and held their breath waiting for the answer. For a minute, Malcolm was frozen. Then his heart told his body to act. He bent down beside the tub, and ignoring the fact his black shirt cost him thirty-five dollars, hugged Kiara tightly. Fully immersing his arms into the hot water, he picked Kiara up and stood her up on the mat. Taking a towel, he dried her off, picked up her panties and motioned her to step into them.

By this time, Kiara had stopped crying and was speechless. She followed Malcolm's request and stepped into her panties. Pulling them up to her hips, Malcolm motioned her to lift her arms up above her head, which she did and pulled her nightgown down upon her body. He then opened the door to the bathroom. Donna and Gloria stepped back, and watched him hoist Kiara into his arms and take her into the bedroom.

"Now that's some *Officer and Gentleman* type shit," Donna said.

"At least they seemed like they are going to be able to talk about what's going on. So I guess I have done my good deed for the day," Gloria said walking toward the kitchen. "As a reward, I call the first piece of pizza. Reuniting parents to be can work up a girl's appetite."

CHAPTER FOURTEEN

Kiara

KIARA AND MALCOLM stayed up most of the night discussing what the next seven months held for them.

"I know this may be the worst thing to say at this time, but I don't want to be your girlfriend Malcolm," Kiara said whispering in the dark. Even though they could hear Donna's snoring in the next room, both felt the situation deserved hush tones. "I mean you are really cool and I enjoy spending time with you but I don't want to be in a relationship with you."

"You know my feelings should be hurt that you are willing to carry my child but don't want to be my girl, but this whole situation is just so backwards. I'm willing to just go with the flow," Malcolm said, spooning Kiara and rubbing her stomach.

Since she was approaching two months, Kiara felt like she could finish out the semester with no problems. She hoped her mother wouldn't be too disappointed to let her come back home. She planned to have the baby in Wilmington and maybe transfer to University of North Carolina at Wilmington and finish her degree.

Malcolm pledged to be there for her through the good and bad times. The first situation to put that to the test was meeting and telling each other's parents. Since his hometown was only an hour away from campus, the two drove down two weeks later.

"So Kiara, where are you from and what do your parents

think about all this?" the Millers asked Kiara. The icy stares the two laid on Kiara matched the chilly temperature outside. The middle-aged couple sat in matching recliners wearing identical looks of distaste.

"I'm from Wilmington and I haven't told my mother. My father passed away when I was in high school. I felt the appropriate thing to do was to tell her in person, just as Malcolm and I are here telling you in person," Kiara said keeping her voice calm and even, though she felt her insides quaking. She had not eaten anything that morning because even though her morning sickness came and went, she didn't want to chance an upset stomach in such a hostile environment.

"I hope that you kids realize how disappointed we are about this. Malcolm had such a good chance to do well on the school's track team. You know he won state titles his junior and senior year in school." Mary Miller drew her words out of a pursed mouth. "I'm sure that with all this, his concentration will be affected. That is just so bad, considering he seemed to have such a promising season ahead of him."

"Well, Mrs. Miller, I can understand how hurt you must be. I'm sure that my mother will probably have the same apprehensions about my future. I'm attending CRU on a track scholarship after going to state all four years I was in high school," Kiara said. She tried to respond as evenly as she could considering this woman was trying to flex on her about how good Malcolm was supposed to be at track. Shit, it's not as if he was up for the Olympic trials or something.

"Well I understand that you have worked out your athletic activities, but how is this going to affect Malcolm academically? I know that taking responsibility and being concerned about your wellbeing will probably affect his grades," Mr. Miller said leaning forward to look directly in Kiara's face.

'Oh hell, now I know this man isn't tripping,' Kiara thought. 'Father, give me the strength to deal with this bullshit.'

"No disrespect Mr. and Mrs. Miller, but I'm sure that your

son should have no problem dealing with this situation. As far as your concern about me, the person who will be suffering the majority of the physical changes due to this pregnancy, I don't expect any problems keeping my 3.4 average. But like Malcolm and I have discussed prior to coming up here, he doesn't have to take on too big of a role if he thinks it will create too much of a problem for him," Kiara said flatly. She could feel her nose start to twitch, a sure sign that it was time to go before she went off on these people. It was an amazing thing about her hormones, the littlest thing could set her off and the holier than thou attitudes of the Millers was just the thing to raise her dander.

"Malcolm, if you don't mind, I'm going to step outside for a minute and go sit in the car. I believe I'm starting to feel a little upset to my stomach and I'm sure that you and your parents need to talk about some things. Please, don't mind me," Kiara said gathering her coat and her purse and walking out of the living room toward the front door. She felt like Sophia in *The Color Purple*. Hell, at least Miss Celie offered Sophie a glass of lemonade. Malcolm's mother didn't even pretend to be hospitable.

"No, Kiara wait, I'm coming with you. If my parents and I have anything else to discuss I'm sure we can talk about it later this month when I come home for spring break. We walked in here together and we will walk out together," Malcolm said getting his coat.

"I'm sorry about my parents tripping like that. They are taking this pregnancy kind of hard and they are just trying to protect me," Malcolm said cranking his car.

"Don't worry, next week we are going to meet my mother and it will be your time in the hot seat to be called out of your name and insulted."Kiara had not told her mother why she was making an impromptu trip to see her, and didn't mention she was bringing Malcolm along for the ride. When the two walked into the lemon colored kitchen, her mother managed to hide her surprise at the guest appearance by warmly welcoming Malcolm.

"Now this is a surprise. Kiara has never brought a boy

home with her. Now I know she and our sorority sister, Donna, have driven down for sorority functions, but she has never brought anyone else home to visit," Dorothy Michaels said hugging Kiara then Malcolm. "Well, that's not true. Her friend Chris did come down Christmas Eve. Kiara, how is your friend doing?"

Sitting down at the kitchen table beside her mother, Kiara blushed and responded, "She is fine, last I talked to her."

"Malcolm, do you know Chris?"

"We met briefly during homecoming," Malcolm said dryly.

Seeking to delay the inevitable, Kiara went to the cabinet to grab two glasses to pour her and Malcolm some lemonade. Even though her face read calm, her stomach felt tied in knots. She would have rather walked across hot coals than face the disappointed stare and hear her mother's deep sigh of displeasure. Kiara's palms were sweaty with nervous perspiration. Wiping her forehead, she felt little droplets of moisture. Grateful for the blast of cool air from the refrigerator, she poured herself and Malcolm drinks and sat back at the kitchen table.

Her mother, seemingly unaware of her daughter's nervousness, inquired about Malcolm's background, asking about his major, where he was from, and what his parents did for a living. Unable to take the internal pressure building inside her, Kiara interrupted her mother's interview with the news she drove two hours down I-40 to bear.

For two minutes, her mother sat silent, eyes downcast as she concentrated on peeling that last potato. She then lifted her eyes and conveyed her disappointment in a very deliberate voice. "Kiara Lenora Michaels, I'm shocked at this news. I can't believe I sent you to that school for this to happen. What will your high school coach think when he hears about this? What will I say to the church members or the sisters when they ask about you? How am I going to be able to hold my head up?" she said.

"Momma, I'm sorry. Malcolm and I didn't plan for this to happen. But it did," Kiara said feeling her bladder tense up. 'Damn, I knew I should have gone to the bathroom before we had this conversation,' she thought.

"I'm sure you didn't plan for this to happen, but I'm just saddened that you put yourself in this situation. As for you, young man, you should be ashamed of yourself for putting my daughter in this position. You young people are so irresponsible and don't think about the consequences of your actions."

"Mrs. Michaels, like I told my parents, we both are upset that this happened. We didn't plan to become parents so early, but we are committed to working together to get through this on our own," Malcolm stammered. It was hot in the kitchen, not only because of the tongue-lashing but it seemed the oven was on full tilt.

"Momma please. Malcolm and I have already talked about this. We have worked out what we are going to do. If we were adult enough to get in this situation, then we will be adult enough to handle it. As long as we are both in school, I can use the services of Student Health or go to the county health department for pre-natal care. We are both going to stay in school and work so we won't have to ask you or Malcolm's parents for anything," Kiara said trying not to get short with her mother.

Kiara's mother replied in a clipped voice, "Little girl, let me get one thing straight with you. Just because you are supposed to be pregnant, don't mean you can come up in here and get sassy with me. This is my house and I'm still your mother."

The two Michaels women sat silently staring at each other until a nervous Malcolm cleared his throat. In a joint motion, the two swerved and looked at him as if to say mind your business.

"Well, there is nothing we can do about this now. All I can say is that I'm disappointed in you. I had hoped that you would achieve so much more in life than this. I'm just glad your father isn't around to see this. It would have just killed him," Dorothy said shaking her head.

Kiara felt even worse at the mention of her father. In her heart, she suspected her father knew about her sexuality. He never pressed her why she wasn't interested in going out with any of the boys who expressed interest in taking her skating or to the movies.

She couldn't officially date until she was sixteen, her mother's rule. Still that didn't keep the boys from calling. Just the thought of her deceased father being disappointed in her current situation, felt in a way, harder to reconcile than her mother's displeasure. Just thinking about her father made Kiara's eyes well up and tears began streaming down her face. Malcolm grabbed her hand and squeezed it. "It's going to be okay Kiara. We are going to get through this," he whispered.

Dorothy stared at the couple for a minute then exhaled. "If you and Malcolm are intent on going through with this, I'm going to do what I need to do to support your decision," she said with a sense of reluctant acceptance. "I'm going to make you an appointment with Dr. Phillips. He delivered you. I will not have my new grandbaby delivered by some third year student from CRU's med school. After this semester is over, you will come home and have that baby. We can decide what to do about your education after that."

"Thank you momma for understanding. Malcolm and I are going to head back now before it gets too dark. He has an interview with the Beta Chapter at seven," Kiara said standing up and motioning for Malcolm to do the same.

"Before you go, cut off some of that ham in the fridge to take back with you and wrap up one of those potato pies on the counter. I made four for the Men's Day program tomorrow, but one less won't hurt anything. Girl, now that you are eating for two you need to put some weight on those hips. If those people get funny about your scholarship, don't worry. We have enough to pay for you to finish out this semester. We are going to have to talk about you coming back home and going to UNCW after you have that baby. I'm not about to have you trying to go to school and raise a child up there."

"Yes ma'am," Kiara said walking past her mother to grab the aluminum foil to wrap up the pies. After the rounds of hugs and promises to call as soon as they got back to Blueburg, Malcolm and Kiara backed out of the driveway and headed north.

"Wow, your mom took the news a lot better than I thought she would," Malcolm said putting a CD in the player.

"Trust me, when I get back to campus, she and I will have the real conversation. What you saw was the front she puts on for company. She reserves the hellfire and brimstone speech of how her children disappoint her for close family. Still, my mom and I both know, once I make my mind up, I don't usually change it. I know while she may be mad about me getting pregnant, she is going to respect my decision to keep the child."

"At least we got the hard part over with, telling the folks. Should be smooth sailing from this point on," Malcolm said grabbing Kiara's hand.

"Yeah, well I will try to remember that when my feet are swollen and I'm feeling like I have the worst case of heartburn known to man. I have been doing a lot of reading up on what is going to happen to me and it's nothing nice, let me tell you. Now let's get you back for your interview. Oh and by the way, just so you know, my brother is a Beta. So if some bulky looking dude calling himself Big Brother Iceberg turns up during one of your sessions, don't be surprised. I'm sure my mother called him up to tell him about you being interested before we backed out the driveway."

CHAPTER FIFTEEN
Kiara/Donna

WORD SEEMED TO spread fast across campus about Kiara's pregnancy. She faced disparaging, muttered comments and hostile stares from sorority sisters. During March's sorority meeting, Andrea suggested Kiara not attend the sorority's regional meeting so she wouldn't embarrass the chapter. "Unwed motherhood doesn't fit the image of the organization," she said. Gloria, forever a source of knowledge, graciously informed Andrea their current Imperial Doyenne, or national leader, was a teen mother herself.

"Sister Swan, if our national leader has made supporting all mothers part of our national platform, the fact one of our own is expecting should not been seen as shameful. I sense you are bitter the chapter did not select you to represent us, but green is not your color. Get over it and move on," Gloria said during the chapter's meeting.

Kiara's sisters weren't the only ones to feel a certain betrayal about her pregnancy. Chris confronted her with less than friendly remarks when they crossed paths at the spring step show.

"I can't fucking believe this shit. Gayle told me about you being pregnant by some boy from the track team. She always told me you were shaky but I didn't want to believe her. No wonder you didn't want anybody to know about us," Chris said looming in front of Kiara. Kiara had come outside for a breath of fresh air during the shows' twenty-minute intermission. Standing on the sidewalk, Kiara sensed step show attendees focusing attention on their conversation. "I never thought you were gay. You're just like those other girls trying out being with girls like it's some sort of phase."

"Listen, you or nobody else has the right to tell me who I am. I am a lesbian who slept with a man and got pregnant. It's not the first nor will it be the last time that will happen," Kiara said evenly in a low tone. "You and your girlfriend need to mind your damn business and keep my name out your mouth. Oh yeah, I heard Gayle and you are back together so I guess you are doing okay."

"Man, fuck you," Chris said dismissively waving her hand and walking back in the building. "I hope you have a good life, you and your baby daddy."

Turning around to go inside, Kiara saw Ruth, Donna, Veronica, and a few other sorority sisters walking toward her.

"C'mon soror, we getting ready to go on and we need all our sorors on hand to help bring the noise," Donna said raising her voice. "Chris is lucky she walked away, or else I would have taken these pumps off and beat that ass. Hell I might still do it after we are done if she is still around."

"Don't worry about it D, I'm fine," Kiara said. She felt shaken up, but the hugs of reassurance from her sorority sisters helped calm her down.

Kiara put the negative reaction of others behind her and finished her junior year with high marks. After bidding Gloria farewell on her summer internship, she and Donna settled in to spend the summer together. Both had enrolled in summer school to allow Kiara to build her course credits and Donna to graduate earlier. Everything seemed to be on track for a good summer until she agreed to do a favor for a friend from her days of dating Chris.

He was a bouncer at a gay nightclub. He was working and had a craving for Chinese food. Since Kiara had to go out to the mall near his favorite restaurant to pick out yet another pair of shoes since her feet had swollen to a size ten from her regular size seven, she offered to pick him up some lo mein and deliver it to him on her way home.

Walking around the climate controlled mall in her sundress and flip-flops, a welcomed relief from the July heat that had made her life sheer hell, she absent-mindedly rubbed her stomach. Malik Joseph Michaels was set to make his appearance on September 18. Malcolm had picked out Malik, while she'd contributed Joseph in memory of her father. Malcolm called her it seemed every day from Columbia, South Carolina, where he had gotten an internship. During the months of pregnancy, they had come to an easy agreement about how their lives would run. He would provide emotional and financial support and be a part of their son's life. He promised her he would not be just one of those guys who 'hit it and quit it.' He respected her and the choice she made to carry his child. He would be as good as father to his son as his father had been to him. Walking to her car, Kiara sent mental thanks she had lucked out with someone who managed not to make a bad situation worse by being an ass. Sometimes, the thought crossed her mind that her father would have liked Malcolm. Then she would feel a sense of sadness about her father never having a chance to meet his first grandson. But she knew no matter what, her father's spirit would help shape the life of her son. She would teach him to be strong and caring, just like the man who'd helped raise her.

Donna and Kiara had spent the summer months shopping and stocking up for the newest arrival. Two weeks prior, Donna coordinated a massive baby shower, with gifts coming in from across the country from former track members and their line sisters. Tomorrow was the last day of summer school, so this time tomorrow, Kiara planned to be sitting at home on her mom's front porch with her feet up, drinking iced tea and eating plenty of fried fish and grits.

Pulling up in the Looking Glass parking lot across the street from the club, Kiara noticed no one was outside. Staring across the gravel parking lot, she noticed a group standing in the far corner of the parking lot. She assumed they were some guys psyching themselves up to go into a gay club. Kiara had seen it repeatedly; taking those first steps toward self-acceptance was always the hardest. Only as she walked toward the entrance and heard some of the conversation wafting in the air, she realized that wasn't the case.

"C'mon faggot, what do you have to say for yourself now? You still want to suck our dicks?" the tall one with the crew cut sneered. He pushed this scrawny blonde guy over to the stocky built one with no neck and a baseball hat on his head.

"Yeah, faggot," baseball hat said, shoving the guy over to someone with greasy black hair who pushed him back to crew cut.

Usually, security would be patrolling the parking lot. But since the club didn't officially open for another hour, no one had arrived. Maybe it was a maternal sense of protection, but Kiara felt the need to step in to stop the bullying since no one else was there. She figured if she said something, they would go away. She was wrong.

Kiara yelled, "Hey, y'all leave the guy alone." When the three turned and looked in her direction, the object of their attention, seeing his chance to escape, ran off in the other direction.

"Fuck you bitch. Why don't you come over and suck my dick you fucking dyke," crew cut said. His fellow hecklers stood shoulder to shoulder with him watching her.

"Ya momma's a dyke," Kiara said, her feet planted firmly on the broken concrete. "Your dick probably so little no girl wants to get with you because they don't like Vienna sausages."

"What did you say to me?" crew cut said walking toward her followed by his friends.

Three months ago, Kiara could have sprinted those 200 yards from that spot to the door in less than twenty seconds. However, carrying another life had clipped her sprinter's wings. She got close enough to door to imagine getting away safely before the three managed to grab her.

"I'm going to show your black ass how big my dick is," crew cut said, dragging her back toward the side of the club where the three had parked their car.

Kiara, having seen self-defense films that were always shown to incoming freshmen girls, knew to drop all her weight and kick and scream and shout fire. But the city's only gay club was hidden among trees in an industrial part of town where factories were constantly making noise. The location proved to be Kiara's disadvantage that night.

Jerking open the back door of his car, crew cut flung Kiara on the back seat while his friends crowded the space behind him, peering into the gloom of the car. With every ounce of strength, Kiara squirmed, scratched and shoved him, but it seemed to only excite him more. Kiara never knew fear tasted dull and flat, like rusted iron. She felt her heart pound in her chest. Her throat, raw from screaming, felt constricted. Crew cut's rough hand blocked her mouth. Feeling her panties jerked down, Kiara began trembling and her bladder released its contents. She was terrified. Nothing was in her control anymore. Not even her basic bodily functions. Crew cut's response, a sharp jab to her closed eye as the bully berated her for soiling his car.

"Oh yeah, this is going to be good," he said, stabbing her with his half-erect penis. Kiara's heart and soul screamed. This wasn't happening to her. Her mind struggled to process what was happening. She wasn't here. She was in her car singing along to the radio, feeling her baby navigating around her stomach. 'This isn't real,' Kiara thought. Lightning bolts of pain ripped through her body. She felt herself floating above the scene. She had heard in her classes how the mind shuts down in times of great trauma. She never imagined she would have firsthand experience.

"Oh yeah baby, you like this don't you?" crew cut said, clenching his hand around her throat while he rammed her on the cracked leather seats. Choking, Kiara struggled to keep herself from passing out. Sensing his prey was drifting, crew cut punched her in the mouth. Blood seeped down her throat.

Every inch of her felt betrayed. Her eyes, filled with tears, begged with her attacker to stop. "Please stop, you are hurting me," Kiara said, her voice cracked like broken glass.

Time stopped as Kiara's mind drifted away from this desecration. Somewhere above it all, she saw crew cut pull out and splatter her sundress with his seed. He backed out of the car and let his friend have his way with her.

"Dude, I'm not going in after you. You know I like it from behind," no neck said as he snatched Kiara up and flipped her over like a discarded piece of trash.

'Hell must feel like this,' Kiara thought. As the blood ebbed down her legs, Kiara forced herself to shout, "Stop, I'm pregnant."

Maybe they heard her over their grunts of glee and just didn't care. Perhaps, they thought she was just saying something. Most people had already commented she didn't look pregnant, just that she looked like she had been eating well.

Salvation came in the form of a 1987 Volvo. Seeing the car pulling into the parking lot, baseball cap yelled, "Danny, there is a car coming."

Her attacker backed up hurriedly. Pulling Kiara out by her legs onto the ground, he jumped in the back seat. Crew cut cranked the car and baseball cap ran to the passenger side. The car pulled away, just as the twin beams of the Volvo shone like a beacon of rescue on Kiara's torn body lying prone in the gravel. She was able to make out the first three letters and a number on the license plate. The name 'Danny' rooted in her mind.

"Oh my God Russell, there is a girl on the ground," the driver shouted. Hearing a car door open Kiara looked up. She recognized the man coming toward her as one of the professors she had in her freshmen year. He looked like an angel of mercy lifting her off the ground.

"Now what do we do? If we take her to the hospital, they are going to ask a bunch of questions about how and where we found her," the driver said standing beside his car wearing a worried look.

Carrying her to the car, her former professor responded. "Well, we can't leave her here. We can say we were driving by and happened to see her on the road. If you don't want to go to the hospital with me, fine, stay here. Try explaining how you got here when one of your students sees you standing in the most notorious cruising spot in Blueburg, alone."

"Fine, fine."

Kiara slumped in the back feeling the car speed away from that place of horror. Bleeding and hurting with every breath, Kiara was grateful she was alive. The car smelled like cigarette smoke and the brakes needed work, but to Kiara it felt like a chariot sent from heaven. Escorting her into the emergency room, the professor apologized but said he couldn't stay with her.

"Thank you, I'm going to be okay," Kiara said. In his eyes, she could tell he knew she was lying. Still, he left her.

The sounds and the lights of the emergency room seemed to intensify Kiara's sense of terror. It seemed to be so much, but she managed to tell the nurse she had been raped. Kiara heard "Code 86 in ER" over the intercom and someone appeared with a wheelchair motioning her to sit down. Soon she was in a room and faced a blonde nurse who looked too young to be out after curfew.

"Ma'am, my name is Kimberly and I'm one of the forensic nurse examiners on duty tonight. I am specially trained to work with persons who have reported being sexually assaulted," the soft voiced woman said moving swiftly around the room. "I will need you to sign some paperwork so that I can conduct an examination. Are you able to sign the paperwork?"

In a daze, Kiara nodded yes, noticing two more people had entered the room. They introduced themselves as well but Kiara was finding it hard to hold on to the details. The room felt hazy. Sounds came through her ears like people were speaking into gauze. Kiara felt Kimberly's gloved hand touch her arm and guide her to lie back on the hospital table where she sat after she signed her name on the forms. She noted in the name field *Jane Doe 12* was already typed.

"Ma'am, by law I have to advise you, you are not required to speak with law enforcement, but I would encourage you to do so. In talking with law enforcement, you are not required to prosecute. But I will tell you, if you decide to prosecute, the authorities will pursue the crime to the fullest extent of the law."

Kiara answered from a place far away she wanted to talk to law enforcement. When asked if there was someone that could be called, Kiara provided Donna's name without thought.

The team of people in the room moved around like a well-oiled machine. Kimberly, offering encouraging smiles and gentle touches, explained the process of what and why the things happening were taking place. Standing on a sheet, Kiara began crying as a shorthaired black woman aided her in removing her clothes. The woman resembled her grandmother. She stared compassionately into Kiara eyes and Kiara felt slightly less terrified. Rationally, she knew she was in a safe space but she could feel the touch of the two men on her skin. If she could rip off her flesh, she would, just to rid herself of that feeling.

When the Blueburg police officer stepped in, Kiara felt her heart stop beating. She recognized the cinnamon colored woman, who paused slightly. Just last week, the two Kappa Alpha Rho sorority sisters had sat side by side at a picnic, laughing and basking in the July sun. Now they stood in a sterile hospital room while Kiara's violation was documented. The officer explained she was there to take pictures and conduct an interview. Kiara felt so ashamed. She wordlessly nodded her head and allowed herself to be adjusted. Following the photographs, Kiara had her mouth, vagina and rectum swabbed for evidence.

"Ma'am, you are doing really well. I'm sorry we are having to do this but we should be finished soon," Kimberly said. "Now I'm going to have to check under your fingernails."

Kiara had always taken such pride in her hands. Chris always said they were so smooth. She kept her nails painted purple and neatly trimmed. Now they were jagged, traces of her attack trapped underneath them. She had been so shaken by the whole ordeal that it wasn't until after Kimberly had bagged all the evidence and was checking her vitals that she realized she was having contractions. She had told the staff she was pregnant, but the staff delayed giving any drugs to deal with the process until her assault exam was complete.

"Damn girl, you look like shit. What happened? The hospital called and said you were here but didn't give my any details. When I checked in, the nurse just escorted me back here," Donna said after seeing her sorority sister. At first glance, Donna felt the need to shriek in horror. She had prepared victims of homicide, car wrecks, and long-term illness, but she didn't know those people like she knew Kiara. Her sorority sister had beaming brown eyes with braids she wore in a high ponytail. Her roommate always smiled and radiated an inner glow thanks to the life growing inside her. Donna didn't recognize this woman as Kiara. This woman lay propped up in bed, bruised face, busted lip, and blackened eyes. This person looked like joy had abandoned her.

"Thank you Donna for letting me know I look bad," Kiara responded angry at the callous greeting. "Having been beaten and violated by three sons of bitches who planned to spend their night gay bashing, I would think I would look a little worse for wear."

"What! I don't understand, gay-bashed," Donna said confused, then recognition dawned about what her sister was saying. "Oh my God, honey what did they do to you? I hope to hell they find them sons of bitches soon and put their asses under the fucking jail. Vengeance may be mine said the Lord, but I would fuck them up if I got my hands on them."

Reaching out for Donna, Kiara said, "Donna I was so afraid. I went to take Sandy something to eat and there were these guys in the parking lot. They were picking on this guy and I said…"

"Sh, sh, you safe," Donna said bending down to hug Kiara. "The doctors are going to take care of you and it's going to be fine. I saw soror outside who is a sergeant with the police department. I was going to speak but I was so intent on getting back here to you."

"Yeah, she came in and talked to me so I guess she is going to be working on this. You know she is hardcore, so if they are out there she is going to find them," Kiara said. "I'm so scared Donna.

I don't know what is going to happen. I think I'm in labor because I'm feeling all this pain and the doctors have been in here. They said they may have to induce labor but it's too soon. I'm only seven months. I don't want to give birth like this."

"I'm right here with you and we are going to get through this. I'm not going anywhere. We are swans and swans swim together," Donna said forcefully. "We will get through this. You are going to have a healthy boy. I'm going to be a godmother and this shit is going to work itself out."

"Promise?" Kiara said. She knew Donna really didn't have any control of the outcome of the rape or the pregnancy. But she needed some sense of normalcy to help her cope. Donna nodded her head and Kiara relaxed, slightly. Feeling her sister's arms around her while she waited for what would happen next.

CHAPTER SIXTEEN
February 2002
Kiara/Gloria

"MA, TELEPHONE." MALIK's nine-year-old voice carried through the house into Kiara's home office.

"Who is it? Unless it's Grandma, Paula, or your dad, take a message," Kiara yelled down the hall. For the past two hours, her focus had been on completing yet another paper as part of her master's program in Industrial/Organizational Psychology at the University of North Carolina at Charlotte.

"It's Tia Gloria. Do you want me to tell her to call you later?"

"No, I'll take it," Kiara said grabbing the phone on her desk. When she heard the phone ring, she assumed it was Malcolm doing his nightly homework check with Malik. Since their son's birth, he had been an active participant in Malik's life and hers. After graduation he moved to Columbia, SC but managed to make the drive to Wilmington and then Charlotte to be involved. Even though Malik had her last name, Malcolm made sure he knew his father and his side of the family as much as possible. Malcolm was the main person encouraging her to go for her masters in psychology. Staring at her unwritten paper, she sometimes wished he could help her with her homework like he did with Malik. Her homework was due by midnight. She hoped to have it done before 7:00 p.m. so she could fix dinner. Still, it would be worth delaying completion of the paper, worth thirty percent of her final grade, to catch up with the elusive federal employee with the swan tattoo.

"Glo, where have you been? I have been ringing your office, your home and your cell for three days."

"It's all gravy; had to take care of some State Department business on a sudden tip, so that's why I was incog-negro for the past seventy-two hours. The job of the youngest undersecretary for Central American Affairs is a job without a time clock," Gloria said leaning back in her office chair. "Got your message, we still on for this weekend? It's been forever since we have seen each other face to face."

"Yep, Malcolm is coming from Columbia to get Malik on Friday for a boys' weekend and Paula has given me permission to leave the city. I should get to D.C. around six Friday night. And girl, I need a break. In between running around Charlotte with Malik, my job, the sorority and my relationship, some days I don't know if I'm coming, going, or already there," Kiara said taking off her glasses and rubbing her eyes.

"I maintain a perpetual state of awe about all you do. Between raising my godson, being a good girlfriend and helping people realize just how crazy they really are, you're Army strong, doing more before six a.m. than most people do all day."

"I try, but between you and me, I'm starting to feel a little bit burnt out. It is just that I'm doing so much and you know I volunteer with the rape crisis center every month and that just wears me down sometimes," Kiara said. "You know Paula and I have talked about it and she suggested I start going back to my therapist. Those two years with that doctor in Wilmington after the attack was such a blessing. It really helped me deal with all the anger and shame I had about the attack. We both know how messed I was afterwards, especially when they told me I couldn't have children because of the damage those fuckers did."

Gloria sat silent. Ten years later and she still found it hard to talk about what happened. One of their Wilmington graduate chapter sorority sisters, a former New Hanover County district attorney, filed a civil suit against Kiara's rapists. Their parents, high-level business owners, settled for an amount that allowed Kiara to fund a down payment for her house in Charlotte and made sure Malik's college education was paid for three times over. Kiara even earned enough to become part owner of the Looking Glass. Kiara's first major decision for the club, install massive lights in the parking lot and hire a security guard to patrol the parking lot.

"I support whatever you need to do to be healthy. We all need to take a break sometimes from being Superwoman. That is why I'm so excited you can come up to D.C. and hang with Donna and me this weekend. So it's cool, she is going to pick you up from Regan, and you stay with her Friday night then stay with me Saturday? It's my turn to host the parish's singles movie and discussion night, so I won't be able to get free until around ten-ish."

As an active lay member of St. Raphael's Catholic Church, Gloria developed a social outlet for single members to view a movie featuring Catholicism, then discuss it afterwards. Kiara knew when Gloria approached the church leaders with the idea two years ago, they had no idea of some of the films Gloria had in mind. Still, it proved to be popular so they couldn't cancel it.

Walking down the steps to head to the kitchen, Kiara asked, "What's on the docket for this week, another showing of *The Exorcist?*"

"No, after the incident with Sister Jude three months ago, I decided to retire it from circulation," Gloria said, multi-tasking by checking and responding to her emails. "No this time, I'm showing *Henry V*. I love me some Kenneth Branagh, even if the haircut he had in the movie was a little busted. I digress. When is the last time you talked to Donna?"

"Last week. She sent Paula a check to support her chapter's Bowling For Babies event. You know it's one of their signature fundraisers for the March of Dimes. I'm not trying to get into Zeta business or my sister's pocketbook, but it seems marrying a marine lieutenant has helped her feel a little bit more generous with her charitable giving."

Motioning her secretary hovering around her office door to come in, Gloria answered, "I know right. I'm just glad she found her someone worth a damn after that shit Peter pulled. I never liked that pretty motherfucker anyway."

"Whatever *New Jack City*, I'm just glad Kevin makes her happy. I know after the divorce she was down for a while and really didn't want to move back home with her mom. Still, it worked out all right. She was able to help out after her dad passed, and if she hadn't been living back home, she may have never met her new baby daddy," Kiara said as she lifted the pot to have her nose embraced by the smells of simmering shrimp, okra, oysters, and crab.

"I know right. I think that is so cute how they met on base at the commissary in Jacksonville. She was reaching for some cereal for the kids and he just got it without asking and handed it to her. Who knew shredded wheat could spark a love affair?"

"Well you know I met Paula in the ER when Malik got stung by a bee and had an allergic reaction, so love can strike when you least expected it."

"Maybe I need to fall out like a fainting goat somewhere and see who I find. My secretary is here with some work for me, but let me share this Intel before I go. You have to swear on your mother's eyes not to tell her you heard it from me. When I babysat India last month, she let it slip that Donna and Kevin have picked out a name," Gloria said. "You know how she named Milan and India after places she always wanted to visit? Well this one is going to be named after one place she is too familiar with, Lejune. I guess since that's where she and Kevin met, why not give their first born the same name."

Kiara's mouth dropped open as she twisted the cap off a juice. She knew black folks could get creative when it came to naming their children, but naming your first son after a marine base was a little bit too much for her. "Girl, you are lying! Lejune?"

"That's what India told me and you know that four year old is like her momma. She gives it to you straight. I trust her word more than I trust my parish priest and you know how I feel about my faith. Let me focus on finishing this paperwork. I will see you later this week. Adios, adieu, and I holla."

Gloria hung up the phone and turned her attention to making sure she read all the papers her secretary had brought to her to resolve. As she read over the briefings, she couldn't help but be struck that so much classified information was just laying bare on her desk, waiting for her to give the up or down. She had been with the department for five years after transferring from the Department of Justice where she started her federal career after graduating. She worked her way up the ladder working twelve-hour days, networking with those in the know and putting her single status out there as an asset. Being on the go didn't allow her to build too much of a romantic future. Sure, she had some dates now and then, but most of the men she interacted were more concerned with advancing their careers, not necessarily supporting hers.

Even though she would never say it, she envied Donna and Kiara. Both had partners who were there for them and children who thought their mommas caused the sun to rise and the moon to shine. All Gloria had was a drawer full of sex toys. Sure, having the gravy parking spot at work was good, but she wanted more out of life. 'Oh well, what can you do?' she thought as she glanced at her watch and realized that yet again, 7:00 p.m. had caught her still in the office.

While Gloria hustled to catch the elevator down to the parking garage to go home, Kiara was hustling in the kitchen to finish dinner before Paula pulled into their two-car garage.

"Hey baby, what smells so good?" Paula asked walking into the kitchen all smiles in her orange nursing scrubs.

"Me," Kiara said offering her cheek up for a kiss. "Since today is Fat Tuesday, I decided to throw something together to mark the occasion. I stopped by and got some Dixie beer that is chilling in the fridge and the bread pudding is in the oven. I know you get homesick sometimes, so I figured I would do something to get you in the N'awlins spirit."

"Between you, one of the doctors on my floor bringing

in some beignets this morning, and me sneaking down to Bayou Kitchen for lunch, I'm going to be as big as house and just as happy as a frat boy on Bourbon Street with a bunch of beads. I'm going to get freshened up so I can enjoy dinner with my two favorite people," Paula said. Within thirty minutes, the Michaels-Malveux household settled down to eat dinner and catch up with each other's day.

On days when Kiara didn't play hooky to work on her graduate school papers, she worked for a local mental health agency. Since she had no work related tidbits to share, Kiara enjoyed Paula's stories about her day working on the cardiac unit while Malik provided them the details of the latest episode of All My Mallard Creek Elementary School children. Kiara loved this part of her day; the domestic bliss of being with the woman she loved, in the house they shared, doing simple things like raising a family and planning for a better future.

After eating two bowls of gumbo, Paula volunteered to clean up the kitchen allowing Kiara to head upstairs to finish her paper. After tucking Malik in and listening to him read a chapter of his favorite nighttime book, Kiara dived back into her academic studies. Hitting the send button with only forty-five minutes before the paper's deadline, she sat back satisfied.

"My love, don't forget to call your mother tomorrow to confirm you will be able to make it to her school program," Paula said, interrupting her reading when Kiara walked into the bedroom. "When I talked to her today I told her I could make it, but I didn't know for sure if you would have to do something with the sorority or the center."

"Oh my God, thank you for reminding me. I will make sure I check the schedule to make sure I'm not on call. I still can't get over how well my mom and you get along. Especially after I told you how she hit the roof when she found out I was gay."

"I would imagine after all that you went through after what happened, you had no problem telling your mom you liked women," Paula said taking a sip from the bottle of beer she was drinking. "Dealing with the rape and Malik having to be in ICU for about three months because he was premature is a lot for a twenty-one-year-old to handle."

"Yeah, Dorothy and I were a really good team for a while. Don't get me wrong, Malcolm did his share. But his job kept him traveling so much he didn't have a chance to be there with Malik like he wanted," Kiara said taking off her glances and then her tank top. "But once things settled down and I started branching out, I had to tell my mom. Trust me, I thought telling her I was pregnant was bad. I think when I introduced her to the girl I was dating back then, she was going to fall out."

"You know, I have to say, every time your mom and I talk, a small part of me remembers the stories you told about how she used to berate you about being a lesbian. Stuff like 'I'm so ashamed of you' and 'I thought I raised a daughter, I raised a fool.' I think it's ironic she didn't start accepting you more until Malcolm's parents tried to take custody away from you when Malcolm told them you and your ex were living together."

"Yep, those sons of bitches must have been smoking some powerful stuff if they thought they were going to take my baby away from me. Malcolm had no problem with me being a lesbian so they shouldn't have had a problem. But obviously, I had cast some lesbian voodoo spell on him to make him have no problem, so they had to step in I guess. My mom is a lot of things, but one thing she is most of all is protective of her children. Malcolm's folk acting ugly really helped her to realize my sexuality didn't impact the way I raised my child or conducted myself. Baby, if you could have heard her tearing them a new one when we had the meeting you would have died. I thought Dorothy was channeling Donna the way she told them off. So by the time you came along, she was ready to accept you and the role you played in my life."

"Well I'm glad to be the one she loves and adores," Paula said to Kiara. Kissing her lover now beside her in bed, she went back to reading her book.

"So Ms. Paula, do you have big plans to live it up since

you are going to have the house to yourself this weekend?" Kiara asked.

"Nope, other than getting my hair done Saturday, I will be sticking close to home and missing you."

"And I'm going to be missing you just as much if not more," Kiara said.

"I seriously doubt you are going to miss me that much. I know how the three of you are when you get together. Donna is going to cook enough food to feed four armies, Gloria is going to get y'all tickets for a fly gallery show, and you are going to have them almost pissing their pants with stories about the people you come across in your job."

"Yep, just another K-Rho get-together session jumping off this weekend. But before I go out of town, let me give you something to think about while we are apart," Kiara said, pulling down the covers.

"Now I understand why I didn't put up a fuss about you going out of town. You always give the best go-away presents," Paula said smiling, raising her left eyebrow.

Despite being in a relationship for close to five years, the sight of Paula's bountiful breasts still set Kiara's mouth watering. Even though the idea of tasting her wetness was thundering in Kiara's mind, she knew her partner liked to take things slow. Kiara began kissing Paula slowly, tasting the cinnamon after effects of the mouthwash she used. Dropping her head, Kiara began nibbling on Paula's neck, prompting her partner to moan softly as the sensation sent shivers throughout her limbs. The two of them fit so nicely, Kiara's still trim track runner body resting on Paula's softness. Content Paula was ready for phase two, Kiara slid her mouth from her neck to her breastbone laying kisses of promise and passion. Kissing the space between her breasts, Kiara murmured, "Paula Justina, I love me some you."

"And I love me some you, Kiara Lenora," Paula said as she lay back on the yellow bamboo blend sheets and received Kiara's attention. After exploring Paula's torso with gentle touches and targeted kisses, Kiara slid between her thighs and teased Paula's clit with the tip of her tongue. Paula's wetness tasted like nirvana as Kiara motivated her to climax. Since Paula liked to be stimulated and penetrated at the same time, Kiara utilized her fingers to help her lover achieve her peak of ecstasy. Feeling her lover tense then release, Kiara smiled in satisfaction. Kiara welcomed the opportunity of being the one doing the heavy licking and welcomed every opportunity to hone her skills. Sure, the couple had some toys to help add spice, but when it came down to it, what nature provided worked just fine.

Getting dressed the next morning, Kiara smiled watching Paula sleep. When the two of them met, she was not in the best of places. The relationship, which prompted her to move to Charlotte, had ended badly with infidelity on both their parts. Never one for one-night stands, she had resolved to be a solitary lesbian, at least until Malik was older. Then she met Paula and that all changed. She often said Paula made her believe in forever. She knew between classes, the sorority, volunteering, and being a mother to Malik, she didn't devote as much time as she should to making Paula feel treasured. Soon, she would slow down and really enjoy the good life she had.

"Key, you need me to get up and make you some breakfast?" Paula murmured.

"No honey I got it. I know you have to work a double tonight so get some rest. I'm going to check on Malik to make sure he is doing what he needs to do, fix him some eggs, and then we are going to head out."

Turning over, Paula promised to call her later and headed back into dreamland. 'Yes,' Kiara thought, 'I love being a lesbian. While I'm glad to have my son, there is nothing like the love of a good woman.'

CHAPTER SEVENTEEN
Donna/Kiara/Gloria

"GIRL, YOU KNOW I'm taking this picture back to Charlotte with me," Kiara said to Gloria four days later, admiring a vivid orange and red acrylic painting of the desert. After dealing with flight delays from Charlotte-Douglas to Regan Airport, Kiara had arrived in the DMV area and spent the night at Donna's. Today, the trio planned to take over D.C. But before they hit the streets, the trio sat enjoying Gloria's interpretation of brunch in her townhouse.

"Take it, I don't mind. I got that piece from a street vendor down in Adams Morgan a few months ago. Now, I would have to cut you to the white meat if you try to walk out with the piece on the wall behind you," Gloria said putting another slice of her collard green quiche on Kiara's plate. "I had it commissioned from an artist I met through one of my co-workers. It took me a few dinner dates, but it was worth it."

At first glance, the photo looked like a typical lush green landscape portrait of a garden. Upon closer inspection, it was a picture of a man covered in green paint with pieces of flower petals glued to preserve the model's modesty.

Looking around her sorority's sister home, Kiara marveled at how much the space summed up Gloria's personality. Native crafts and pictures that reflected the diversity of the Caribbean and

African American experiences served as her decorating theme. She scattered her collection throughout her home saving her seriously pricey pieces for the room where they would have a rapt audience, the bathroom.

Gloria had expensive taste and the bank account to back it up. Kiara and Donna teased her about how when she heard about the death of Gianni Versace, she called to have her credit limits bumped up so she could snap up his clothes before they increased in price. Her credit card companies accommodated her gladly.

"I see you still dragging around Totally Screwed. I'm surprised, especially after I read about your boy who did that having some big show in New York," Donna said taking a bite of her pancakes.

"Yeah girl, I thought about selling it. Then I thought nah. It reminds me of a simpler time. Plus, having that piece is like an in case of emergency break glass fund. You can call it my very own Jean-Michel Basquiat picture, only it's hardware."

"Gloria, what is that song your phone is playing?" Kiara asked after the air filled with a blast of salsa.

"Oh, that's Celia Cruz, so that means Carlos is calling me. That's his favorite singer. Hand me the phone."

Kiara and Donna exchanged knowing looks while Gloria chatted in Spanish. The two had discussed the Carlos situation many times before. Each of them swore Gloria was cheating herself out of a good thing by maintaining just a "friendship" with the fine six-foot-three Cuban with a nice tight butt and sexy green eyes. Kiara had met him three years ago when she came up for a girl's weekend. Carlos could discuss rap lyrics and foreign policy just as fluid as Gloria. He even caught most of her sorority sister's cultural references. Kiara felt like he would be a perfect romantic match for her single sorority sister. Donna had met him when Gloria brought him to her wedding in Kenansville. At the time, the newly minted Donna Bofield remarked to Kiara how easily Carlos managed to fit in. He charmed her mother, sisters, and she even caught her gay cousin making eyes at him.

"So how is your 'friend' Carlos doing? You still just hanging out with him, nothing serious?" Kiara asked.

"He is fine. He just called to tell me about this date he went on last night. The girl acted like she was auditioning to be a dancer at the ta-ta bar when they went to the club," Gloria said refilling Kiara's juice glass.

"I think it's cute the two of you compare dates," Donna said sarcastically. "You know, I think the only date the two of you should be discussing is when the two of you are going to go on one. I mean come on. He got a good government job, going to law school at Howard and his ass is like great god I reckon. If I was single, I would be like ay papi every day."

"How many times do I have to tell you, Carlos and I are just friends," Gloria said. "Let me make it easy for you to understand. One, he's in law school; I'm working on my doctorate so our free time is like none. Two, we value our friendship and would rather not complicate things. And, three, he likes ABC girls: Asian, brainy, and competitive. I am talking 1600 on the SAT, full ride to the Ivy League, got their doctorate at twenty-five."

"So, 1560 on the SAT, full ride to Cornell of the South and getting her doctorate at twenty-nine is a little too lowbrow for him? His stock is falling rapidly," Donna said, pursing her lips as she drank her cranberry juice.

"Don't be so hard on Carlos. He has been a good friend to me and he is a good person. Yes, it would be nice to have someone special in my life, and yes, he does have a lot of things I would love to have in a man, but we are really just friends," Gloria said emphatically.

Kiara and Donna shrugged their shoulders and continued eating. Gloria sat watching them, then deeply sighing, shared while she enjoyed living the good life, she did miss having a significant other in her life. What she didn't share was that she had considered Carlos a possible candidate.

"Y'all haven't been in the game for a minute. It is Run

DMC, tougher than leather out here for a single girl who works seventy hours a week. I have dated a few guys I have met through work functions and enjoyed some after classes coffee dates with some guys from my program, but no one is clicking."

"Well do you think your standards are too high? I mean I know we are in D.C., but there are some good men out there who don't have high level government jobs or advanced degrees," Donna said. "There are plenty of city employees, regular business owners and just plan working brothers that could appreciate you."

Clearing the table, Gloria rinsed off their dishes and put them in the dishwasher. She told her sisters she aimed to be an equal opportunity dater, but, just like in college, she tended to date men who crossed her path.

"I'm not saying I don't feel complete because I don't have a man, but sometimes I would like to be able to call someone other than you guys or my mom with good news or if I have had a bad day. Sure, Carlos has been a good source of conversation when I feeling like chatting."

"See that's what I am talking about. What you just said is confirmation the two of you need to, like the Bible says, be equally yoked. You mentioned him in the same breath as your momma and your girls," Donna said. "But you are grown so you know what you need to do and who you need to do it with. Now, as much as I love sitting around and listening to you complain, I'm ready to hang out with my girls. It's not that often I have a day to myself and I aim to enjoy it."

For the next seven hours, the trio toured museums, checked out sales at boutiques and people watched on U Street.

"Goddess bless, I needed this day," Gloria said to Donna and Kiara. The three had spent the day riding the Metro around town to avoid paying for expensive parking. "I forgot how much I miss having you guys around me just to hang out and keeping me from stressing out so much about stuff I can't change."

Rubbing her stomach, Donna chimed in, "I know, this has

been just what I needed. It is bad enough trying to find time for me with Milan and India pulling me in different directions. Then with the baby coming, my time is really going to be gone. As much as I love my family, I wish sometimes I was back at CRU worrying about making it to class on time, not what I'm going to have to cook for dinner."

Turning to face her sorority sister, Kiara remarked, "You know what Donna, listening you today, this is the longest I have ever been around you that you haven't said a curse word. What gives?"

"Check it, a few months ago I'm heading upstairs to put laundry in Milan and India's room and I hear them fussing. India, who has yet to get all her permanent teeth in, is telling her big sister she is going to whoop her ass until she rope like okra and smell like onions. I wanted to laugh so bad because you know that's my favorite way to talk about jumping off into someone's ass. Then I realized I am a mother and those girls look up to me. I have to be a better role model. If that means I need to hold my tongue better around my children so they don't sound like Def Comedy Jam, then so be it. The Bible says, it is not what goes into the mouth that defiles a person but what comes out the mouth that defiles a person. I guess I don't want to do dirty no more when it comes to how I talk."

"Well honey, I'm proud of you and I support you for wanting to get a handle on your words," Gloria said. "While I have to admit, your curse word vocab was tight, there are so many other ways you can use your mouth."

"Maybe if I had used my mouth in a different way, I wouldn't be in this position right now," Donna said walking onto the subway platform behind her sorority sisters. "Hey, at least I didn't curse. A girl can't give up all her vices at one time."

Sharing a laugh, the three headed to the steps to continue on their adventure. Gloria caught sight of a couple clinging to each other, apparently deeply into each other. Inwardly she sighed. Listening to Kiara and Donna talk about their families today brought home to her how truly alone she was. Maybe she needed to listen to her sisters and give Carlos a chance. Nothing ventured, nothing gained as the saying goes. 'Perhaps,' she thought rushing to catch up with Kiara and Donna.

CHAPTER EIGHTEEN

Donna

AFTER A WEEKEND filled with catching up, laughing and promising not to let too much time lapse between seeing each other again, the three women returned to their respective lives. Soon, the chill of winter gave way to the blooms of cherry blossoms as March brought the first days of spring. Donna, who planned to go on maternity leave at the end of the month, struggled at work to tie up all the loose ends before she left. Being a military wife helped her land the job as director of the agency that trained veterans to become educators. She wanted to make sure when she left for her three months, her staff wouldn't be left adrift.

The Tuesday of her final week, her cell phone buzzing broke her concentration. Looking at the display reading Peter Darden, she grimaced.

"Hello," Donna said flatly.

"Hi sweetness, how are things?"

"Busy, how can I help you Peter?"

"I was calling to let you know that I'm driving down to Richmond this weekend to visit my brother and wanted to know if I could get Milan and India. He has been asking about them and I figured it would be a good time for them to meet their new cousin."

"Yeah, they sent me a card when your niece was born. I didn't even know they had my new address because I sure didn't give it to them. Milan has Girl Scouts and India has a swim meet. I don't want to disrupt their schedule just because you have a whim to be a father."

"Donna," Peter said exasperated. "I didn't call to start anything with you. I just want to know if I can spend some time with my kids. Please."

For a half moment, the old Donna, who would have rained hellfire and brimstone on him for making such a last minute request, threatened to emerge. Instead, she took a deep breath and counted to ten.

"Fine, I will let India's coach and Milan's troop leaders know not to expect our daughters. Is there anything else I can help you with?"

"That's it. How is the man who is helping raise my daughters doing?" Peter said in pleasant voice.

Leaning back in her chair, Donna thought, 'this motherfucker is really trying to have a conversation with me.'

"My husband is doing fine. How is that unemployed housewife you married doing?"

Somberly, Peter replied, "She filed for divorce last week, so life at the house is a little bit strained. It's partially why I am heading down to Virginia. Her folks are coming in this weekend to help her pack and I don't want to be bothered. I will go ahead and save you the trouble of saying 'payback is a bitch isn't it?'"

"I wasn't going to say that," Donna said not trying to hold back the glee in her voice. "I'm sorry the two of you didn't work out. How are you holding up?"

"I'm fine, even though I'm sure you really don't care," Peter said in a voice heavy like the tenth hour of a twelve-hour shift. "I'm sure you have a busy day so I will let you get back to it. Call me tomorrow with the details so we can work out how we can coordinate this weekend. I know this weekend isn't my usual one and if I have to give up one so I have my children two weekends in a row fine. I just want to spend time with my kids and my family."

"Fine, fine. They get home around four so you can come get them then. I will talk to you later," Donna said disconnecting the call.

Turning back to her work, Donna's head churned with conflicting emotions. Yes, she was glad the man who cheated on her received walking papers of his own. On the other hand, divorce was not an easy process to endure.

During their senior year, Peter stuck to his guns about Donna being his one and only girlfriend. After the Titans drafted him, the couple married in a large wedding and moved to Nashville to live happily ever after.

Three years later on a frigid Tuesday while a pregnant Donna tried to cook dinner, a deliveryman came knocking with divorce papers. Turns out, Peter's philandering was only on hiatus, not retired.

Donna took small comfort in the fact that a year after the ink dried on the divorce decree, the Titans tired of him as well. The team cut Peter after he suffered a career ending shattered knee during a game against the Seahawks.

A year after Donna moved to Virginia with her new husband, Peter found a job coaching at Bowie State. While she appreciated that the move allowed him to spend time with their children, sometimes she wished she could banish him to the cornfields for screwing her over. Still, he helped give her two of the biggest blessings of her life, so she had to cut him some slack.

"Dang Donna, you look ready to pop, but pregnancy always seemed to agree with you," Peter said, smiling broadly three days later.

"Yeah, yeah, come on in. I thought I told you Milan and India don't get home for another hour," Donna said ushering him into her Woodbridge home.

Handing her a blue wrapped present, Peter smiled bashfully. "I know, I came early so I could give you a present for the baby and chat with you for a minute. This whole thing with the divorce made me think about how I treated you when we were married, and I just want to say I'm so very sorry."

Donna almost swooned from the shock of her ex-husband bringing her a gift and being apologetic. She thought, 'I better run out and get a bunch of lottery tickets because today must really be my lucky day.'

Offering to get them drinks, Donna retreated to the kitchen to regroup and get her emotions in order. Coming back, she settled on the couch and told Peter she accepted his apology. Still, she could not resist digging. "So what happened?" she asked.

"I guess the life of a college defense coach doesn't quite compare to being a NFL wife. I found out all these trips back home to Philly to see her family was not about her being homesick for cheesesteaks. Her new man plays for the Eagles. All this time, I thought she was with me because she loved me."

Donna tried to disguise her chuckle as a cough then decided to abandon the pretense. She burst out in a full body laugh.

"Peter, are you serious? You thought that blonde weave wearing, boob job having, barely graduated from beauty school trick was with you because you are a nice person? Negro please. Like I told you in college, those crumbs just wanted you for your cheddar. When it was gone, it would be just a matter of time before they would be as well. She saw a football player that she could wrap her legs around and take away from his family and you fell right into that trap. If you had kept your dick and the rest of you at home, you wouldn't be in this position," Donna said.

"You're right. I should have never left you and the kids. I had a good woman who worked her ass off for me, for her family and for herself. I was so stupid," Peter said quietly. "I'm so sorry, so very sorry. I'm sorry it took something like this to make me realize how much I hurt you."

Donna, known for always having a retort for every situation, was speechless. As much as she wanted to gloat that the mighty had fallen, the girl that had fallen in love with Peter wanted to wrap him in her arms.

"I forgave you a long time ago for the shit you pulled before we got married. I got over how you dogged me out after I delayed going to grad school so you could be a big time football star," Donna said, her voice rising a little until she caught herself. "I mean, sure I was pissed for a while, then I realized I couldn't be a good wife and a mother if I'm busy carrying a grudge about what went wrong with us. I have moved on, and I know it may not seem like it now, but you will be able to move on from this. You just have to focus on the things that make you smile instead of that trash that is going to try to stick you for your paper. Like the Bible says, shake the dust off your feet and keep it moving."

Grinning Peter replied, "I'm sure Jesus did not tell anyone to keep it moving."

"Well that second section came from the Book of Donna. If Ruth and Ester could have their own books, then I can create my own gospel with as much bullshit I have put up in my life."

The two shared a laugh then fell silent looking at each other with rediscovered eyes. The sounds of children's chatter and Donna's husband announcing the trio's arrival interrupted their reflection.

"Daddy, you're here," Milan said running into the house and into her father's arms.

"Hi dumplings, did you two have a good day in school?" Peter said, appearing to Donna to transform from a mournful man to a joyous father. "I know your aunt and uncle are going to be so excited about seeing you and introducing you to your new cousin," Peter said. "What's up Kevin, how are you doing?"

"I'm good, nice to see you again. Babe, I'm going to head upstairs and change. Peter, take care on the roads. Milan and India, you have a good time and remember what we talked about in the car," Donna's man of few words said, covering the bases of social niceties in dealing with his wife's ex and asserting his role as the current father figure and spouse.

"Good seeing you again as well. Donna, we are going to

get on the road so we can beat some of this traffic. I will call you when we get to the hotel."

"Sure, sure," Donna said getting up and getting the girls' suitcase that she had packed and brought downstairs. "Now drive safe and have a good time. Milan and India mind your father and don't think just because you're not home you don't have to do your homework."

Watching Peter's car pull down the driveway and away, Donna felt a tug in her heart and in her stomach. She knew the feeling in her stomach was her son making his presence felt, but the pain in her heart was a little bit more difficult to explain. She had a good life with Kevin. He respected her and would give his right arm for the kids. He encouraged her when she went back for her masters. All the things Peter didn't do. So, why was she standing there reminiscing about her old life with Peter? She had a good life. Although Kevin did not make her toes curl, he was her husband. They took vows to have and to hold. Still, Peter did look good in those khakis.

"Donna, telephone," Kevin's baritone voice called out. Walking into her home, Donna smiled at the man fixing her favorite meal and took the cordless phone into the living room.

"So tell me he looked like death eating a saltine. Raggedy clothes, unshaven, and eyes red rimmed like he been peeling onions," Gloria said gleefully.

"No, he was clean shaven, smelled like Sunday morning on the way to church, and wearing those black framed glasses that make him look like he's some famous novelist," Donna said shaking her head. "You know Peter always did clean up well."

"Curse his hide. The least he could do is look pitiful. Serves his tail right after the hell he put you through with the divorce."

"I know Glo, but hating on Peter is not going to change what happened between us. The Bible says to let all bitterness be put away and to be kind to one another. Now as much as I wanted to dance a jig when he told me about the divorce, I had to get my mind right and let it go. And get this, he came up in here apologizing for the way he treated me. I tell you karma is something all together good."

"Damn, those are some serious hormones churning through your body. You are mellow like wine. I miss the ass kicker I pledged with, who would have torn him a new one and told him where to stick his apology. But alas, maturity comes to us all. Listen, I'm not going to stay on the phone long. I'm planning to drive down to Hampton tomorrow to do a workshop with the graduate chapter. Do you want to ride? I know since the kids are gone you may want to get out the house."

"Girl, another sorority trip? Between you and Kiara, y'all eat up the road for K-Rho. I'm good to pay my yearly dues and make it to a meeting or two."

"Yeah, I guess," Gloria said reviewing the forms scattered on her dining room table. "It seemed like a good idea running for regional community service coordinator last year, but now that I have to surf a sea of paperwork every quarter, it don't seem like a good thing. To be fair, Elder Swan Samuels told us when we crossed being a Rho was about working for the community. Trust me, they are getting their money's worth. So, how about it? Are you down for being my co-pilot tomorrow? I promise we can stop at the country buffet you like on the way back."

"Thanks for the offer but I think I'm going to pass. I'm looking forward to sleeping in tomorrow and spending time with my husband. In fact, why am I talking to you? My man is in the kitchen after working a ten-hour day cooking my pregnant behind smothered pork chops and gravy since I mentioned this morning I was craving some home cooking. Let me let you go so I can properly show him how much I appreciate his efforts."

"Well excuse me. Don't do it too hard that you go into early labor. I will call you tomorrow and let you know how the session goes."

Donna walked in to find her burly husband, who spent his

day molding Marines, wearing an apron and putting what looked to be a pan of macaroni and cheese in the oven.

"Baby, why don't you turn the pork chops on low and meet me in the bedroom? I have some tactical maneuvers I would like to discuss with you since we got the house to ourselves."

CHAPTER NINETEEN

Kiara/Gloria

"PAULA I WILL be home as soon as I can. No, I don't know how long this is going to take," Kiara said holding her cell phone to her ear. Instead of heading home after a hellish day of work, complete with co-workers' attitudes and computer shutdowns, she was stuck on the John Belk Freeway on her way to put out a proverbial fire. "Baby, I appreciate you and all that you do. I know it was my responsibility to pick up Malik from Boy Scouts tonight, but I have to go to this meeting with the dean of students. If I could avoid having to go I would, but I can't. Traffic is picking up so I'm going to have to put both hands on the wheel. I will talk to you later."

Today was not the day for this to happen. She and Paula had been going through some tense times lately. The week prior, they had gotten into a shouting match when Kiara interrupted date night to rush a payment to the printers for a sorority program. The month before that, they broke one of the cardinal rules of relationships when they went to bed angry at each other. Looking for a phone number, Kiara found a text message on Paula's phone from one of Paula's ex-girlfriends. She had dismissed it as being an idle just-saying-hello message, but Paula had added a barbed, "You know if you weren't so busy being Ms. Purple and Platinum, I wouldn't have had a chance to respond."

Tonight should had involved them sending Malik to a friend's house to spend the night, Kiara fixing a nice meal, and Paula leaving her exhausted from a vigorous round of lovemaking. Instead, Kiara was on her way to the city's only historically black university to prevent the school's Kappa Alpha Rho Chapter from being removed due to hazing allegations.

"So how did it go?" Paula asked Kiara. She and Malik were eating dinner when Kiara arrived home.

"P, that is K-Rho business so you know I can't tell you. But I will say, don't be surprised if the campus is a little less purple and platinum next year," Kiara said opening the refrigerator and grabbing a soda. "Honestly after reading the report, we are lucky there will be any Rhos on campus next year. It just makes me so angry sometimes how these girls twist the process to bully and berate those wishing to be their sisters. I didn't go through that and neither did anyone who came through Lambda Mu. I don't get why it's so hard for the girls to grasp the concept of what sisterhood really means. I mean hell, look at Gloria and Donna and all we have been through together. That is what sisterhood is about and we didn't get paddled or punished. For seventy years, Kappa Alpha Rho had stood solo as the only sorority never to face a lawsuit for hazing. Now this new generation comes along and all kind of bullshit has been popping off."

"Kiara, I know you love your sorority and I respect all that it has meant for you. but every K-Rho is not Donna or Gloria," Paula said placing a plate of pasta in front of Kiara. "What the three of you have is special and honestly goes beyond your letters. I mean, you know one of my line sisters and I crossed without speaking to each other. The line that crossed after us got into a knockout, drag out during the step show my senior year. The bond the three of y'all have is unique. Didn't you tell me Gloria took vacation time to make sure she was in court with you every day during the rape trial? And didn't you max out your credit cards to help Donna get furniture for her apartment when she moved out from Peter?"

Kiara nodded her head in agreement. She and her line sisters had been through a lot together since that winter's night at the student center. Through ups and down, joys and pains, they had been there with a shoulder to lean on, a joke to tell to lighten the mood, or a word of advice to hopefully prevent heartbreak later on.

"Don't let the misguided actions of a few of your sorority sisters make you stop being dedicated to your organization. But don't let your dedication prevent you from doing what you need to do to make sure everything in your life gets taken care of," Paula said looking at Malik.

"I hear what you are saying, but you know how much I value being active. I feel that being an out K-Rho forces our members to see lesbians are part of our organization and that we are just as dedicated as the next sister is. Granted some of the sisters seem to have an issue with it, which saddens me, but I'm going to keep doing what I do," Kiara said spearing a piece of sausage.

"I think it's good you haven't hidden the fact you are gay. I remember you telling me about the members' reaction when you pulled up with that split license tag with both of our sororities on it. I am your partner, and I support whatever you want to do with your life. All I'm asking you is to remember there are other people in your life you have to consider."

The two lovers sat looking into each other eyes. Malik, sensing a change in the air, silently got up from the table and put his plate in the dishwasher. Announcing he was going upstairs, he left Paula and Kiara.

"Baby, I just worry about you sometimes. You're working, going to school, and volunteering. And I know sometimes you still have nightmares about what happened with those guys at the club," Paula said, her voice dropping lower. "I don't want you to get so burnt out between everything you got going on that's there is nothing left for your family or yourself. Finish eating dinner and come to bed soon."

Receiving Paula's kisses, Kiara promised she would. Sitting

at the kitchen table, Kiara reflected on the choices she had made and the ones she would be facing soon.

Kiara tossed and turned that night thinking about Paula's words. The next day under the guise of writing a clinical assessment for a new client, she emailed Gloria for her feedback on the situation.

Gloria, I don't know what I need to do? I love Kappa Alpha Rho, but I can't sacrifice my family or myself. Shit, I remember my dad's face when my mom used to be running in and out the house with Kappa stuff when I was younger. I swear I don't want to see the same expression on Paula's face.

I feel you. Kappa Alpha Rho can do many things for you, help you get a job, a good deal on a house if your realtor is a soror. But it for sure can't keep you warm at night or show you off to its friends during Career Day.

Multi-tasking as always, Gloria was typing away with Kiara while comforting a friend crying over yet another imploded relationship on her work phone.

So what do you think I should do? Pull back from the sorority and spend more time with Paula and Malik? I know that is the logical thing to do, but I really enjoy working for the organization. Paula should understand being dedicated. She went through her process twice before she crossed and she is active in her chapter.

I know, but on the Kappa crest, Ms. Libra, you can sometimes not be balanced in what you do. I know I'm the one to talk, but you spend a lot of time with K-Rho and you are just the chapter's assistant treasurer and one of the members of the undergraduate committee. Maybe you need to back away from the light Carol Ann and chill a bit. You have a great family and I don't want you to get burnt out trying to do everything for everybody. Just remember like ABC daytime, you only have one life to live.

True, but after that situation with Andrea in college, I vowed nothing was going to keep me from being active in my organization. But maybe I

179

need to pump my breaks some. Elections are coming up and I don't plan to put my name on the ballot for anything. I'm going to do it Donna style next year. Make sure my check clears so I can wear my paraphernalia with a clear conscious.

Got to love that deuce of ours. Gloria glanced at the clock on her desk. *¡Ay dios mio, look at the time. I have a meeting in ten minutes. I will talk to you tonight.*

Hitting send, Gloria quickly disconnected from her friend on the phone with promises to meet her for lunch tomorrow and refocused her mind. Rushing down the hall toward the conference room, she mentally metamorphosed, switching from supportive sister-friend to steely, smart State Department up and coming superstar. Her supervisor's email inviting her to this meeting provided sketchy details. Garrett said only to report to the conference room at 2:00 p.m. to discuss a joint project between Justice and State. Walking in, she was pleasantly surprised to see Carlos sitting there with his supervisor. Taking a seat beside her supervisor, Gloria raised her eyebrows at the friend she had spoken with the night before.

"Ms. Allen, pleased you could join us. I was saying to Garret and Carlos a few minutes ago, I'm excited about this project with Justice and State coming together to address illegal immigration," Carlos' supervisor said from the other side of the table. "We are all aware of the issues with illegal immigration concerning those crossing the Texas/Arizona border. Every year there is a flood of activity in Florida from those seeking to enter our country without the benefit of a visa. What we hope to do is address issues such as human smugglers here and in those countries to stem the flow."

"Sounds like something I would be interested coming aboard and working with. I would love to hear more about this," Gloria said, scrolling through her mental file cabinet of contacts that could help with this project.

"Good. That is why I asked Carlos Domingo to join us. He

is heading this project up for us and will be the best person to lay out the roadmap."

Taking his cue, Carlos slid the already copied binder over to her and launched into a full discussion of how his team would work with U.S. contacts while Gloria's team would be responsible for locating contacts in the Caribbean.

Gloria listened to Carlos with a sense of admiration and awe. She thought, 'he is so soft-spoken I forget sometimes how smart he is.' Carlos was a first generation Cuban American whose family came to this country to escape Castro. In fact, the 'Wet Foot Dry Foot' policy brought them together as friends. Gloria was debating with a co-worker about the policy, which allowed Cubans who had made it to dry land to remain in the United States while other migrants from Caribbean countries were often forced to go back home. Listening to her passionate discourse on how racist the policy was— Haitians who landed on dry land were often sent back home or languished in detention camps— Carlos interjected and said he agreed with her, but different situations often merited different solutions. She had been impressed with how calmly and skillfully he made his arguments then, and she felt the same professional swooning now. Mentally adjusting her thinking, she refocused on his words.

"So Ms. Allen, that's basically the nature of the project. We would like you to pull together a team of co-workers to coordinate the State Department's responsibilities, and I will do the same for Justice. I would suggest we hold weekly meetings to maximize the potential of success. If that is agreeable," Carlos said.

"I feel I can establish and maintain a standing meeting space and time for this project. Let's plan to circle back next week at Justice to discuss our team building and next steps," Gloria said.

"Great, I will be sure you have all the information we have by EOB tomorrow." Carlos stood up and extended his hand across the table to Gloria. The two shook hands, as professional co-workers do, and parted ways.

However, most professional co-workers, when delivering

packages, do not bring along takeout Thai and Asian beer to their co-worker's home.

"Damn Gloria, I thought you were never getting home. I think your neighbor was going to call the police," Carlos said.

Unlocking her door and waving to her eighty-six year old neighbor, Gloria replied, "Please, you have been here enough times that if she thought you were really a threat, she would have called them in the first ten minutes of you being here. And why didn't you use the key I gave you for safe keeping?" Gloria said.

"I knew this being Wednesday you were going to confession. Since you haven't had a date in a couple of weeks, I figured it wouldn't take you that long so I just waited. I had only pulled up a few minutes ago."

Shouting from the bedroom while she changed into a pair of purple sweat pants and a white tank top, Gloria said, "Oh, and don't think I have forgotten about you letting me walk into the meeting Ray Charles style. You could have let me known what was up."

"Yeah, I know, but it's always so much fun to see you enter a room, assess the situation and take control. I had no doubt you would be the perfect fit for the project," Carlos said walking into the living room with their food arranged on purple plates.

Scrunching up her face to keep from smiling, Gloria said walking into the living room, "Well, all is forgiven if you managed to remember to get my favorite dish from Bangkok Palace."

Moving over on the couch to make room for Gloria, Carlos replied, "Yes, I made sure to get the green curry tofu with two summer rolls. Now can we get into the movie?"

For the next two hours, the two laughed and caught up with all that had taken place in their lives since they last saw each other. The two had a standing agreement to get together weekly to share a meal and gripe about their respective workplaces.

"Oh my God, I needed this tonight. Work this week has left me feeling like Anne Sullivan in *The Miracle Worker*. I'm pumping water, signing the word water, and pushing people's hands under a fucking fountain and they are still not getting the concept of why their hands are wet," Gloria said.

Gathering up the plates and taking them in the kitchen, Carlos said over his shoulder, "It sucks being the smartest person in the room doesn't it?"

"Exactly, I mean I can't help it that I'm sexy and smart. They just hating."

Carlos entered the room, shaking his head at Gloria's mock pouting. He kissed her on the forehead and said, "I'm sure if you have managed this far, you can make a few more months. I know you said you are going to take an extended leave later this year to concentrate on your dissertation. Maybe a few months without your smiling face and sharp mind will cause your co-workers to straighten up and realize what a treasure they have in their midst."

"I was going to let the smartest person in the room comment fly, but now I get the sense you are mocking me," Gloria said, assuming a wounding tone she managed to maintain until breaking out in a giggle.

"I was being sincere. One of the reasons I pushed for this project is to let you have something to focus on, so that your boss won't be so hard on your back expecting you to do everything and be everywhere. You could do this project in your sleep. You do some work on this, focus on getting your papers done, and then you can take your leave on a high note."

Looking at Carlos, Gloria could have sworn she sensed something more than just simple friendship behind his words. Then again, maybe she was projecting. Since her conversation with Donna and Kiara, she had been thinking more about dating Carlos. Sitting on her sofa beside him, she felt maybe this would be a good time to say something. 'Nah, why mess up a good friendship?' she thought.

"Gloria, it's been a long night so I am going to head home. I will bring the records to your office tomorrow so we can get this officially started. Buenos noches dulce princesa."

Walking toward her bedroom after walking Carlos to his

car, Gloria inhaled the traces of Carlos' cologne lingering on her clothes. 'Is it really worth it to suffer in single sorrow than make a move and risk not having my feelings returned?' she thought smiling. Still feeling Carlos' lips on her forehead, she drifted off to sleep leaving the question unanswered.

CHAPTER TWENTY
Kiara/Donna

'OH MY GOD, is this meeting ever going to end?' Kiara thought to herself as she fought not to yawn from boredom. She had given her report almost two hours ago. However, before the chapter could close the books on yet another year, there was the issue of selecting those to lead them into the next two years. The doyenne position required the holder to devote time being the face of the chapter on local, state, and regional levels. The woman selected for the position served as chapter leader and chairperson of the sorority's non-profit foundation, and bore the responsibility of supervising and inspiring the chapter members and the thirty undergraduate members of the organization's two college chapters. Sitting at the table facing the chapter, Kiara could read boredom on many of the fifty-five faces in front of her.

"Elder Sister Swan Johnson, I respect and honor the fact you would have no problem serving as doyenne for another two years. Your leadership has been exceptional. But, our constitution clearly states no member can serve more than two terms, even if the terms are not consecutive," Renée Lincoln, the chapter's outgoing parliamentarian said.

"Sister Swan Lincoln, you are correct, but I feel like the chapter needs a steady and experienced hand as we go into the

next two years," Geneva Johnson said, her tone chiding her younger sorority sister for her perceived ignorance about what was good
for the chapter. "As you are aware, our chapter will be hosting the
regional conference next year, we are breaking grounds on a new
community outreach center and we are set to pay the mortgage
off on this very house. As we embark on such monumental tasks,
it would behoove the chapter to have the right person leading the
way."

Feeling a tickle on her thigh, Kiara knew without looking at
her phone it was Paula. Today, May 7, was their anniversary. Paula
had booked a room at an upscale bed and breakfast across the
street from Duke University, a three-hour drive from their home.
Check in was at 3:00 p.m. and it was fast creeping up to noon.

*Nee— I'm going to have to bail. Your sisters are taking too long to
get themselves together and P and I are heading out of town. Text me and let
me know what happens*, Kiara wrote on a piece of paper and slid it to
her left to Renée.

Glancing down at the paper then up at Kiara, Renée smiled.
"Swans, I would like to propose we close this debate to allow us to
complete the process of selecting our leaders for next year," she
said standing up. "I would like to nominate a candidate who has
demonstrated the leadership and commitment this chapter needs
to take us forward. She has served on this chapter's executive board
for the past four years and has been a member for more than a de-
cade," she said. "She recently completed our national leadership
academy and helped coordinate our partnership with NAMI. I
would like to nominate Kiara Michaels as the next doyenne."

Kiara fought her first instinct to drop her mouth in shock.
She couldn't believe Renée just did that. The two of them had
talked about there being a need to take the chapter in a new direction, but she didn't expect this to be her solution. 'In fact, when we
talked before the meeting about possible candidates for doyenne,
Renée didn't mention nominating me,' she thought. Half of her
felt honored and thrilled, but the other half of her worried about
the impact it would have on her relationship. 'Wasn't it just a few

weeks ago,' Kiara thought, 'I was saying to Gloria I was going to dial back my involvement? But doyenne, that would be something to go before my name,' Kiara mentally smiled.

Truly, it would be like mother, like daughter for the Michaels' women. Her mother had served as her graduate chapter leader for three terms and later served as state director. Kiara hoped to follow her example. Surveying her sisters sitting in front of her, Kiara noticed the nomination appeared to make some of the members uncomfortable. If approved, she would be the first out lesbian to hold a prominent leadership position in the state, if not in the entire organization. Perhaps her climb wouldn't be as smooth.

"Sister Swan Lincoln, while I agree Sister Swan Michaels has been a valid asset to the chapter, I don't feel she is an appropriate choice to lead our chapter," Geneva drawled out in an accent thick as buttered grits. Kiara saw other sisters nod their head.

"Why is she not an appropriate choice? According to our constitution, she meets the requirements. She has attended at least one national convention; she has been a member of this chapter for at least five years and has been a member for at least ten. She was also one of the first graduates of our national organizational leadership program," Renée said. "She would be ideal to help us plan for what lies ahead."

"Traditionally, the doyenne of our chapter has been a little bit more seasoned. I don't think Sister Swan Michaels has reached thirty yet. Then there are others things we have to consider," Geneva said. "While Sister Swan Michaels' sorority accomplishments are stellar, her activities outside the sorority may not cast our organization in the best light. I would never attempt to pass judgment on how members conduct themselves when they are not about the business of Kappa. I leave that to my Heavenly Father. But, I can't support having a sister who has been known to engage in certain behaviors represent my organization in the community."

Kiara's face hardened. She thought, 'so I'm good enough to work on the chapter's books, but not good enough to represent the chapter in public? I guess because my role is strictly internal. And when no one really wanted to do the job, it was fine to have me do it.'

Kiara smirked slightly about that 'seasoned' line Geneva tried to pull. She knew it was to cover up what she really wanted to say. 'No bull dagger is going to represent my organization'. It was this kind of lack of sisterhood that bothered Kiara. She gave her time, talent and treasure, but some of the sorority members couldn't see beyond her taste in partners. Donna had often said, "No one can hurt you like family, and being in a sorority is like having a hell of a lot of sisters."

During her years as a member of the graduate chapter, members' reaction to her sexuality had varied. Two years into her joining the chapter, she had been "re-assigned" from the committee working with the nine to fourteen year-old girls due to the committee's chair feeling uncomfortable with her working with young girls. The first time she took Paula to the sisterhood dinner, limited to sisters and spouses, there were some stares and whispered comments from her older sisters seated at their table. Of course, Paula wore a royal blue, one-shoulder dress with her sorority pin fixed prominently above her heart, so it could have been her attire in a sea of purple and platinum causing the stares.

On the other hand, several of the chapter members, including many of the older sorority sisters, made her feel welcomed. The doyenne prior to Geneva appointed her to the undergraduate committee because she felt the younger sorors needed to know that Kappa Alpha Rhos came from different kinds of backgrounds and lived diverse lives. All that should matter was their commitment to the organization. Another member, with over fifty years of membership, nominated her to be Sister of the Year and had insisted Paula pose in the picture with her during the ceremony. Kiara remembered Geneva looked like she had a serious case of heartburn standing next to them.

Her sisters' reaction to her sexuality often saddened her, but she refused to back down. The check she wrote for dues was cashed just like everyone else's, and she wasn't going to let anyone bully her out of being the best Rho she could be.

"Sister Swan Michaels has always been devoted to supporting our chapter programs in person, something I unfortunately can't say for a lot of our members," Renée implored to the members, who seemed visibly torn about her nomination. "She has worked hard for Kappa Alpha Rho and that is what we need to be concerned with, not what she does and who she does it with. We are all adult women who live and breathe and act like adult women. Unless they have a criminal record, I don't think we need to adopt a morals clause in selecting our leaders. Our national constitution doesn't have it, and we shouldn't try to add something that isn't there."

"Sister Swan Lincoln, you are correct. Our constitution does not address morality in our founding documents, but I'm sure such perversions that have invaded our fine organization did not exist in the times of our Eternal Emeralds," Geneva said, pursing her plump burgundy painted lips at Kiara.

Sitting there while members danced around the issue of whether she was qualified to serve as doyenne, Kiara felt like she was back in that meeting room on Groundhog Day with Andrea. This time, however, she wasn't going to excuse herself to go to bathroom while her sisters implied she wasn't fit to be a Kappa Alpha Rho leader. 'I am K-Rho and we always rise to the top,' she thought standing up.

"Swans, I know the hour is getting late and we all have our lives to lead. I would like to make a statement and suggest we move ahead and vote," she said. "I will admit Sister Swan Lincoln caught me off guard with the nomination, but just like we sing in our national hymn, when Kappa Alpha Rho requires our action, we don't hesitate a fraction. I stand here ready to serve my sisters to the fullest capacity. I realize some of you may have trouble with my age, but I am dedicated to our causes. I have worked beside many of you and I stand here sure no one of can speak ill of the work I have put into making sure the legacy of our founders is honored.

189

If the body doesn't chose to elevate me to doyenne, I will continue to be a committed member of this chapter and serve in whatever capacity I am needed. I encourage us to consider the oath we took when we became members, and how the vote we cast today will reflect to our younger sorors where we intend to take our organization and the traits we support in choosing our leaders."

Sitting down, Kiara felt nervous about how her words would be received but satisfied she had stood up for herself. True, this time she really did need to pee, but she was going to hold it until she knew which way the vote would go.

"Well-spoken Sister Swan. Because of the nature and significance of this vote, I will request we deviate from our standing ballot vote and move by a show of hands vote. Those voting no need to raise their left hand, and those voting yes vote with their right hand," Renée said. "Elder Sister Johnson, as the outgoing doyenne, I would ask for you to serve as the official tabulator of the votes. If all hearts and minds are clear, may I have all my no votes first?"

While the sisters cast their votes, Kiara looked out the window at the passing traffic. She refused to face her doubters but felt the energy of her supporters.

In a voice strained with resentment, Elder Sister Johnson said, "Sister Swan Michaels, your sisters have selected you to be the next doyenne of the Xi Kappa Chapter. Do you accept?"

"I do Elder Sister. Thank you to those who believed in our sisterhood and me. Today marks a new day for our organization. I'm glad to be sharing it. I know some of our members chose not to support me. Please don't let the fact I am a lesbian distract from the fact I am also a member of Kappa Alpha Rho. Our sisterhood is built on recognizing the traits of finer womanhood, which exist within all of us, and our goal and mission is to let our light of leadership shine."

Kiara waited until the meeting adjourned to text Paula with the news about her election. Her lover's response: *I'm sure this is going to make for an interesting anniversary weekend.* Kiara hoped she meant that in a good way.

"Sister Swan Michaels, as the incoming doyenne, you need to call a meeting of the executive board within the month so that we can start planning for next year. I would be glad to offer any assistance you will need," Geneva said stiffly.

"Thank you for your kind offer Elder Sister. I feel confident with the help of the incoming board, I will be able to establish a program for the upcoming year. You have served the chapter well these past years. I only hope I can be as good of a doyenne as you have been. Now, if you will excuse me, I have an obligation I have to keep. Enjoy the rest of your Saturday," Kiara said, giving her a big sisterly love hug.

'Amazing,' she thought, walking into the May sunshine. Twelve years after feeling fear about her potential sisters finding out about Chris, she was leaving now to celebrate her anniversary with her partner after being elevated to head up the sorority's largest graduate chapter in the state.

"Momma, you will never guess who you are talking to?" Kiara said gleefully. "Your only daughter is the new doyenne of the Xi Kappa Chapter of our illustrious and glorious organization."

"Oh my word. Honey, congratulations. I'm so proud of you. Wait until I tell your aunts the news. I guess our sisters recognize the fine sister they had in their midst," Dorothy said. "I remember you telling me about how some of the sorors were less than sisterly to you. I just knew sooner or later they would have to get with the program."

"I know. Momma you should have seen Elder Swan Geneva's face. You know she was the main one not supporting me. If she knew like I knew about her niece Purusha, that came through at St. Aug, she would sing a different tune about lesbians in the organization. But I'm not one to gossip, so you didn't hear it from me," Kiara chuckled while she turned the ignition in her car. "Momma, I don't know what to feel. I'm excited but I'm also so nervous. You know leading a chapter is no easy task and a lot of the sisters didn't support me."

"Baby, I'm just down US 74 if you need me. I know I haven't said this to you Kiara, but I am really proud of you. I'm glad you have stayed active in the organization, but I'm more proud of the woman you have become. No matter what life has handed to you, you have rolled with the punches. I'm glad you are my daughter, and if your father was here I know he would say the same thing."

Sitting at the stoplight, Kiara felt tears forming. Hearing her mother say she was proud of her meant more than words could express. She had started this journey toward sisterhood because of her mother, and now that she had reached this level it made the achievement ever better.

"Momma, you are going to make me cry. I'm proud of you and how you have supported me with everything. I know you were disappointed by some of the choices I made, but you have been by my side throughout it all."

"Baby, we are swans and swans swim together through good and bad times. Baby, I'm going to call you later. I was getting ready to head down to the church to help decorate for service tomorrow. You know we are honoring the graduates, so we are decorating the pews. I wish Paula and you could make it down, but I know she told me y'all were going to Durham this weekend, so I hope to see you soon. I love you."

"I love you too," Kiara said.

Still bursting with her good news, Kiara hit the speed dial for Donna. Gloria was in Costa Rica, so she would have to settle for an email.

"D, guess who is the newly elected leader of the largest grad chapter in North Carolina," Kiara said merging into interstate traffic.

"I'm going to go ahead and say you are because I'm going to need to cut the conversation short. Kevin and I are on way to the hospital. My water just broke. I will call you later," Donna said and rushed off before disconnecting.

Surprised her sorority sister had answered the phone, Kiara shrugged. 'I guess everyone is having a new beginning Saturday,' she thought.

Driving up the highway, Kiara replayed the meeting for Paula, varying her voice to mimic Geneva's Charleston drawl and Renée's Midwestern twang. Her lover nodded her head at the appropriate places, shook her head in disdain when the story called for it, and beamed broadly when Kiara ended the story.

"I'm so happy for you baby, my Kiara, the doyenne of the K-Rho graduate chapter. It's amazing how something like this could happen, especially after you told me last week that you were going to be pulling back on your involvement," Paula said dryly.

"I was buttercup, I really was. Then Renée up and did this, and seeing how those biddies noses turned up like 'oh my God,' I had to see it through. If the chapter hadn't elected me, I would have been fine. At least I wouldn't have backed down," Kiara said, grasping the wheel and turning quickly to meet her lover's eyes. "But the chapter elected me. It wasn't even a close vote. My soror that is the first lady at the mega-church on Tyvolva, voted for me, which I didn't expect."

Paula looked out the window and said, "Like I said, I am happy for you, but I don't want you to get so caught up in being about the business of Kappa you forget you have a family. You know I bleed blue and white, but you can't let your sorority life overshadow your real life."

Grabbing Paula's hand while she guided the car along I-85, Kiara promised her she would make sure the life they had created wouldn't take a back seat to Kappa Alpha Rho.

"Baby, I make a pledge to you today I will never put the sorority over our family. I am going to be there for Malik and you. I realize last year was hectic and I apologize for that. This is my last year in grad school, and you know we talked about me starting my own consulting business so I will be able to set my own hours," Kiara said earnestly. "This year is going to be the year of us. I promise I'm not going to disappoint you."

"You say that now and I'm going to hold you to it. Just remember Kappa can do a lot of things, but I don't think it can do this," Paula said, leaning over and whispering in Kiara's ear.

Eyes widened, Kiara looked at her lover who smiled and winked. "Damn girl, I'm glad I decided to give you those yoga lessons for Christmas. I hope our room at the inn is soundproof because I expect I'm going be lifting up my voice and singing tonight."

CHAPTER TWENTY-ONE

Gloria/Donna

WHILE KIARA SPENT the summer attending sorority committee meetings, and Donna adjusted to being the mother of three, Gloria struggled with her feelings about Carlos. Lately, she noticed more and more how his cologne sent her silently swooning. More than once, she felt her train of thought slowing down as she felt his presence. She discovered the Caesar haircut she ribbed him about actually heightened the impact of his deep chestnut eyes. Then it was the matter of his voice; she never noticed how it resembled the low thunder of an approaching summer storm, deep and charged.

All these thoughts ran through her head the Wednesday following the Fourth of July. Tonight, the weekly get-together was at Carlos' apartment. Gloria sat crossed legged on the floor with briefing papers spread out around her while Carlos sat on his couch with his laptop sitting on his lap. Lifting his head, Carlos asked, "Penny for your thoughts?"

"I was thinking, while I'm sitting here with you studying, I could be out on a date. The father of that student I mentored last year called this week and asked me to go out with him for dinner."

"What student? You know you always had at least three in rotation. I know you must be volunteer of the year working with the kids at that middle school and keeping an eye on the chapter at Morgan State. Sometimes, if I didn't know better, I would think you were actually two people," Carlos said.

"My sweet, I'm just one woman who knows her way around a day planner. And you know you put volunteer hours in also at Our Lady of Lourdes. Anyway, the kid in question is Kyle. He is the one that thought it was so amusing to practice the curse words his older brother brought back from his tour in Korea. Little did he know, the principle was a Korean War vet who had brought back the same words when he came back," Gloria said, stretching her arms, a little self-conscious that maybe in trying to cram thirty-six hours of work into a twenty-four hour day she may have forgotten to put on deodorant.

"Yeah, I recall him. You told me he helped out in the language lab sorting tapes. So how did daddy get the number? You want something to drink?" Carlos said in a strange tone walking into the kitchen. Watching Carlos' back, Gloria thought, 'is that jealousy I hear coming out his mouth?'

"Since I would be spending time with their boy wonder, I gave my number to Charles and his ex-wife in case they needed to reach me. I got their numbers as well, in case I needed to call and explain why I had to smack their child for getting fresh. At any rate, daddy is interested in discovering more about D.C. Since I'm not working with their son anymore, and he recalled some conversations we had about various galleries in town, he called me and asked if I could show him some nightlife. I was thinking we could check out that new spot on U Street."

"Oh," Carlos' voice floated into the dining room. He entered bearing a cuba libre for Gloria and a bottle of beer for himself. Handing her the glass without making eye contact, he sat into his chair. "So when are the two of you heading out on the town?"

"I was thinking this Friday. I know you are going to be going out of town for your sister's birthday party. I figured since el gato is going to be away, I get a chance to get a breather from work and have a chance to shake my money maker," Gloria said, taking a sip of her favorite drink. 'Damn, that boy knows how to make a drink just like I love it,' she thought. He was the only one that got the blend of cola, rum, and lime just right, causing her taste buds to rumba.

In the back of her mind, Gloria hoped Carlos would act a little bothered, but he just shrugged his shoulders and went back to his books. The truth of the matter was Gloria really wasn't that interested in going out with the boy's father. He was beyond her ten years older rule, and if memory served correctly, a dues paying member of the Hair Club for Men. Still, it had been a while since she had ridden a horse. She was ready to get back into the saddle. If she couldn't get a wild mustang between her toned thighs, she would make do with a comfortable stable horse. Gloria and Carlos fell back into the studied silence until Carlos surprised her with an admission.

"I'm glad you are getting out there Gloria. You are too cute to be single. I know work and school has been weighing on you. It is good you are dipping back into the pool of dating. I know Carolyn would love to get you married with some kids."

"When did you and my mother get so tight? Oh, that is right, you and her connected last spring when she came up here to attend that conference on immigration law. I'm surprised she confided in you about her concerns about my personal life."

"She worries about you and wants to make sure you are safe. I told her I'm keeping my eye on you to make sure you are not getting into too much trouble," Carlos said smiling at her. "You know, now that you mentioned it, I actually planned to start getting back into the swing of things myself. I was thinking about asking out Laura Lee. You remember her? You introduced us at the CRU alumni fundraiser we attended last year. We have emailed back and forth a few times and she mentioned she is a baseball fan. I am thinking about taking her out to see the Nationals play. What do you think?"

Despite every fiber of being throbbing with how much of a bad of idea she thought it would be, Gloria replied she thought it would be a good idea for him to ask her out. After all, who wouldn't want to date a researcher short-listed for a MacArthur Fellowship, who was frequently mistaken for Lucy Lui?

"Good deal. Maybe if you and your date hit it off and Laura and I connect, we can hang out sometimes."

"Sure," Gloria said. Just how she wanted to spend her free time; somewhere having to make nice while one of the few women in the DMV area she could view as worthy competition chatted up her crush.

Gloria kept her feelings of growing attraction to herself until finally she couldn't hold it anymore. Sharing a juice with Donna a month later, she shared her feelings.

"Donna, it's killing me. I want to say something to him so badly, but I don't want to make a fool out of myself. I don't know what has happened to me. I have never been tongue tied around a guy," Gloria said to Donna. India and Milan were away with Peter, and Kevin was upstairs bonding with his son, leaving the two to chat in the kitchen.

Next week, Donna would be heading back to work after three months maternity leave. She and Gloria had spent the afternoon sorting through her closet to find clothes to fit her post pregnancy body. Since her official first day was August 8th, the goal was to find something professional but cool.

"What, Ms. I Got Something To Say For Every Occasion don't know what to say? Honey, I have to write this down."

"I'm serious, when I'm around him I get all flustered, like I'm some high school girl. Hell, I never even got flustered around dudes when I was in high school. It is the damndest thing. We have been friends for so long, and I never had any thoughts beyond Carlos is nice and I like spending time with him. Now, I keep thinking about being more than just friends and it is screwing with my head. I blame you and Kiara for putting that thought in my head in February."

"Swan please," Donna said shaking her head. "You know you have been thinking about the boy long before Kiara and me tagged-teamed you. Now I know our resident psychotherapist is in Charlotte and can't be here to give you her twenty-four cents, but I would say, perhaps getting close to sealing the deal on getting that long piece of paper, you are considering sealing the deal on other things as well. I know I may give you a hard time about jumping on Carlos, but I respect the friendship you have. I would never encourage you to rush into something just to satisfy my desire to see everyone I love matched up like Noah. My advice to you is to follow your instincts. When the time is right for you to say something to him you will know it, and you will say the right thing. Don't rush anything or else you will end up regretting it."

Kevin walked in on the tail end of the conversation and handed their son to Donna.

"Great Hera's ghost, you could have warned me you were getting ready to whip your boob out," Gloria shrieked when Donna lifted her shirt and began nursing.

Scrunching up her face into a smirk, she said, "Like I said, before you say something to old boy, make sure you are prepared for the consequences of your actions. Say the right thing and sooner than later you will be sitting somewhere with someone sucking the life out of you, and you'll be happier than anything to have it happen."

CHAPTER TWENTY-TWO

Kiara

DRIVING UP I-40 toward Cary for the Kappa Alpha Rho state meeting a week before Halloween, Kiara kept playing Paula's parting words in her mind.

"Kiara, maybe we should take a break for a while," Paula said. "I know my timing sucks with you leaving today for your meeting, but this is the first time in weeks I have managed to catch you in one place for any period of time. Usually I'm at work when you are home and when I'm at home you are somewhere else. I told you on our anniversary I needed you to make the family more of a priority, and you said you could do that. But you haven't and I refuse to keep covering for you."

Despite her best intention, Kappa Alpha Rho had taken up more time than she expected. Between making sure all the necessary contracts had been signed for the regional conference, to overseeing and attending chapter events, Kiara often found little time to just be. If she wasn't at work, she was at UNC Charlotte attending classes. If she wasn't at the university, she was at the sorority house. If she wasn't at the sorority house, she was running by Malik's school. No matter what day it was, the place she most likely would not be was home.

She and Paula did manage to sneak away for her birthday

weekend to Asheville. But even then, she had to tear herself away from admiring the fall foliage to call in to the sorority meeting. Paula took it in stride but Kiara knew she wasn't happy about the intrusion.

Prior to Paula's announcement, she and Kiara had been eating breakfast while silently staring at each other around Kiara's dying birthday flowers. Malik, a grown up fifth grader, had left for school an hour before, leaving Paula the opportunity to speak the words she had been carrying around.

"Paula, why are you saying this? If this is about last week, then I apologize again. I know I should have been there for you when the car broke down, but I was inside the convention center trying to work out the setup for the conference and didn't have any reception. I said I was sorry," Kiara said, forcing herself to sound contrite. 'Damn,' she thought, 'how many times does she want me to apologize for that?'

"Kiara, this is not about last week. I'm over that. This is about the week before that, and the week before that. Fuck, this is about the past year of you standing Malik and me up so you can be super Rho," Paula said angrily. "Baby, you have your letters and no one is going to take them away from you. Your momma is so proud of you that I'm sure she danced the electric slide during her grad chapter meeting when she announced you were the doyenne for the chapter up here. But I know for a fact your mother is more proud of how you came back from the rape, finished school and got on with your life. Didn't you she tell you that in May? You don't have to prove anything to anyone. Even though you have been somewhat slack lately, you have made an excellent life for Malik. That boy doesn't want for anything but your time. And I can say the same thing. I miss my girlfriend and sometimes I think she doesn't miss me."

Kiara saw tears forming in Paula's eyes. Stretching her hand across the table to comfort her, her face fell when Paula withdrew her fingers.

"Listen, I'm going to be late for work and I know you have

to get on the road," Paula said getting up from the table. "I'm thinking about Malik and me driving down to Columbia tomorrow for Allen U's homecoming. Since Malcolm and his wife live down there, I may call and see if they want to do dinner. I know Malcolm and you had an agreement he would see Malik monthly. Since you have not been able to find the time to drive him down there, I figured I would do it."

Watching Paula walk to the door, Kiara's voice cracked. "I know if you go down to South Carolina you are going to have to come back. Have you thought about how long you are going stay here with us?"

Hand on the doorknob Paula answered, "I guess that depends on you," and walked out. Sitting alone at the kitchen table, Kiara took the last bite of her omelet and mused, "deja fucking vu."

All during the drive, Kiara reflected on the path that had lead her to this point. She realized she joined Kappa Alpha Rho so that she would have something in common with her mother. She hid her sexuality in order to be more acceptable by her soon to be sisters, then dealt with rejection and scorn because of it once she became a member.

Still, she had found sisterhood in the form of Donna and Gloria. Then it was the fact her sorority sisters elected her, an out and proud lesbian, to be their leader. So much had changed since that winter's night, but had she? She had made so many decisions in her life in order to please others or to prove herself worthy. Seeing the *Welcome to Wake County* sign, she realized Paula was right. She didn't have to prove anything to anybody. Just the fact she was here, a rape survivor, a sorority chapter president, a mother, a partner, and a sister was enough to consider her life an achievement.

'I guess this is what Donna would say is my Road to Damascus moment," Kiara thought to herself, pulling into the hotel parking lot where the state conference was being held. 'Just like Saul getting thrown from the donkey and deciding to follow Christ, I'm going to start living my life differently. No more stressing about doing everything to get other people's acceptance. I'm going to start cherishing the things and the people I love and those that love me. Damn, that Christian cussing soror has really worn off on me. Got me thinking in Biblical terms about life's situations.'

Walking into the lobby, Kiara's eyes found comfort in the sight of purple and platinum splashed everywhere. She planned to grab her registration bag, go to her room and take a nap before the afternoon session. Fate, however, had other plans.

"Chris!" Kiara shrieked when she saw the face of the Alpha Delta Rho graduate chapter member helping with registration.

"Kiara, it's so good to see you. What has it been, ten years?" Chris asked, giving Kiara a big smile and a hug across the purple covered table.

Taking the purple bag containing her registration papers, Kiara stepped to the left of the table and allowed the sister behind her to step forward. "Yeah, something like that. When did you become a soror?"

"I joined about two years ago during grad school. I know, crazy huh, considering the hard time I gave you in school," Chris said. "Listen, I would love to catch up and find out how your life's been. I am giving the welcoming address during the evening reception, so maybe we can get a drink or something afterwards."

"We'll see. Well I'm not going to keep you. I'm going to head up to my room and I will see you later," Kiara said backing away.

Waiting for the elevator, Kiara struggled to understand why she felt happy to see Chris. After all, their last face-to-face encounter had not been pleasant. Still, she couldn't help but notice how good her ex looked.

"Girl, you are not going to believe who I just ran into?" Kiara said on the phone to Gloria. "Chris. Heifer is a fucking sister."

"What! I'm shocked and a-Paul-ed and a Peter too for good measure," Gloria said walking briskly toward Carlos' office. "Of all the people I would have thought to be a sister, she would be next to last on the list."

"What?"

"You know shocked and a-Paul-ed and a Peter too? Don't worry, it's a Catholic thing. So how did she end up crossing your path?"

"She was working at the registration desk. She said she joined two years ago, and I was like that's nice. Then she had the nerve to ask me if I wanted to get together this evening to catch up."

"The sheer audacity of it all," Gloria said pushing open the glass door with her behind. "I know you told her no, right?"

Hesitantly, Kiara said she didn't deny or confirm, just delayed.

"Iris, I'm not Paula or Elder Swan Michaels, and in the words of Donna, everyone is grown and knows what they should do. I would advise you to stay away from Chris. Just because we all wear the same colors, we are not all sisters. Now you know, I'm usually light and love with everyone, but I don't like the way she came at you, and I think that is a door best left closed."

"Well, she did send me some flowers after she heard about the rape and a savings bond for Malik, but you're right. No need to bring up old shit. I'm just going to give her a sisterly hug when I see her this evening at the reception and keep it moving."

So why did 11:00 p.m. find Kiara feet curled up on Chris' couch?

"You know I heard you had been elected doyenne of the Charlotte chapter, but I didn't expect to see you this weekend. I wasn't planning on attending the conference, but one of our sisters got sick, which left a space that needed to be filled. Since I was off today, I volunteered to fill in."

Sipping her wine, Kiara murmured, "Lucky for the chapter." Then in a louder voice Kiara continued, "You know it just blows my mind that you joined Kappa Alpha Rho. You were so anti-Greek in college."

"I was a lot of things in college that I have outgrown. I just want to apologize again for the way I handled the break-up. I was hurt that the sorority seemed to be taking more of a role in your life than me, so I acted like an asshole," Chris said. "Now I was pissed about you taking up with dude, but I guess you figured out I was cheating on you with Gayle and hooked up with him out of spite."

Kiara raised her eyebrows. She hadn't known Chris cheated on her with Gayle. That explained a lot, now, in hindsight.

"But you know, I didn't invite you over to dwell on the past. So you got boo'ed up in Charlotte? That Paula must be a lucky woman," Chris said filling up Kiara's wine glass.

"Yes, she is," Kiara said, "and I'm sure the right woman is out there waiting for you. I mean look at you, MBA from FAMU, still got that tight body you had in college, you own this nice townhouse and you are a K-Rho woman to boot. Honey, I'm surprised you not beating them back with a stick."

Leaning close enough for Kiara to inhale her scent, Chris answered, "You always knew how to make a girl feel good."

"Thank you," Kiara said smiling back at Chris. They chatted about non-threatening topics like family, friends from college and the state of affairs in the world, but as their mouths moved, their eyes carried on a very different conversation.

Watching Chris' full lips form words, Kiara flashed back to the feeling of those lips on her lower back, her inner thigh, the hollow space behind her knees. Watching Chris' fingers fondle the wine stem, she recreated the feeling of those digits caressing her neck, stroking the arches of her feet, and exploring her inner valleys.

"You know Kiara, I have an extra bedroom if you don't feel like heading back to the hotel tonight," Chris said, breaking into Kiara's thoughts. "I have to be at work at six, so I can make sure you are back at the hotel in time for you to freshen up before session."

All Kiara had to do was say yes, like the song from the British female duo playing softly in the background. After all, it was getting late, but as much as her loins wanted to lie down and let Chris rekindle the magic, she knew it was time to end this re-union. Even though it would give her great pleasure feeling her former lover's hand on her body, she knew the impact it would have on her soul couldn't be repaired. She had been unfaithful to Chris with Malcolm and unfaithful to the grad student she dated in Wilmington with some random woman. There would be no third time charm when it came to her sleeping around. She had agreed to spend the evening with Chris to get closure about the way their relationship ended. There was not going to be any opening of legs.

"Thank you for your offer, but I think I owe it to the chap-ter to spend the night in the room they are paying for. It's been great catching up tonight, but I'm ready to head back to the room," Kiara said, pushing her full glass away.

"Sure, sure. I understand. Let me get my keys."

"No, it's late and I don't want you to have to drive there then back here. Just write down the directions and I can find my way back."

Finally, it was done and the two of them were standing by the door looking at each other.

"It was really good seeing you again Kiara," Chris said, her lips just inches away from Kiara.

"Yeah, it was nice. You should look Paula and me up if you are in Charlotte. Maybe we could find you someone to call your own."

"That would be nice."

Then with a chaste hug suitable for a church function and a kiss on the cheek, Kiara was in her car heading back to the hotel. Even though she had moved on from the break-up with Chris, it still felt good to be able to formally say good-bye to her first long-term girlfriend face to face.

Sorority sessions went well the next day. Kiara felt inspired by all the hugs and smiles she received from sisters who had a chance to meet the doyenne who made sorority history in the Queen City. There were a few less than sisterly looks from members who felt like her kind didn't belong in their chapter. All the dirty looks faded in her mind after a shy UNC Pembroke student stopped her as she walked out of the bathroom between sessions.

"Excuse me soror, I just want you to know it may not seem like a lot to some people, but I think of you as one of my role models. I had always known I liked girls, but I didn't want to let our sorors know," the brown skinned girl with the oval glasses said. "Over the summer, my aunt who belongs to the grad chapter in Lincoln County and I were talking. She mentioned the fuss about you being elected and that she didn't see what the big deal was. To her, as long as you were about the business of Rho, it shouldn't matter who you loved. I guess hearing her say that gave me the courage to come out to her. I had never come out to anybody. I just wanted to say thank you for giving me the courage."

Kiara felt herself welling up. She never thought anyone would see her as an inspiration, especially when she struggled with revealing her sexuality when she pursued her dream of sisterhood. Now, here was a young woman saying she gave her courage to be herself.

"Sister Swan, I want to say thank you for sharing that with me," Kiara said enveloping the girl into a hug. "If you need anything in terms of Rho, or just someone to talk to, you can always call me. Here is my card with my email address and phone number. Feel free to use it whenever you need it. By the way, what is your name and your aunt's name?"

"Oh, I'm Karen Cannon and my aunt is Patricia Kemp. She actually said she was thinking about transferring to the Charlotte chapter so you may get to meet her."

"I will keep my eyes open, and Sister Swan, thank you again and be strong."

Taking her seat in the graduate chapter intake training, Kiara smiled to herself as she reflected on the encounter. Even though her dedication to her sorority had taxed her relationship, she was glad that in a small way it had hopefully helped someone avoid the shame she had felt.

Kiara carried the good feelings about her encounter with the UNC Pembroke student for the rest of the day. Getting to her room, she rushed to share her satisfaction with Paula. Her call went to voicemail. Slightly worried, Kiara shrugged it off and got dressed for the formal dance that night. When she returned to the room Paula had not returned her call. That night, Kiara drifted off with a sinking feeling in her stomach.

The next day, smiles and hugs from her sisters masked Kiara's tension about what waited for her at home. Leaving the hotel, she tried Paula again for good measure. Voicemail again. Kiara struggled not to cry driving home. 'In hindsight, maybe I should have slept with Chris,' she thought then quickly dismissed the thought. Whatever happened next, she was not going to complicate things.

Pulling into driveway and seeing the car with the vanity license tag, Kiara squared her shoulders and settled her stomach.

"Hey baby, how was the conference?" Paula asked pleasantly, stirring what smelled like turkey chili.

"Good, I called you Saturday to tell you about this swan I met from UNC Pembroke, but the phone call went to voicemail and you never called me back," Kiara said putting her bags down in the kitchen. "Where is Malik?"

Turning the stove down, Paula came and sat down at the kitchen table. "He is at the neighbors. Honey, I'm sorry I missed your calls. I don't know what was going on with my phone. While we were in Columbia it worked just fine making calls, but for some reason everyone that called me went to voicemail. I didn't realize it was a problem until I got home last night and had about six calls from my mom, your mom and work. I spent about twenty minutes on the phone this morning getting an adjustment on my bill because of it."

"Paula, what you said Friday was in the back of my mind all weekend, and I think I had a breakthrough trying to figure out why I focus so much on the sorority. A small part of me, that was that girl afraid to be herself, but wanting to please her mother and be a K-Rho, still exists, even though I have been a member for almost twelve years," Kiara said staring into Paula's eyes. "I hid who I was, not only because I didn't feel I needed to share everything about myself, but because I really didn't feel I could be a lesbian and a good sorority member. Once I crossed and had to deal with the bullshit with being the assistant gracious guide in college, it seemed that maybe I was right to feel that way. But this weekend, when I had a chance to be truly out and proud among my sisters, I felt accepted."

"The only validation you should ever hope to have in life should come from within. It's good that other people prop you up and make you feel alright, but what counts is how you feel when you look in the mirror. If my words caused you to look deeply inside, then I'm happy to know. But the key is what you plan to do moving forward."

"First thing is I'm going to get us both new phones with better coverage so we won't have to worry about one of us not being able to get a signal or receive a call when we need to talk to each other. Second, I'm going to be more proactive about not taking calls at all times of the day and night," Kiara answered. "You and I are going to schedule monthly just us days. No sorority, no school, no work. Just two lesbians in love. How does that sound?"

"I love a lesbian with a plan. For what it's worth, I did some thinking too and I couldn't leave you and Malik. So I guess we are stuck together, even if you do wear the wrong colors," Paula said, kissing Kiara's cheek before heading back to the stove.

CHAPTER TWENTY-THREE

Donna/Kiara/Gloria

"ARE YOU FUCKING serious? Peter spent Thanksgiving with you, Kevin, the kids and your in-laws?" Kiara said while eating her third helping of turkey salad. It was the Saturday after Thanksgiving and she was carrying on a phone conversation with Donna in between bites.

"I know right. I really didn't plan it that way. Then I remembered what it was like that first family holiday after the divorce. You want to be with your family, but there is always that family member who didn't get the memo about the split and asks where is so-and-so. Sometimes you don't feel like being bothered. Since I knew he didn't have any concrete plans for Thanksgiving, I figured why not," Donna said. While Kiara lounged on her living room sofa, she sat on a cold aluminum bleacher watching India's swim meet. Cheering at the appropriate time, Donna kept one eye on the child in the pool and one eye on the child cooing in the carrier.

"You have to tell me how that came to be, because I know when I talked to you Monday you didn't mention anything about *Guess Who's Coming to Dinner* action taking place at the house."

"It really didn't occur to me until Tuesday night. He called me when I was in the grocery store and sounded so poormouthed I couldn't help myself. Well, you know when I brought the topic up to Kevin he was all 'hell naw,' but after some serious bedroom bargaining he was cool with it. Key, you should have seen it. Now you know my baby stands six-four in his bare feet and is a cool two hundred. Well, he is the baby of the family. All his brothers look like Titans, and I'm not talking about Peter's former teammates. Peter looked like a little boy next to Kevin's brothers. But, Peter got along with everybody, so it was all-good, especially when they realized he was a former NFL player. Then it was really on."

"I just can't get over it. It wasn't that long ago when you spat fire every time you heard his name called. I guess time does change things."

"The Bible says if you forgive others the Lord will forgive you. I'm not about to let some grudge block my blessing. I had to realize there was no need for me to carry around hateful thoughts about Peter. I loved him enough to marry him and bear his children. That boy made me a happy woman many times over. I just choose to focus on the positive instead of the bullshit. Enough about my life, how goes it with you? I know I'm looking forward to coming down to regionals in March to see how Xi Kappa is going to handle things," Donna said.

"Honey, it has been a headache and a half with securing hotels, handling registrations, coordinating vendors and making sure the sisters have plenty things to do to keep them occupied when they are not about the business of Kappa," Kiara said walking into the kitchen with her plate. "The undergrads have been such an asset, especially your sands, Leslie. You know, working with these girls reminds me of how we were as undergrads. Just hyped about being Greek, like we were the Beta line of the organization, wearing nothing but purple and platinum and giving the call every chance we got."

Shaking her head in agreement, Donna continued Kiara's train of thought. "Life seemed so simple then. If we made two hundred dollars from a party, we were stoked. Now, with all the scholarship pageants and graduate step shows, and trying to make sure the mortgage is paid for the sorority house, it is as if we are running a business for sure, not a sisterhood. I don't see how Gloria and you do it. You are the doyenne for the grad chapter and she is the community outreach chair for Chi Xi Kappa chapter up here. All I can do is to pay dues and attend a meeting or two."

"Don't get it twisted. It's a struggle to keep everything balanced, but we all make room in our heart and schedule for Kappa as it allows. I have to confess, Kappa has caused some tense moments between Paula and me. We even talked about splitting up last month," Kiara said quietly. Paula and her mother had gone shopping. While she was in the house alone, it pained her just saying the words aloud.

"Yeah, Gloria told me. I didn't want to bring the subject up, in case you weren't ready to talk about it," Donna said waving to India climbing out of the pool. Her middle child waved and smiled before heading with the rest of her team to the locker room.

"I figured as much. I'm sure Gloria also told you about me running into Chris at state meeting last month."

"She did, and I sent plenty of prayers up you wouldn't slip and do something you would regret. But that is behind you, and now that you have officially closed that door you can move on with a clear path. Key, I'm going to talk to you later. India is getting dressed and we need to stop by the grocery store before I head home. Kevin's parents are staying until Wednesday and they are some eating people. You wouldn't believe all the food we cooked for Thanksgiving; it is almost finished. Now, I have to get food for next week so my babies can have lunch. I tell you, this grown up stuff is for the birds sometimes."

Donna's version of a blended family worked well. India and Milan spent the Christmas holiday with Peter's folks in North Carolina, while she, Lejune and Kevin spent the holidays with his parents in South Carolina. The New Year came in and Donna couldn't wait to see what it would bring—until her cell phone rang that January morning as she headed home from picking up Milan from Girl Scouts.

"Donna, I'm so sorry to have to call you, but there has

been an accident," her neighbor Melinda said high-pitched and hysterical.

It was as if time stopped and the world came crashing around Donna. Struggling not to stop in the middle of traffic, she listened to the words coming out of the phone.

"Calm down Melinda, just calm down and take some deep breaths," Donna said, her mind split with the absurdity of her trying to calm down her neighbor while her heart tapped a frantic rhythm in her chest. Her neighbor managed to shriek out that India had been hit by a car while crossing the street from a sleepover at her house. The driver, who appeared to be texting, managed to slam on the breaks, but it wasn't enough to prevent the unthinkable.

Her neighbor, standing in her front yard, saw the whole thing, and was on her way to the hospital in the ambulance. Donna fought back the urge to yell at her neighbor for letting her child cross the street by herself, after she'd clearly told her she would pick India up. Instead, she registered the hospital information. She knew, without knowing, she had to remain calm for Milan, Lejune and herself.

Donna's heart pulsated with pain for her child. She felt like running every car off the road that stood between her and the hospital. Realizing she had to get herself together before she caused an accident, she saw the sign for her favorite grocery store. Seizing the chance to park and get her thoughts together, Donna pulled into the crowded parking lot.

"Milan, I need to run in and pick up some things. Do you think you can look after your brother while I run into the store?" Donna asked.

Locking her car, Donna walked inside the store on trembling legs. Instinctively, she grabbed a shopping cart, hoping that grasping the plastic handle would help her fight back the urge to collapse on the floor. Realizing she needed to call someone to help her cope, her first call was to Peter but it went to voicemail. 'Fuck,' she muttered. 'Why didn't the son-of-bitch pick up?' He was supposed to take the girls to the movies that afternoon, so she expected him to call within minutes after he saw the urgent text and voicemail. Chest tight with anxious feelings, Donna dialed Kevin's office next. She knew he was on base, so it would be hard for him to drop everything and come, but he needed to know. The Marine who answered promised to ensure the master sergeant knew the circumstances behind her call, which gave Donna some relief. She knew her husband would soon be there to comfort her, but she needed some reassurances now. Hands shaking, she hit the number four button on her phone.

"What's shaking, bacon?" Gloria answered, strains of Afro-Cuban jazz playing in the background.

"India has been in an accident. I'm on my way to the hospital. Can you meet me there?"

"¡Ay dios mios, Donna. I'm on my way, soon as you tell me where I'm going."

Giving Gloria the details, Donna felt herself calming down. Assured her sorority sister was on her way, Donna felt calm enough to walk back to her car.

"Momma, I thought you needed to get something for dinner. They didn't have what you wanted?" Milan asked. Donna paused before turning her key and turned to face her eldest child in the backseat.

"Baby, I'm sorry I told a fib. I went inside because I needed to make some phone calls that I didn't want you to know about. That was Ms. Melinda on the phone. India has been in an accident and they are taking her to the hospital."

"Is she going to be okay?" Milan's shaky voice asked.

"Yes baby, she is going to be fine. We are going to head to the hospital right now so buckle your seatbelt," Donna said, adopting a motherly tone to cover up her terror.

Melinda met her in the Douglass Turner Children Hospital lobby, and after hugging her, the two walked back to the pediatric emergency room. Walking down the halls, Donna remembered the graduate chapter fundraiser to purchase teddy bears for the hospital's initial patients the year prior. Irony could be such a bitch sometimes. She had no idea her child would be on the receiving end of her sorority's philanthropic generosity.

Melinda offered to stay but Donna sent her home to comfort her own daughter, who had also witnessed the accident. After checking in, an orange clad nurse escorted Donna into a second waiting room to await news. India had been taken to the surgery once she arrived, but the nurse promised someone would be out to talk to her soon.

For fifteen minutes, she sat silently staring back at parents sharing her suffering. She was not supposed to be here. She was supposed to be home getting ready for date night. Peter was going to keep Milan and India overnight. Kevin's sister was going to babysit Lejune. It was the first Saturday in a while that she and her husband could be a couple without midnight feedings, nighttime bedtime stories, or late nights on base.

"D, any news?" Gloria rushed in with Carlos on her heels. "I hope you don't mind that Carlos came with me. We were at his place finishing our presentation. He insisted on driving me here. I told the nurse up front I was your sister and Carlos was your attorney so they would let us back here since it is reserved for family members. I mean, I am your sister and Carlos is going to be passing the bar soon, so it wasn't like we were totally lying," Gloria rambled.

"At a time like this, I could give less than a fat baby's ass what you said to get back here. I'm just glad you are here. India is in surgery and they will be out to talk with me soon. My daughter, my child is being operated on because some motherfucking son of a bitch asshole decided to drive and text," Donna whispered.

Gloria squeezed her line sister's hand as she struggled not to erupt in tears. Quietly, Carlos asked if he could take Milan and Lejune downstairs to the cafeteria to get something to eat. Nodding, Donna gave her consent.

"Donna, I'm going to ask you something I never asked you before. Forgive me if this isn't the best time, but you told me not too long ago, when the time is right, I will know what to say. Will you pray with me?"

Slowly turning her head, Donna looked at her sorority sister. Gloria and Donna's faiths were as different as fish on Friday to honor Catholic teaching and fried chicken on Sunday— common after church meals.

"I know we have different ways of worshiping, but you and I both know our faith has helped us get through a lot of things. Even I get at a loss for words sometimes, so I feel praying can help get us through this," Gloria said.

"Hell, the Bible says when two or three have gathered together in My name, I am there in the midst. I guess it don't matter how we get to the foot of the cross as long as we come united," Donna smiled sadly.

Nodding her head, Donna dropped her head and clasped Gloria's hand. Taking a breath, Gloria started with a simple prayer of healing she had learned from her parish priest when she was a child. "St. Gerard, who, like the Savior, loved children so tenderly, and by your prayers freed many from disease and even death, listen to us who are pleading for India. We thank God for the great gift of her, and ask Him to restore India to health if such be His holy will. This favor, we beg of you through your love for all children and mothers. Amen."

Donna picked up: "Father, I come before you on bended knee and heavy heart to ask you to stop by and bless your humble servant, who is standing on your word to claim a healing for my precious daughter. Lord, you say all we need is ask in your name and it is given. You are the doctor from whom all blessings flow. Lord, my sister and I touch and agree that you will not take away the gift you have given me in the form of India Andressa. I'm claiming the blessing because you are a wonder working God and by your stripes, we are healed. I ask, Lord, for a blessing on my child and I ask you guide the hands of the surgeons and the nurses, so that through them, your will be done. All this I ask in your humble name."

Watching the clock tick, Donna reflected on her life and realized trouble really hadn't touched her. She was raised in a loving home with parents who showed her, and her sisters true love endured and adapted. She finished college, married her college sweetheart, and when that marriage didn't last, was lucky to find another man to make her heart sing. She had three lovely children who were the light and joy of her life. Was this God's way of bringing some sorrow in her life? Shaking her head at such crazy thoughts, Donna focused on willing the door to open with good news from a medical professional.

"Mrs. Bofield," the nurse said coming into the waiting room. Looking up with tears in her eyes, Donna nodded and stood up. The nurse's smile was the answer she sought. "Your daughter is out of surgery and is being taken to her room. She did fine. I will be back in a moment to get you and take you back."

Donna burst out in tears again, only this time it was for joy. Gloria joined her and the sisters hugged tightly as Donna felt faint with relief. Her India was going to be fine.

"Baby, I got here as fast as I could. Is she alright?" Kevin said rushing in followed closely by Peter.

Donna clasped Kevin and told him the good news. Peter overhearing, got so caught up in the moment he grabbed Gloria in a bear hug. Any other day, Gloria would have tongue lashed him for touching her, but given the circumstance she let it ride.

The nurse observing the scene asked if the parents wanted to go back to see their child. Three heads nodded in unison and with a shrug, the nurse asked them to follow her.

"Donna, I'm going to go downstairs and find Carlos and the kids. If you are cool with it, I'm going to take them back to my house. Just call me when you can," Gloria said.

"Thanks soror. You have been a godsend, Carlos as well," Donna said turning to hug her sorority sister.

"No worries chica, that's how swans do things. We swim together and help keep each other afloat. Kiss my god daughter for me and I will talk to you later."

CHAPTER TWENTY-FOUR
Gloria

GLORIA NEVER SAW it coming, but in hindsight, all of the signs were there. Ever since the situation at the hospital with India, Carlos had treated her differently. After leaving the hospital, the four of them had stopped by the local grocery store to get items to make homemade pizzas.

Watching Carlos guide Milan's hands to make a perfect ball of dough and spread it out, Gloria felt touched in a way she had never felt. She could see in Carlos the image of a father she craved. Her father had tried to be there for her, but the distance between Detroit and D.C. was sometimes hard to manage. Her heart really melted when he told Milan and Lejune an off the top of his head bedtime story shortly before giving Gloria her standard good night kiss on the forehead. But since that day, almost two months had passed and he hadn't been able to find the time to spend with her. At least, not like before. She chalked it up to the fact he was in his final year of law school and she was preparing to defend her thesis. Still, those Wednesdays when there was no Thai take out to share or jokes to make worried her. Had she sent out a signal to him she was interested? Did he feel it best to avoid her unless it was work related?

The two of them still met to work on the project, which they started less than a year ago, but it seemed Carlos no longer wanted to share tidbits about his dating calendar. In return, Gloria reigned in her desire to share details about her escapades.

Riding the Metro back home on President's Day, Gloria texted her dilemma to Kiara. *It's the damndest thing. I miss him and he really hasn't gone anywhere.* She agreed to meet a lobbyist for dinner, drinks, and dancing, but his dullness diminished her desire midway through the dim sum. Gloria claimed an early meeting and decided to head home, order in and drown her sorrows in chocolate milk and cereal. Thankfully, the subway car was half-empty, allowing her to put her feet up without too many people looking at her strangely.

Did he say why he was giving you a wide berth?

No. I would say something but I don't want it to come across I'm sweating him.

So what do you think it is?

I don't know. Maybe he has found someone and doesn't want to make me jealous because I can't find anyone to wrap my legs around. Damn it, being a single straight girl sucks.

Maybe you should switch teams. I know a couple of cunning linguists that could appreciate a bi-lingual girl like you.

Gloria laughed out loud, triggering a few stares from the other riders. Shaking her head, she texted her regrets. She wasn't ready to swim in the pool of ladylove just yet.

Even though their personal connection seemed to have weakened, Gloria and Carlos' professional relationship was still on point. It was no surprise once all the work was done on their cross agency project on immigration they received high marks from their supervisors.

"Sure, when the team met for drinks after we made the presentation, he gave me a big hug and said how great of a team we are, but it wasn't like the hugs he had given me before," Gloria said sitting on Donna's living room couch, watching Donna braid India's hair. It was St. Patrick's Day and Gloria paid full homage with a green and orange shirt demanding a form of affection in honor of her assumed heritage. "Something is up. I just know it, but I don't know what it is. You remember me telling you he went to Detroit last weekend? He said it was to interview for a firm who scouted him during a Hispanic National Bar Association meeting last summer. And yes, he did come back with the pros and cons of what the firm had to offer, but something in my spirit tells me something else was on the agenda during his trip to the Motor City."

Dipping her finger in the jar of hair grease India was holding, Donna nodded her awareness of Carlos' trip. "Didn't you say your dad took him out while he was in town to show him the real Detroit?"

"Yeah, daddy said he asked questions about the cost of living and different parts of town. When I asked Carlos about the trip, he said he liked the city, but he wasn't ready to give up East Coast living."

"I hear that," Donna said, finishing the last braid. "Done. Go tell Milan I'm ready for her. She needs to come on downstairs so I can finish y'alls hair and get you ready for your daddy to pick y'all up."

Sitting back on the sofa, Donna listened to Gloria reflect on Carlos' action and inaction. She actually had some insider knowledge of the situation, but he had sworn her to secrecy. Donna thought to herself, 'Carlos better get his act together soon or else I am going to have to break my word and sing like Mahalia.'

"I mean, if he has found someone else then it's cool. I love him like a brother and I want him to be happy. Now, I would have rather had a chance to say my peace about my feelings for him before he runs off into the sunset. But if it is not to be, then so shall it be written, so shall it be done."

Rolling her eyes, Donna replied, "Yul Brynner from *The Ten Commandments*, I need you to pump your breaks. You have the boy married with kids just because he's not all in your face. Honestly, you have been busy with the sorority, work and school, so maybe he is just hanging back."

"True, and if that is the reason, then I appreciate it. If it is something else, I will get to the bottom of it, Blondie style, one way or another."

"I thought you gave up metaphors for Lent. Backsliding already?"

"No, I gave up similes. See, simile is a metaphor, but not all metaphors are similes. A metaphor is a form of speech that transfers the sense or aspects of one word to another. A simile is similar but uses the word like in the process."

Raising an eyebrow, Donna asked, "Really?" then sighed and yelled, "Prototype, I'm on a schedule."

"Prototype?"

"Yeah, Kevin came up with the idea of giving the kids P nicknames. Since Milan is the oldest, she is the Prototype. India is Phoenix since she had the accident, and as you can tell, bounced back without a hitch, and Lejune is Promise since Kevin always wanted to have a son and he got one straight out of the gate."

"Wow, and you think I get Prince "Let's Go Crazy" with words. Listen, since you are Madam C.J. Walker today, I'm going to say adios. I need to drive over to Morgan State to help with the girls scheduled to do their probate show Monday. They had twelve girls come through and they are supposed to be introduced to the university by doing the usual stepping routine. Remember our show? You know when Kiara broke out with *Back to Life* by Soul II Soul a cappella? Those folks were just blown away. Then I'm going to meet Carlos, international man of mystery, for drinks at this bar on U Street."

"Well, be safe and don't drink too much green beer. And I'm sure your Kiss Me I'm Irish shirt will prove very successful."

Walking into the bar, Gloria marveled how for one day, everyone black, white, Hispanic, and census box left unchecked became descendants of the Emerald Isle. Today, Gloria was Shannon O'Mallory, or at least that is what her nametag said handed to her by a red-haired leprechaun. Carlos was supposed to meet her here so they could check out the band, Unlady Like Behavior. The lead singer had been a part of Tragic Mulattos back in college. When

Gloria had seen them advertised to play a free show at the pub, she convinced Carlos to take a break on a Saturday and come out.

"Chica, I'm so sorry I was late, but I got caught up on a last minute errand," he said sliding into the booth after giving Gloria a kiss on the check as she took a swig of her second beer.

"It's rice and gravy. I have been entertaining myself people watching and sucking down beers. You are right on time, the band just kicked off their set."

Motioning to the waitress hustling by, Carlos ordered a beer and soon joined Gloria enjoying the quintet with a violinist, bassist, drummer and two lead singers. The two sat and grooved for about two hours as acts came and went on the stage playing hip-hop revisions of Irish classics. Gloria noticed, for some reason, Carlos seemed nervous. He kept checking his phone and she could have sworn his mouth kept twitching in a nervous smile. He even ordered a third drink, which was truly out of character. He was usually a two drinks maximum drinker.

"Carlos, is there something going on? You seem to be a little bit on edge for a Saturday," Gloria said putting her left hand over his.

"You have such beautiful fingers, has anyone ever told you that?" he said, not directly answering her question.

"Actually yes, you did last month when we had lunch at the Ethiopian place near Howard. You remember? I had left my college ring at your house and as you handed it back to me, you said you never realized my fingers were so small. You know, I still can't figure out how I left the ring at your house. I usually never take it off, but then again, I probably took it off when I was washing dishes after your big Super Bowl shindig. But enough about my digits, you seem edgy. Is everything cool?"

"Everything is good, just got a lot of things on my plate. In fact, if you wouldn't mind, I need to shove off," Carlos said.

Trying not to sound too disappointed he was cutting their evening short, Gloria nodded okay and motioned for the waitress.

"I got this Gloria," he said pulling out his wallet. "But I do have a favor to ask. I'm feeling a little bit more buzzed than usual. Maybe I shouldn't have had that third Guinness milkshake. If you wouldn't mind, could you take me home?"

Walking toward her car, Carlos and Gloria compared thoughts about what their future held. Carlos had made the decision to stay in the area and get on with a local firm that did a lot of pro bono work with the immigrant community, and Gloria was considering going into the world of academia.

"Dr. Phillips at Morgan State said there is a chance I could get on with their Poli Science Department if I wanted to do some teaching. Nothing heavy, just a night class or two. I'm thinking I may take her up on it," Gloria said. "I love being a federal employee with the holidays off and it has given me an opportunity to travel. But I get so much enjoyment being around the next generation. I want them to see that you can still be fly and have your doctorate. It's not reserved for ancient specimens."

"I think you would be an excellent professor if that is what you decide to do," Carlos said pulling out his phone. As he appeared to check his text messages, his facial expressions swerved from furrowed brows to a half smile and finished with an embarrassing chuckle.

"Must be some good info you're receiving," Gloria said, pulling into traffic. "You're heading home right?"

"Actually, I need to make a stop if you don't mind. I have been bragging on the pan suave at Ollie's to my neighbor and I promised I was going to bring her some. Would you mind stopping by?" Carlos said.

"My pleasure, I may have to pick up some desert to take home. Good call."

Ollie's was her and Carlos' spot when they first met. Located midway between their two offices, the two used to go and swap stories over ropa vieja and lechon asado con arroz on their lunch breaks. The two frequently stopped through together, and separately, to sample the tried and true menu items cooked by the Ramirez family. In fact, they had a standing "anniversary" lunch every June 1 to mark the first time they met during a new hire luncheon.

Driving down New Hampshire, Gloria reflected. They had been friends for over nine years and had shared highs and lows professionally and personally. They had shared a bed together more than once when one of them was too drunk or sleepy to drive home after late night catching up sessions. Each of them maintained at least three changes of clothes at the other's home. When Gloria's apartment was broken into before she moved last year, Carlos arrived at three in the morning and comforted her as she filled out the police report and stayed the night with her when she was too jittery to sleep. His sisters called her for fashion advice and his co-workers knew her by face. She even helped him win a lip sync contest at his job when they performed *"Criminal"* by Fiona Apple, complete with handcuffs in a mock interrogation scene.

'Damn, we have everything for a relationship but the name,' she thought pulling up in front of the restaurant.

"C, maybe we should have called before we drove down here. Usually this time on a Saturday, the place would be filled with customers, but it looks like nobody is home," Gloria said. "The Cuban flag is not even flying, so you know he must be closed for business."

Smiling, Carlos lifted one shoulder and suggested the two of them go investigate. Ignoring the sign taped to the door about limited hours due to a private party, the two walked into the restaurant.

"I was starting to get worried. Everything is set up in the back like you asked," the owner said giving them a wink.

Gloria looked around confused. 'What is going on?' she wondered.

Grabbing her hand, Carlos walked Gloria to the back of the restaurant usually reserved for family gatherings. Entering the room, Gloria felt her heart rate accelerate as she saw her and Carlos' families sitting around looking at her. In slow motion, she saw Carlos pause in front of her and drop down to one knee.

"Gloria Irene Allen, would you do me the honor and privilege of being my wife?" he asked first in English, then in Spanish. In his hand, a box with a one-carat, pear cut diamond with her birthstone on both sides.

For a minute, Gloria's mouth didn't move, and she could register the fear that he had overshot himself grow in Carlos' eyes. Knowing that words had failed her, she could only nod yes. Hugging her newly created fiancée, she heard applause from her parents, family, and Donna and her brood. Gloria felt tears running down her face.

"This is so unreal Carlos. How did you manage to plan all this?" Gloria sputtered as Ollie came before her with a chair lest she fall down.

"Thank Donna for encouraging me to do this. Right after India's accident, I called Donna to check on her and she invited me out to lunch, her treat. We came here and she gave it to me straight: I need to be about my business. She could see that we really had something special, but we were both too pig headed to say anything to each other. She asked me to write down everything I wanted in a wife, and for twenty-four hours, every time you did something on that list to cross it off. If, at the end of the day, I had more items crossed off than I had left uncrossed, then I should ask you to marry me." Ollie brought in a tray of champagne glasses for the adults in the room and ginger ale for Milan and India.

"You suggested he ask me to marry him right off the bat? No asking me out on a real date, no let's go steady first and see what that's like?" Gloria said looking at her sister with a big smile on her face.

"Glo, you and Carlos had been around each other too much to play that getting-to- know-you routine," Donna said shaking her head. "I mean, I peppered him with questions to see how much he knew about you and he told me some stuff even I didn't know. And you know that is saying something."

"True, true. So, Soror Matchmaker put the bug in your ear to do this? So when was this magic twenty-four hour period?" Gloria said turning to her soon to be husband.

"The Sunday before the King holiday. It started off with you calling me after early morning Mass, asking me if I wanted any breakfast because you knew I was getting up early to study and probably was getting hungry after drinking my usual two black coffees with no sugar. There went my wanting a woman who was strong in her faith, but still could take care of me and help me take care of myself. You came over, cooked breakfast and watched the usual news program. You knew what was going on and had an opinion. There went my woman with a good head on her shoulders. While all this is going on, you are wearing a pair of my sweats and t-shirt, which I must say, you looked rather good in," Carlos said, slightly blushing as Gloria's father gave him a look.

"After we had breakfast, I stayed for the pre-game show and some of your buddies from work came over. Since no one had thought to order food beforehand, I just ran out to the store and got some groceries and made some eats," Gloria said. "I remember how much your boys loved those papas rellenas I made."

"Nothing like a woman who can cook," Kevin said, squeezing Donna, who shook her head in mock exasperation.

"You stayed for the game and kept up with the score even as you were returning emails and dealing with sorority matters on your phone. A woman who can work and play with the same dedication. After you went home, I started checking off things and I realized everything I wanted, you had. All I had to do is figure out how to propose to you."

"And having me leave my class ring at your house last month gave you a chance to get my ring size for the engagement ring?"

"Actually no, that would have been too easy," Donna interrupted. "Carlos actually asked me to go with him to help him pick out a ring and I volunteered my hand to help him get a good fit. So, if it fits a little bit snug I apologize."

"Well thank you and your digits for their service. So, I understand how you made up your mind to ask and how you picked out the ring, but how did you manage this?" Gloria said, gesturing around at her parents, who despite living in two separate area codes were sharing a table.

"Well of course I had to ask your father's permission. That was the real reason for the trip to Detroit. While I was there, we got your mom on the phone and she gave her consent," he said. "The hardest part was trying to pick out a day when the two of them would have advance notice to get here. When you called last week about going to the show, I took a chance and sent them an email to see if they could make it."

"Honey, I would have moved heaven and earth to get here, so I talked one of my buddies who works at the airlines into to getting me a discount on a ticket. I flew into RDU last night and your mother and I drove up this morning. You know, your grandmother is working on the Celebration Sunday dinner, otherwise she would have been right here," Gloria's father said grabbing her in a hug.

"Oh my gosh, I just can't believe this. I'm getting married," Gloria said returning the hug.

The happy couple made their rounds and enjoyed the post proposal meal, but soon Gloria managed to maneuver Donna into a corner.

"You are too, too much soror. I don't know whether to hug you or hit you for keeping something like this from me," Gloria said smiling broadly. "You had me sitting on your couch this morning, just unaware of what was going to happen."

"Anything for you. You are so smart about everything in the world plus one, but you couldn't catch on to the fact that Carlos was crazy about you as well. Didn't you ever wonder why he was also game to go to any K-Rho function you asked him to attend, and always seemed to keep a stash of salt and vinegar chips plus chocolate syrup at his place? I still can't understand how you enjoy eating them together," Donna said. "He told me when we had dinner, he had been on to you for years, but didn't want to say anything because he didn't want to mess up your friendship. I tell you what, the two of you would have probably gone on for years not opening your mouths to speak the truth. The Bible says the truth will set you free, or in your case, get you married.

"Oh, and Kiara and Paula send their love," Donna continued. "They would have come up, but you know they are on a cruise for Paula's birthday. Just imagine, no more "Me, Myself and I" for you. Now, it's all "Let's Get Married.""

"I guess I'm going to have to practice my Oprah voice because you know as soon as the preacher finishes, I'm going to burst out with your favorite line from *The Color Purple*."

"It wouldn't be a Gloria function if a movie reference wasn't involved. I tell you, you are one piece of work sister girl," Donna said.

CHAPTER TWENTY-FIVE

Kiara/Gloria/Donna

"EXCUSE ME, ARE you here for the Kappa sorority meeting?" the familiar voice said to Kiara's back as she stood in front of the Sanford Student Center.

Hugging Gloria, Kiara smiled and said, "Echo, you need to stop playing with me. I have been standing here for close to thirty minutes, feeling older by the minute watching these undergrads mingle around." Donna stood slightly back smiling as she rubbed her protruding stomach under the clear October sky.

"It has not been that long, Iris. Well, maybe it has. On the way from the parking lot, I ran into one of my professors who I had to catch up with about the world of academia. You know, now that I'm on staff at Morgan State, I can actually contribute to the conversation better. Then, Donna had to stop to use the bathroom at one of the dorms. Then just as we turned the corner to get here, ran into that neo-soul singer, Phoenix, coming out the bookstore. You know, he performed last night at the step show. I hate we missed it, but Donna and I had to get a picture with him. Imagine, when we were undergrads, Dwayne Samuels was just some skinny boy that always stole the show when the gospel choir performed. Now he is opening for Badu and up for four Grammys. If I had known then, like I know now, I would have been nicer to him. You know I heard he is supposed to donate money to the music department to create some type of scholarship. Maybe I should look into doing that. Not that I have long money like that, but Carlos' friend, Angela Rodriguez, said it's a great way to lower your tax responsibilities. You know she is a tax lawyer?"

Donna shook her head as she looked at Kiara. "I knew I shouldn't have let her have all that coffee on the road. She is wired and rearing to go. We got in about an hour ago and checked into the hotel. In hindsight, maybe we should have left last night, but you know India performed with her Indian dance troupe last night at some festival and I wouldn't have missed it for the world."

"No problem Donna. I haven't been waiting that long. In fact, I thought I was going to be late. The ceremony honoring Coach Anderson didn't end on time, and of course, I couldn't find a parking space. One of the parking attendants recognized my purple triangle sticker though and helped squeeze me into a space. Sometimes it pays to be a lesbian."

The trio was back at Copper Road University for homecoming, seven months into Gloria's engagement. Paula and Malcolm's wife were tailgating with mutual sorority sisters. The plan was for Kiara to connect with the two of them, along with Malcolm at the football game. But the morning belonged to her sorority sisters.

Walking into the redesigned student center, the trio marveled about how much things had changed since they last walked the beige carpeted floor. For Kiara, what remained the same occupied her thoughts. Gloria still talked a mile a minute. Only this time, it was about how she was balancing planning her wedding, writing her dissertation, and coping with Carlos' crisis about passing the bar. Donna, while not asking for a light for her cigarette, still expressed dryly the need for people to hurry up. Only this time, she directed it toward people in front of them getting breakfast.

"My sweet swan sisters, can you imagine this is the first time in five years we have all managed to attend homecoming at the same time?" Gloria said as they entered the spacious cafeteria humming with students and alumni. Grabbing three trays and handing them out, she continued, "Between the three of us, we have attended every homecoming since graduation, but there were times life kept us from showing our school and sorority pride. One year, I was out of the county. Another year, Kiara's mom was in the hospital and the third year, oh what was the reason?"

Donna answered, "I was giving birth. That would be the year when Andrea's wig blew off during the half-time show when she was presenting a check on behalf of the alumni association. Oh my God, I would have loved to see that."

"Stop playing Donna, you know you and Gloria have laughed about that ten thousand times since Gwen tapped it and sent to you," Kiara said stepping up to the omelet station. While she got her food, Gloria loaded her tray down with fruit and oatmeal and claimed them a table. Donna was the last to sit down with a plate loaded with turkey sausage, grits, hash browns, and pancakes.

"Are you going to eat all that?" Gloria asked.

Pouring syrup over her short stacks, Donna replied, "I am. Rio and Cairo couldn't make up their mind what they wanted to eat this morning. I figured I would get something for everybody."

"D, every time you mention the names you have picked out for your twins, I just have to say wow. You should give them middle names of Melbourne and Base Esperanza and have all seven continents covered," Gloria said.

"No, middle names are Kevin's territory. I gave him first naming rights to Lejune and you see what happened. He is thinking about naming them after my mom and his dad. We will have to see."

The trio's voices mingled with others around them catching up with old friends and meeting new ones. Halfway through the meal, the trio heard a familiar voice at the table beside them. Turning quizzically, Kiara faced the last face she expected to be attached to the voice that had provided the soundtrack to her college years.

"Excuse me, are you Cassandra from *Cassandra's Confession?*" she asked the blonde haired slender man sitting at the table behind them.

"I am, but my real name is Cassidy. I just used Cassandra during my radio work," he said. He added in reaction to Kiara's surprised face, "Don't feel bad, everyone assumed I was a thick black girl. Blame it on the late nights and the cigarettes," he said laughing.

Kiara joined in and complimented him for giving her a lot to talk about when she was a student. Donna and Gloria chimed in and shared stories about the dedications still stuck in their heads. Kiara noted that Donna didn't bring up the infamous Marvin Gaye declaration.

Finishing their breakfast, Kiara looked around the table and felt a sense of belonging. Her time at Copper Road and afterwards had been marked with all kinds of tears, fears, and triumphs. For most of it, a girl who resembled a gazelle— slender shape, beaming brown eyes and a direct gaze— and a girl who looked like an African queen regarding her subjects who had failed to amuse her, had been by her side. Sure, she had three other line sisters and hundreds of sorority sisters who had crossed her path, but for her, Donna and Gloria were the Kappa Alpha Rho sorority experience.

"Listen sorors, I know we are supposed to catch the bus to the stadium at eleven and it's about fifteen till, but I got to pee. I'm going to find a bathroom and be back. Don't leave me," Donna said, hoisting herself up and waddling with her tray toward the door.

Agreeing they wouldn't leave her behind, Gloria and Kiara gathered their purses and walked outside. Sitting outside on the low brick wall, catching the sun, Gloria echoed Kiara's thoughts of how the three of them bonded over the years.

"You know Donna and I were talking on the way down about all the stuff we have went through from the time we met at the interviews. It's almost like that Hugh Grant and Andie Mc-

Dowell movie. Only we have three weddings and a funeral. Donna's two, my upcoming and then Donna's father dying. That is unless you have something you are not sharing about Paula and your plans for the holidays," Gloria said raising her eyebrows.

"No, we have no plans of jumping the broom anytime soon. We are just leading our regular lesbian life in the Queen City. We are content to know neither one of us is going anywhere anytime soon."

Seeing Donna approaching them, Gloria responded, "Good, I like Paula and I hate having to break people into the circle that is our sisterhood. Not everyone can understand what it is like being a Goddess of Greatness. I mean, people don't realize when you take the oath of sisterhood it really means something. You are saying you are going to be there for the highs and lows. Like I was telling my undergrads during our retreat last weekend, being a sorority sister is more than just letters and calls. It's about being strong for each other when you don't feel like you have it in yourself, and being each other's strength in time of need."

"Yes, like the Bible says, as each has received a gift, use it to serve one another," Donna said as she joined them.

"And have unity of mind, brotherly, or in our case, sisterly love, and a humble mind," Gloria said. "Just because I usually quote movie lines don't mean I can't dabble into Donna's territory of relating everything to the Bible. Here is the thing; we have helped each other in so many different ways from the time we crossed. This sisterhood stuff sustained us through some serious stuff."

"Gloria, you know my hormones are touch and go. Don't have me crying and I just touched up my makeup," Donna said.

"If you go, I will be right there with you D. I love the two of you so much, and I couldn't imagine what life would have been like if we hadn't been on line together," Kiara said as the sun caressed her face. "To coin one of your phrases Gloria, Goddess bless indeed."

"Oh hell, now I know we have been friends for too long.

You are starting to sound like Gloria with all that fate and the universe stuff. Gloria starting to sound like me with dropping scripture. And then again, there was that situation with the cheerleader with the tight ass and open mind when Peter and I were trying to save our marriage."

Stopping in their tracks and speaking in unison, Gloria and Kiara said, "What thing with the cheerleader?"

"Successful swans swim serenely silent, so she shall succeed. You remember we had to learn that during the process about the values of not sharing everything all at once? But hell girls, we have been friends and sisters for long enough, I guess I can tell you."

"Well for this, I guess we are going to have miss the bus. Don't worry, I will drive us to the game. I hope you don't mind, but my car is a little junky," Kiara said.

"And the circle is complete," Gloria said as the three continued to catch up and indulge in the sweet taste of sisterhood.

ABOUT THE AUTHOR

La Toya Hankins

La Toya is a native of North Carolina and currently resides in Raleigh, NC. A graduate of East Carolina University in Greenville, NC, she earned her Bachelor of Arts degree in journalism with a minor in political science. During her college career, she became a member of Zeta Phi Beta Sorority, Inc. and later served as second vice president for one of the largest graduate chapters in North Carolina.

After working as a regional reporter and features editor in the Charlotte metro area for seven years, she entered the world of banking, where she worked for the fifth largest bank in the country. Presently employed with the State of North Carolina, she divides her time between being a proud pet parent of terrier named Neo and volunteering in the community.

Currently serving as the chair of Shades of Pride, organizer of the annual Triangle Black Pride, La Toya is an active supporter of LGBT issues and addressing health disparities that affects her community. Her literary influences and loves include Zora Neale Hurston, Walter Mosley, Anne Rice, and Pearl Cleage. Her motto, borrowed from Hurston: "I do not weep at the world, I am too busy sharpening my oyster knife."

Website: LatoyaHankins.com

CPSIA information can be obtained
at www.ICGtesting.com
Printed in the USA
FFOW04n1325291015
18156FF